JENNIE MARTS

This book is a work of fiction. Names, characters, places, and incidents are the product of the author's imagination or are used fictitiously. Any resemblance to actual events, locales, or persons, living or dead, is coincidental.

Copyright © 2016 by Jennie Marts. All rights reserved, including the right to reproduce, distribute, or transmit in any form or by any means. For information regarding subsidiary rights, please contact the Publisher.

Entangled Publishing, LLC
2614 South Timberline Road
Suite 109
Fort Collins, CO 80525
Visit our website at www.entangledpublishing.com.

Select Contemporary is an imprint of Entangled Publishing, LLC.

Edited by Allison Collins
Cover design by Syd Gill
Cover art from Shutterstock

Manufactured in the United States of America

First Edition September 2016

*This book is for Todd-
The one who stole my heart
And loves me as wide as the big Montana sky*

Chapter One

Cash Walker pushed up his sleeves and cocked his head as he heard a car pulling down the dirt driveway of Tucked Away. Taking a last look at the laboring ewe he'd been watching, he stepped out of the barn.

He took off his cowboy hat and swiped a sleeve across his forehead. The scents of autumn filled the air, and the nights had started to cool off, but the days still felt like Montana summer. Shading his eyes from the noonday sun, he spied a car heading toward the barn.

A woman sat behind the wheel of the old beat-up blue compact, and a black-and-white goat stood in the passenger seat next to her.

What the hell?

He recognized Clyde, the resident Tucked Away goat. He was a pain in the butt, often getting into trouble and wreaking havoc around the farm.

But who was the woman, and why was Clyde riding shotgun in her front seat?

He couldn't exactly ask her because she was stuck in her

car, her path blocked by Tommie Lee, the farm's cantankerous two-ton bull.

This wasn't the first time the bull had escaped through the fence and pulled this particular trick.

Chuckling, Cash replaced his hat and took a step forward, ready to help another woman in need.

She rolled down her window and laid on the horn as she inched her car forward. "Go on, you brute. Get out of the way."

The laughter died on his lips. Hmm. Maybe this damsel wasn't actually in distress.

The bull gave her a fleeting glance of interest, but apparently didn't think she was worth the annoyance, and wandered toward the corrals next to the barn.

He raised a hand to the woman as she got out of the car. "Hey, there. Something I can help you with?"

She took a tiny step back, a frightened look on her face. "I thought this was Tucked Away—Charlie Ryan's farm."

"It is. I'm Cash Walker, her lead ranch hand." He offered her one of his most charming grins, but her expression stayed wary, and she shrank back slightly at his outstretched hand. She reminded him of a skittish colt, with her chestnut-colored hair, pale skin, and large brown eyes dark and sunken in an otherwise pretty face.

Keeping the car door between them, she ignored his hand, looking to the house as if hoping Charlie would appear. Clyde clamored across the seats and hopped out the open door.

"I know who you are," she said. "I'm Emma Frank. I'm staying at my dad's farm down the road, and he said he thought this was your goat. I was just trying to return him."

"I imagine so. Nobody would want to keep that ornery old cuss on purpose." He gave the goat a nudge. "Get on back to the barn, Clyde."

A small grin tugged at the corners of her mouth, and the

start of a couple dozen butterflies fluttered in his stomach.

Dang. When was the last time he'd had butterflies? It was more likely the chili he'd slathered on his burger at lunch. "What's so funny?"

"My dad's name is Clyde, too." The grin spread and lit her eyes. "And he can sometimes be a bit of an ornery old cuss himself."

"Well, knowing Gigi, she just might'a named him after your dad." He still missed Gigi—she'd been the mainstay of Tucked Away, and her recent death still hit him hard at times.

"You're right. She could have. They've been neighbors for years." A wistful expression crossed her face. "I miss Gigi. She was always good to me."

He hated to see her smile fade, but instinctively knew he couldn't come on too strong by teasing her too much. Just like he would with a wary animal, he stayed where he was, trying not to spook her. "I remember you now. We went to school together, right? You were a couple years behind me?"

She nodded.

He tried again, doing his best to put her at ease. Usually he had a way with the ladies, flirting and pouring on the charm, but this one was different. It seemed as if even her own shadow might scare her.

Something about her tugged at his heart. She reminded him of—well, never mind—he pushed that thought aside. "Nice job with that old bull. He trapped Charlie in her car like that earlier this summer, but she was stuck for hours. You didn't even bat an eye at the big son of a gun."

She shrugged, a tiny look of pride crossing her face. "I'm pretty good with animals."

Not so good with people, it seemed. But he kept that to himself.

Instead he nodded toward the open barn door. "Listen, you came along at just the right time. I just happen to need someone who's good with animals. I've got a ewe getting ready to drop a lamb. It's the first time she's been in labor, so I'm trying to keep an eye on her." He gestured to the bull. "Would you mind looking after her while I get Tommie Lee put away?"

He watched her look from him to the barn, the indecision apparent on her face.

"It should just take a few minutes. I can usually lure him back to the pasture with a bucket of oats. I think the big oaf gets out on purpose now just because he knows he gets rewarded with an extra bag of chow."

The corners of her lips tipped up again, and his heart warmed at the small victory of earning even a tiny smile. He held up his hands. "I promise I won't bite. But I'm not making any promises about that goat."

He turned his back to her and headed for the barn to get a bucket of oats. He grinned as he heard the creak and clunk of her door closing and the crunch of gravel as her footsteps followed him.

After filling an old coffee can from the feed sack, he turned to point her in the direction of the ewe's stall, but she'd already found it and was leaning over the side of the fence cooing encouragement to the mama sheep.

Her faded jeans were loose fitting as if she'd recently lost weight, but he could still admire her assets. The soft pink T-shirt she wore hugged her ample bust, and her hair fell in long loose natural curls down her back. The scuffed cowboy boots on her feet told him that she was a true country girl.

Tearing his gaze away from her, he headed outside to chase down Tommie Lee, wondering what it was about this woman that had his hands sweating and his heart pounding a little harder in his chest.

His mom had always accused him of having a soft spot for injured animals, and this woman had "wounded sparrow" written all over her.

Best to focus on the animal that he *could* manage with a simple can of oats.

It took him about five minutes of coaxing the old bull to get him secured in the pasture, and he stepped back into the barn just in time to see Emma climbing over the rails of the fence and into the ewe's stall.

"Hey, wait. Don't go in there." Rushing forward, he saw her lean down and pick up a newly born lamb and cradle it against her chest. "What are you doing?"

She turned to him, and he saw the thick film of membrane covering the lamb's head. "He can't breathe." Heedlessly disregarding the bloody mess covering her shirt, she pulled the membrane free of the lamb's face and was rewarded with a deep breath and tiny bleat from the baby's mouth.

Emma looked up at him, a victorious smile breaking free. "He's okay."

This woman was full of surprises.

Too skittish to shake his hand, but not afraid to go up against a two-ton bull or get her hands dirty peeling birthing membrane from a baby lamb. He had a feeling animals weren't the source of her fear. At least not the four-legged kind.

Before he could answer, the ewe cried out with a painful maw. A tiny face appeared and the ewe pushed another lamb out, its head slowly sinking to the hay, followed by its body flopping after it. The new baby wriggled and mewled, and Emma set the other lamb down next to it.

They watched in silence as the lambs squirmed and struggled, adjusting to their surroundings, as the ewe licked and cleaned their skinny bodies. Bits of hay stuck to their wet, wrinkled skin as they nuzzled against their mother's side.

Within a few minutes the babies got their feet under them and found their mother's teats, their tiny mouths noisily suckling for milk.

Emma's hand covered her mouth as she watched in amazement. "They're so sweet. Look at their ears."

"You did pretty well with them. I'm awful glad you were here. How'd you know to do that thing with the membrane on its face?"

She shrugged. "We had a few sheep on the farm growing up. I had a couple that I was in charge of for a 4-H project."

He grimaced. "Yeah, that's what these started out as—a 4-H project for our neighbor girl, Sophie. Then somehow we ended up with a dozen, and now I'm in charge of them."

"I'm surprised you're having lambs in the fall. Don't sheep usually have their birthing season in the winter?"

He arched an eyebrow at her and passed her a clean handkerchief from his pocket. "You do know your sheep. You must have done well in 4-H instead of dropping out like me. And yeah, you're right, most sheep do lamb in the winter, but we purposely do ours in the fall. With so few, it's nice to have it done while it's still warm, and we can keep an eye on them."

After wiping her messy hands clean on the handkerchief, she folded it up and apologetically passed it back to him. "Sorry."

"No problem. That's what it's for." He held out his hand to help her from the stall, but she ignored it again and climbed over the fence railing on her own. He nodded to the baby lambs. "They are cute little boogers."

Her face broke into a smile, transforming her features, and his heart did a tiny thump. Dang, she was pretty. Not drop-dead gorgeous, but pretty in a natural way. She wore no makeup, but her cheeks were tinged with color from helping the baby lamb, and her smile reached all the way to her eyes, turning her face radiant.

"I don't recall seeing you around much. You back home for a visit?"

Her open smile shut down, and he instantly regretted his

words. "I just moved back in with my dad. It's only temporary, until I can find a place of my own." She stared at the fence railing as she picked at a small splinter of wood. "I recently got a divorce."

He knew she looked familiar. It just took him a while to remember. "Oh, yeah, I know you. I was at Taylor and Cherry's engagement party." No sooner had he said the words than he wished he could take them back. She'd been a guest at the party, and her ex had shown up, drunk and sloppy, and took a shot at her father. He'd heard Leroy Purvis was currently cooling his heels in county lockup for attempted murder.

"I remember seeing you there." She peeled another splinter from the fencing. "It's so embarrassing."

"Hey, now. You've got nothing to be embarrassed about. Except maybe poor taste. Leroy is responsible for his own actions. That's on him. Not on you."

She sighed—breathed out as if the weight of the world was on her shoulders. "Tell that to his family. His brothers blame me for everything."

Yeah, he knew the Purvis boys, and all of them were bad news. "Not a one of them has a lick of sense between 'em so I wouldn't put too much stock in what they think anyhow."

She looked up, offering him another small smile, and all he wanted to do was keep that smile on her face. "Thank you. That's nice of you to say."

"I mean it." And he did. He'd had his share of run-ins with bullies, and the Purvis boys were a nasty bunch. And he knew all too well the courage it took for a woman to walk away from a man who abused her.

Now he understood the skittish behavior and the wary looks. "You were really brave to ask him for a divorce. That took guts."

"I don't feel very brave. But I keep trying. I've found two different jobs and been laid off from both, thanks to Leroy's idiot brothers."

"Leroy's brothers? I don't get it. How could they could get you laid off?"

She let out another heavy sigh. "First, I tried working at a fast food place, you know that Happy Burger on Tenth Ave? In Great Falls?"

"Yeah, I know the place." Great Falls was the closest town to theirs, and it was forty-five minutes away. Their small town of Broken Falls had a population of a little over twelve hundred people, and everyone knew just enough of everyone else's business.

"Well, within a few days of me starting there, Earl and Junior started showing up, ordering small stuff, then hanging out in the lobby and making general nuisances of themselves. You know how they are, mean and kind of intimidating. I'm sure the boss figured it was easier to find a new employee than go up against them."

"Asshats. Pardon my language." He offered her an apologetic grin and was rewarded with the slightest of smiles in return. That small upturn of her lips was doing funny things to his gut, and all he wanted to do was keep that smile on her face.

"The second job was worse. Not the job itself—that was great. I got hired in a little drugstore downtown and for the first few weeks, everything went smoothly. The manager liked me. I worked hard—cleaning up the shelves, organizing, offering to work extra hours—trying to be a model employee. Ya know?"

He nodded, imagining Emma giving the job her all, working hard to please the manager who'd offered her a chance at a new beginning.

"I think it must have taken Earl and Junior a couple of weeks to find me, but eventually they did. My heart sank that first day when I heard the bell ring above the door and looked up to see them walk in. They pulled the same stuff, but worse. Angie, the manager, offered to call the police. But I didn't want to cause her any more trouble. Calling the police would only make it worse, and I knew it would be easier on her if I just quit."

"That's too bad. It sounds like that was a good fit for you."

"It was. I loved that job. I didn't want to leave. But I didn't want Angie's business to suffer because of me. So I saved her the trouble of firing me and quit. She was really nice about it, said how sorry she was and all, but I could see the relief on her face."

"I bet," he said.

"I don't know why I told you all that stuff." She looked at the ground, her cheeks flushed with embarrassment. "I don't usually talk this much."

"It's okay. I'm happy to listen. But if you're back living with your dad, does that mean you're looking for a job in Broken Falls?"

She shrugged and rubbed at a white line of scar tissue that crossed her lower arm.

He wondered if Leroy had given her the scar. He'd take a bet that he had.

"I guess. I don't know where to look though. It's not fair to the business to have those two—what'd you call 'em—asshats—showing up and causing them to lose customers." The corner of her lips curved up again at the slang term.

"You just need to find a place that won't put up with that nonsense. A place where you feel safe."

She blinked back sudden tears, and it almost tore his heart in two. Maybe that hadn't been the best word. Did she really feel *safe* anywhere? Having Leroy behind bars should have given her some peace, but instead his two idiot brothers were now following her around and intimidating her.

A notion sparked in his mind. "I have an idea. You free

later this afternoon? Can you come into town with me say around three o'clock or so? I might have just the place for you to work. It might only be part-time hours, though."

"That would be okay. I'd take anything right now." Her look of fear turned to one of barely disguised hope, then changed to an expression of wariness. "Why would you want to help me? You barely know me."

His chin dropped, and he raised an eyebrow, ready to lay on the charm and the slow grin that came so naturally to him when it came to pleasing women. But something in him held back, kept his flirty smile in check.

He knew his charm worked on women, young and old, gorgeous and plain. Hell, he'd been using it since he was a teenager and realized a well-placed compliment and a seductive smile could open doors for him and literally charm the pants off some women.

But Emma wasn't some woman. He'd only been in her presence less than an hour, but he recognized something in her. Not just the fact that they'd gone to school together—he barely remembered her from then—but the fear in her eyes was something he knew. The way she tried to be brave, but shied away from trouble, smoothing things over and not causing waves.

Those were things he recognized—things he remembered from a past long ago—from a time that he'd put behind him, sealed up in tight boxes and shut behind a locked door.

No, this woman didn't need the charming role he usually played—didn't need to be flirted with and teased, complimented or seduced. She'd touched him, stirred something in his heart, something that made him want to help her.

What Emma Frank needed right now was a friend.

Chapter Two

Emma dug through the pitiful choices in her closet—half a dozen shirts, a few good dresses for church or a funeral, and one semi-nice pair of black pants—and wanted to cry with frustration.

But she wouldn't cry. She was done crying. In fact, she'd cried so much that she didn't believe there could be a tear left in her body.

No, the time for crying was done. She'd made her choices—finally broken free of the beast that had tormented, shamed, and beat her for the last eight years of her life. Now was the time for action—for taking back the life that Leroy Purvis had stolen.

He may have beaten her body, stripped her bare of dignity, isolated her from her family and friends, but he hadn't taken her soul. And she had a kernel of courage left.

And as long as she had that ounce of courage, she could make it.

She didn't know why Cash Walker had offered to help her—didn't even know what the job interview was that he was taking her to—but something inside her wanted to trust him. Something in her gut told her she could trust him.

And right now, trusting her gut and that tiny bit of bravado was about all she had to go on.

With that in mind, she pulled out her newest top and the black slacks and pulled them on. The slacks hung loose on her hips. She'd been losing weight—not on purpose—she just wasn't hungry. Losing two jobs in the last two months and moving out of the studio apartment she could no longer afford just hadn't done much for her appetite.

Checking her reflection in the mirror, she noted the way her cheeks looked sunken and her hip bones jutted out. The outfit looked okay, presentable at least, and the long sleeves of the shirt covered the evidence of Leroy's abuse. Her body was riddled with scars, white lines that traced a map of violence across her skin.

The red welts and the bruises healed, and those were Leroy's favorites. She cringed as she remembered the first tight painful pinch he'd given the back of her arm when she'd told him a story about a male coworker—the first sign that something wasn't right with this man. The first warning of his jealous temper, his spiteful nature, and the violent rage that simmered just below the surface.

She should have gotten out then. Should have packed her suitcase and left.

But they were newly married—hadn't even unwrapped all of the wedding gifts—and he was so sorry, so apologetic, promising it would never happen again.

But it did.

Little things at first, and not all the time. Sometimes he'd go months without laying a hand on her—just long enough for her to settle in and think maybe they still had a chance. Then there'd be a little incident one week, then something else the next.

Weeks turned into months, then months into years and before she knew it, seven years had gone by. Seven lonely years of abuse. But she survived. And she finally got out.

She traced the line on her abdomen, shivering as she remembered the night he'd come home drunk and caught her watching a romantic comedy and eating a bowl of popcorn.

He'd thrown the popcorn across the room, knocked her off the sofa, and accused her of all sorts of terrible things. He'd screamed that she must have been watching those movies because she was dissatisfied with their life and with him, that she must dream of running off with a guy like that, handsome and rich. His accusations had turned filthy and foul, and she'd cowered in the corner of the room, praying that he'd tire of his rampage and stumble off to pass out in bed.

But he hadn't. Instead he'd torn the room apart, breaking furniture and tossing the lamp across the room. She'd tried to run, but he'd grabbed her hair, pulled her back, then kicked her in the back, sending her sprawling forward, and she'd landed on the broken glass of the lamp, tearing a sharp gash across her stomach.

The amount of blood must have scared him — probably more scared he'd get in trouble than concern for her health — but he'd taken her to the emergency room, allowed her to get stitches, stayed with her and acted like the doting husband as he spun an elaborate story about how clumsy she was and how she'd fallen and cut herself.

That was the night.

The first night that she knew — knew that she had to escape, had to find a way to leave him. It had taken her another year and two more trips to the emergency room, but she'd finally done it.

She dropped her shirt back in place, covering the scars. It wasn't like anyone was going to be seeing her skin again for a long time.

Even the thought of being with another man—trusting another man—turned her stomach.

Except she'd been with a man today.

Cash Walker.

And he hadn't turned her stomach.

Instead, he'd caused flickers of desire to sputter to life inside her. At least she'd thought it was desire. It had been so long since she'd felt any sort of attraction to a man that she wasn't sure she really recognized the signs. It could have been hunger pains or gas.

But she *had* felt attracted to him. How could she not?

She'd have to be dead or comatose not to be affected by the handsome cowboy's dark good looks. His strong jawline, muscled body, and that thick black hair that looked just a little too long—like he was overdue for a haircut and needed a woman to take care of him.

And she knew plenty who would be willing to take on the job. Cash had a reputation for being a ladies' man, a charmer. She hadn't heard of that many women who he'd *actually* slept with, but she knew his masculine appeal and flirty nature was fodder for plenty of women's fantasies in Broken Falls.

And today wasn't the first time she'd fallen prey to his rugged good looks. He'd been drop-dead gorgeous for as long as she'd known him. She cringed as she remembered the terrible crush she'd had on him back in high school. Not that he'd noticed someone like her—a shy, mousy, wallflower.

She'd seen him a few times since she'd been back—once at the diner in town and once at the engagement party where Leroy had shown up and made fools of them both. She could have died of embarrassment that day.

But today was the first time she'd actually talked to him—spent time with him. And he wasn't at all what she'd expected. She'd been waiting for the easy charm, the flirty seductive grins she knew he was famous for. But he hadn't been like that at all.

Well, his grin had still been enough to have her mouth go dry and her palms begin to sweat. But he hadn't been lecherous or vulgar. In fact, he'd been just the opposite.

He'd been nice. And kind.

And now he was helping her to get a job.

Why? Why was he helping her? What was in it for him?

She had no idea. But she didn't want to miss the chance to find out.

The sound of a truck coming down the gravel driveway startled her out of her musings, and she slipped her feet into a pair of plain black flats and grabbed her purse.

Stepping out the front door, she stopped as she took in the sight of him climbing out of his truck.

He'd changed clothes to go to town and no longer wore the faded blue T-shirt and straw cowboy hat he'd had on earlier. His snug-fitting jeans and square-toed brown leather cowboy boots were the same, but he'd put on a clean button-up shirt and traded the straw hat for a black felt one.

Catching sight of her, he smiled, and everything inside of her melted into a puddle on the worn wooden slats of the porch. She swallowed, trying to find something to say; any words that served as a greeting that she could make come out of her mouth right now would be good.

Instead of speaking, she raised her hand in acknowledgment and concentrated on willing her legs to move, to walk toward him.

"Hey there," he said, approaching the porch and holding out a hand to help her down the stairs.

The man was a gentleman. She'd give him that.

Ignoring his hand—there was no way she was sticking her sweaty palm into his outstretched one—she nodded and walked down the steps and toward his truck.

He followed, pulling open the passenger door for her.

"You look real nice."

"Thank you," was all she could manage to say before he slammed the door, circled the truck, and slid into the seat next to her.

He must have just showered, because the masculine scent of soap and aftershave filled the cab of the truck, and the ends of his dark hair curled along his starched collar. She tore her eyes away from those black curls, focusing on getting her seat belt on, then clasped her hands tightly together in her lap.

She stared out the window as he turned the truck toward town, realizing that she hadn't yet asked him where they were headed. She must have trusted him a little bit, otherwise she might have just gotten into a truck with a serial murderer who was driving her to her death in a Dodge Ram pickup.

"So, where are we going?"

"Into town. You remember Cherry Hill—well, Cherry Johnson now? She's the feisty redhead who went to school with us. You know, the one who had the engagement party that—" he let the last words linger in the air, obviously embarrassed about bringing up the subject.

"Yes, I know Cherry. Sort of. I mean I know who she is and all. But it's not like we're friends or anything."

No, not like that. Because she didn't have *any* actual friends. Leroy had made sure of that.

"Well she runs Cherry's Diner there in the middle of town, and she's been talking about taking on a part-time waitress. She's a mom now and wants to scale back a little at work and spend more time with Sam. Apparently becoming an instant mom of an energetic eight-year-old boy takes up a lot of time."

"I can imagine it would. Sam is so cute—and Cherry and Taylor seem like a great couple. I was only at their engagement party because my dad is friends with Taylor's dad, and he dragged me along. Probably just to get me out of the house.

I'd just filed for divorce and been holed up in my old bedroom for several days."

A few weeks before, Leroy had put her head through their glass shower door, and that had been the last straw. She fingered the scar hidden just below her hairline as she'd remembered that the party had been the first time she'd ventured out in public.

But he'd found her. Just like he said he would. He claimed he would always find her. That it didn't matter what a piece of paper said, she'd always belong to him.

A shiver ran through her, even though the cab of the truck was warm. Pushing thoughts of Leroy from her mind, she tried to focus on the conversation at hand. "I knew that Cherry and Taylor had married and had heard they were really Sam's biological parents. Is that true?"

Cash grinned as he turned down Main Street and pulled up in front of the diner. "Yeah, it's true. Isn't that the craziest thing? You'll have to get Cherry to tell you the whole story sometime." He slid out of the truck, circled around to open her door for her, then flashed her an encouraging smile. "You ready?"

She nodded, her heart pounding against her chest.

"You'll do fine. Don't worry." He glanced down at her lap, and she realized her fingers had turned white and purple from twisting the strap of her purse around them so tightly.

She pulled her hands free and shook the circulation back into them. "I guess I'm a little nervous."

Cash slammed the truck door, causing her to jump. She took a deep breath, aware that his hand barely grazed the small of her back as he guided her up the sidewalk toward the diner. The heat of his fingers on her back seemed to burn through the flimsy fabric of her shirt as she could feel the lightest pressure of each pad of his fingertips.

"Don't be nervous. Cherry's a smart-ass, but she's a real

sweetheart. You're gonna love her."

Yeah, but what will she think of me?

Emma swallowed back the nerves building in her throat and pasted on a smile as she and Cash walked into the diner.

Cherry caught sight of them and flashed Cash a gorgeous grin. The redhead was beautiful, with her curvy figure filling out the pink waitress dress and her strawberry-colored hair pulled up in a messy ponytail.

She gestured to the row of booths along one side of the restaurant. "Have a seat. I'll be over in a sec. Can I get you all some iced tea? Or coffee?"

"Iced tea for me." Cash looked down at Emma.

"Water's fine." She thought about the few crumpled bills she had in her wallet. Water and air were about all she could afford right now.

"And water for Emma," he called, then led her to an empty booth.

She looked around the quaint diner as they crossed the room, the red vinyl and the pink and white checked tablecloths giving it a cheery retro look. A long counter ran along the back of the restaurant, an old-fashioned soda fountain on one end, bringing up childhood memories.

The diner had been around as long as Emma could remember; she'd been here many times when it had been run by Cherry's grandparents. But she hadn't been back since she'd married Leroy and moved to Great Falls and hadn't seen the diner since Cherry had taken it over.

She liked that Cherry kept the nostalgic feel. It was homey and laid-back and offered all the comfort foods like macaroni and cheese and pot roast with mashed potatoes.

At three in the afternoon, the diner was mostly empty, except for one middle-aged guy in a suit sitting at the counter reading the paper and having a cup of coffee and an elderly couple sitting at a table sharing a piece of pie.

Emma scooted into the booth, and Cash slid in next to her. She caught her breath as his muscled thigh pressed against the side of her leg for a moment, then moved away as he adjusted in the seat.

He leaned down, his breath warm against her neck. "Don't worry. You'll do great. Cherry seems tough, but she's a real softie."

Cherry slid into the seat across from them, setting down two glasses of tea and a water. She offered Emma an encouraging smile as she took a long swig of tea. "Lord a mercy, what a day. My feet are killing me. I'm Cherry. Cash tells me that you're looking for a job."

Okay. This one didn't mince words. She got right to the point.

Emma nodded, picking up the red plastic tumbler and taking a small sip of water. "Yes. I don't know if you remember me, but we went to school together." She thought it best not to remind Cherry that she'd also been the one responsible for wrecking her engagement party.

"I do remember you. You were a few years younger than we were," she said, indicating herself and Cash. "I wasn't super social in high school. I feel like I was either helping out my grandparents here at the diner or hanging out with my boyfriend."

"Who is now your husband," Cash said, shaking his head. "Who would've thought you two would end up gettin' married?"

"Me," Cherry said with a mischievous grin.

"Congratulations," Emma told her.

"Thank you. Now let's talk about you. Do you have any waitressing experience?"

Slipping her hands under the table, Emma wiped her sweaty palms on her pants and tried to focus on making a good impression.

And breathing.

Which was kind of hard at the moment, because her breath was currently caught in her throat as she felt Cash's warm hand ease across her leg and squeeze her hand in silent support.

She couldn't look at him. Couldn't acknowledge that he might know that her hands were shaking and her underarms were filled with sweat. Instead, she took a deep breath and squeezed his hand. Hard. As if his rough callused palm were a lifeline and she were drowning.

"I've always been good at customer service and treating people well," she explained. "I've worked retail and fast food, and spent nine months waitressing at a chain restaurant in Great Falls." It had taken her months to convince Leroy to let her start working again. It was the perfect job for her plan to escape, allowing her to bring home a steady paycheck and squirrel away a small amount of her own money. Just enough to be able to afford a security deposit and a first month's rent.

"That should be enough experience to work here. But I'm only looking for a part-time waitress. Someone to help out with the breakfast crowd and give me time to get my son, Sam, ready and off to school in the morning. Would that work for you?"

"Y-yes, that would be great. And I would be willing to cover other shifts if you had something come up at the school that you needed to do."

Cherry smiled at her. "Thank you. That's very thoughtful, and I'll keep that in mind." She spent a few minutes explaining the schedule and salary and looked at Emma for confirmation. "Does that sound good?"

Emma nodded, her next words caught in her throat. She should just be quiet. Take the job and hope for the best. But she couldn't.

Cherry was taking a chance on her—this could barely be

considered an interview—she hadn't even really asked her any questions. She was taking her on Cash's recommendation, and Emma knew she had to be up-front about her situation. "There's just one thing."

"Oh, what's that?"

Emma couldn't meet her eye. She stared at a spot of dried ketchup on the table and squeezed Cash's hand tighter. "I'm recently divorced, and my ex-husband's brothers have caused some trouble at the last few places that I've worked. I would really like to accept this job, but I want to be honest about my situation, and I'll understand if you don't want to hire me."

Cherry laughed. A low chuckle. "You think I'm afraid of those Purvis boys? I can certainly handle a couple of bullies, and they won't cause any trouble in *my* establishment. I can guaran-dang-tee that."

"Really?" Tears stung her eyes as Emma looked up at the feisty redhead. "You still want to hire me?"

"Of course."

"You're not worried about Earl and Junior?"

"Heck no. Those yahoos don't worry me a bit. Are you forgetting that I'm married to the sheriff? They won't cause any trouble here, or they'll have Taylor to deal with."

"Thank you," Emma said, her voice barely above a whisper.

"You can thank me by doing a good job here and giving me peace of mind that my customers are being well taken care of when I'm not here."

Emma nodded. "I will. You can count on me. I'm a hard worker. I promise I won't let you down."

"It's settled then." Cherry smacked the table, causing Emma to jump, and she let go of Cash's hand. "I'll introduce you to Stan." She gave a yell, and a cute Asian guy wearing a tie-dye shirt and board shorts walked out of the kitchen and sauntered toward their table.

He appeared to be in his mid-twenties and had a wide friendly grin and an easy manner about him as he held a hand up to Cash. "Hey dude. What's up?"

Cash gave his raised hand a high-five. "I'm bringing you a new employee. This is my friend Emma."

Emma's heart gave a little flutter at the way Cash introduced her as his friend. It was silly and probably no big deal to him—lots of people easily used that term. It had just been a long time since she had anyone resembling a friend in her life.

She snuck a glance at Cherry who offered her an encouraging smile. Maybe she just might have made two new friends.

That was a little much to hope for. She was just happy with the offer of a job.

"Hey, Emma. Nice to meet ya." Stan gave her a little wave, his smile full of white teeth and charm, and she instantly liked him.

"Hi," was all she could manage to say, overwhelmed at the amount of niceness happening around her.

Cash stood and dipped his head toward the shorter man. "Listen bud, Emma's had a little trouble with her ex-brothers-in-law showing up at her work and harassing her. I need you to have her back. You can take care of these guys if they give her any trouble, right?" He made a karate chopping motion in the air.

Stan raised an eyebrow at him. "Dude, that's just racist. You think just because I'm Asian, that I know karate, or judo, or whatever kind of tai chi move that was?"

Cash shrugged and gave him a good-hearted jab in the side. "Yeah. That, and I know you've been taking a karate class with Sam for the last month."

Stan's stern look turned into another toothy grin. "Ok, you got me." He turned his gaze toward Emma and offered her a friendly wink. "And don't worry, Emma. My karate skills might not be that great, but I know how to throw out unruly customers, and I'm not opposed to calling for backup from the sheriff if we need it. Besides, Taylor's in here almost every day for lunch anyway."

Cash looked down at her and gave her an encouraging smile. "See, it's all gonna work out fine."

She smiled back, her heart lifting in what almost felt like hope. It had been so long since she'd felt it, she wasn't sure she recognized the emotion.

But she knew it felt good. She felt good.

And for the first time in a long time, she dared to look to the future with anticipation of something good to come.

• • •

Cash turned to his side, the sheets twisting in his restless legs, as he struggled to fall asleep that night.

The clock on his nightstand crept close to eleven, but he was still wide awake. He was normally sawing logs within minutes of his head hitting the pillow, his mind and body too tired to do anything except drift right off.

But tonight sleep eluded him.

Instead, his mind was full of thoughts of a doe-eyed woman. And it had been a long time since thoughts of a woman had kept him up at night.

But he couldn't get Emma out of his mind. The way she stared in wide-eyed wonder at the birth of the new lamb, the way her hair fell across her shoulders, and the way she gripped his hand in terror under the table at the diner.

She was different than any other woman in his life. Special. Something about her touched his heart and made all of his protective instincts kick in.

Most of the women he'd been with knew what they were

getting into with him—a fun evening or two, but no strings attached. There were a few women that he'd see off and on, but they knew the situation for what it was. They could have his body, his attention, and his time, but they couldn't have his heart.

Sure, he liked them. He wasn't a total heartless bastard. Most of them were great—funny, gorgeous, sexy—tight jeans, big hair, and bold in the bedroom were his favorites. There had been women who had made him laugh, who he'd had a good time with, and had a general affection for, but no one had captured the elusive heart of Cash Walker.

So, why did half an hour in the presence of a quiet, almost painfully shy woman have his heart feel like it was being pinched in a vise? A nice, sweet woman who had no business hanging out with the likes of him, and who he had no business getting involved with.

But something drew him to her, and he couldn't get her out of his mind.

He told himself he was just being hospitable, helping her out. He was just being neighborly when he gave her his number this afternoon as he dropped her off, and she told him her dad was out of town, helping to take care of his brother in Nebraska, who'd just fallen off a windmill and broken his leg.

Yeah, right. Neighborly, my foot.

But he did want to help her. Felt *compelled* to help her, in fact. But just because he introduced her to Cherry and assisted her in getting a job didn't mean she owed him anything or that he had to see her again.

In fact, he should probably stay away from her.

She had enough on her plate just getting back on her feet without having an old tomcat like him around.

The sharp ring of his cell phone startled him, and he grabbed it off his nightstand.

Aw hell.

Nothing good ever came from a late night phone call. Pushing up in bed, he squinted at the tiny screen—he didn't recognize the number, beyond that it was the Montana area code—as he tapped the screen and held it up to his ear. "Hello."

"Cash?" She only spoke one word—softly, barely above a whisper. The terrified trembling in her voice was different than the quiet shyness he'd heard earlier in the day, but he knew it was her.

"Emma? What's wrong? Are you all right?"

"I'm sorry. I didn't know who else to call."

"Don't worry about that. What's going on?"

"Earl and Junior. They're outside." She choked on her words, and he could tell she was trying not to cry. But he could still hear the terror in her voice.

Chapter Three

Cash was already pulling on his jeans and the pair of boots that lay next to his bed. He grabbed his keys and headed for his truck. "Tell me what's happened. Are they threatening you?"

"I was asleep. I don't know how long they've been here. They threw something through the front window and shattered it. And they're driving around the farm, revving their engine and yelling terrible things. I think they're drunk." Emma's voice choked on a sob. "I'm sorry to call you, but I'm scared."

"It's fine. You did the right thing. Did you already call the cops?"

"No. I've called the police before, and it didn't help. It only makes things worse. They haven't come inside or actually threatened me, so I know the police won't do anything."

He knew that wouldn't be the case with Taylor, but it wouldn't help to argue with her. And he could be there before the police anyway. He just needed to get to her now. "Where are you?"

"I'm upstairs in my room."

"Do they know you're there?"

"I don't know."

"Okay. Stay where you are. I'll be there in two minutes."

"Y-you don't have to come."

"I'm already on my way. If they try to come inside, call the sheriff. Otherwise, just stay out of sight. Hang on, Emma. I'll be there soon."

He clicked off as he jumped in his truck, started the engine, and threw it in gear. His cabin was behind the barn and as he rounded the corner, he saw a familiar truck sitting in front of the main house and Charlie and her boyfriend, Zack, sitting on the front porch swing.

Cash, Zack, and Cherry's now husband, Taylor, had all been friends since high school, and Zack was already off the porch and heading toward his truck as Cash pulled to a stop in front of the house.

"Get in," he said as Zack pulled the door open.

He must have recognized the urgency in Cash's voice, because Zack didn't hesitate as he climbed into the pickup.

Charlie was right on his heels and squeezed in next to Zack as she pulled the door shut behind her. "What's going on?"

Cash put the truck in gear, and gravel spun behind the tires as he raced down the driveway and turned onto the highway. "The Purvis brothers are over at the Frank farm. They're terrorizing Emma—threw a rock or something through the front window and are tearing up the place."

"You remember Emma Frank? She went to school with you guys," Charlie told Zack.

Cash had told her about what was going on with Emma earlier that night when he was showing her the new baby lambs. She knew about Leroy from the shooting at the engagement party, and he'd explained that his brothers had been harassing Emma.

Charlie knew what it was like to be scared and how alone it felt to start over. She'd told Cash that she would do what she could to help Emma and had offered to have her over for dinner later that week.

A dinner party was the last thing on Cash's mind as he turned into the driveway of the Frank's farm. He'd been there before, helped out with branding a few times, back when Clyde still had livestock. The farm was fairly small, made up of a barn, a couple of corrals and outbuildings, and an old white farmhouse.

Barreling down the driveway, he could already see a beat-up old car spinning donuts in front of the house. They must have seen him, too, because they suddenly turned around and came speeding toward Cash's truck.

"Holy shit," Zack yelled as they flew past the pickup, barely missing the side mirrors and causing Cash to hug the edge of the road to avoid going into the ditch running along the side of the driveway. "Crazy bastards."

Cash didn't care about the idiots or that they almost crashed into his truck. He was only focused on one thing. Getting to Emma.

He skidded to a stop—the engine barely off before he was climbing out of the truck and running up the stairs of the porch.

"Emma!" He called her name as he rattled the front door then slammed into it with his shoulder. The flimsy lock gave way, and the door flew open. He'd fix that later—and put in a new deadbolt.

Broken glass crunched under his boots as he stepped into the living room.

There was no sign of her.

Charlie and Zack followed him into the house.

"I'll get this cleaned up," he heard Charlie say as he took

the stairs two at a time, climbing to the second floor and calling Emma's name.

The room to the right held a four-poster bed with a light bedspread and feminine décor. Cash assumed this was Emma's room and charged through the door. The moon offered enough light to see the spread thrown back on the empty bed.

His eyes searched the room, his gaze falling on a huddled form on the floor in the corner beside a wingback chair. Her back was to the wall, her head tucked down, as she hugged her knees.

In two strides, he was next to the chair, bending down and reaching for her.

He touched her shoulder, and she slapped at him, crying. "Whoa there, Emma. It's me, Cash."

Her hands stilled, and she looked up at him, silver tear stains on her cheeks. "Cash?"

His heart broke as he knelt beside her. Moving slowly, as he would with a skittish colt, he rested one hand gently on her knee. "It's all right, darlin'. I'm here."

She blinked up at him, fear still on her face. He knew that fear, had seen it and felt it before. "You're here," she whispered.

"Come on, now." He slid his hands around her back and under her knees, and cradled her against his chest as he lifted her in his arms.

She curled against him as he carried her across the room and sat down on the edge of the bed. Stroking her back, he spoke soft words into her hair. "You're okay now. You're safe. They're gone. It's gonna be all right."

She sighed against his chest, a deep shuddering sigh that tore his heart in two. "Thank you. Thank you for coming."

"Think nothin' of it. That's why I gave you my number. In case you needed me." And she had needed him. Which was a bad idea. He knew it, knew he shouldn't give her the idea that he was someone who could be counted on.

Her head jerked up, and she clawed at his chest at the sound of footsteps on the stairs.

"It's okay. It's just Charlie. She's a friend," he said as she appeared in the doorway.

"Everything okay in here?" Charlie asked, her voice filled with tender concern.

"Yeah, we're good," he said as Emma scrambled up from his lap. She wore a knee-length white sleeveless nightgown, her long hair loose and falling around her shoulders, and the sight of her standing in the moonlight had butterflies swirling and careening in his gut.

She was beautiful.

"Emma, this is Charlie Ryan. She runs Tucked Away. She and Zack came with me. You remember Zack Cooper?" He knew she'd remember Zack. Everyone knew the good-looking blond quarterback who was now the town veterinarian.

Emma nodded. "I met you this summer. At Cherry's engagement party. You gave me your Snickers salad recipe."

Cash shook his head. How the woman could be thinking about a salad recipe right now was beyond him. But maybe it was good. Good to have her thinking about something normal. Like a recipe. Get her mind off being scared.

"I remember. Although anything with that much whipped topping and cut-up candy bars in it should not be deemed a salad," Charlie teased, obviously trying to lighten the tense atmosphere.

She walked slowly into the room and laid a hand gently on Emma's arm. "I cleaned up the broken glass downstairs, and Zack is gonna try to find some plywood or something in the barn to patch up the hole. Why don't I help you put some things together so you can come back to my house with me tonight?"

Emma's hands flittered nervously in front of her. "Oh no, I couldn't. They're gone now. I'm sure I'll be fine."

"I insist. None of us will be able to sleep thinking about you out here by yourself. I had my own run-in with Earl Purvis earlier this summer when he assaulted me and Zack's daughter, Sophie. I know how dangerous he can be, and we'll all rest easier knowing you're safe and sleeping in the guest room at Tucked Away."

"Are you sure? I don't want to be any trouble."

"I am."

Cash could have hugged Charlie. She was so gentle with Emma, and if she hadn't talked Emma into coming back to the farm with them, he would have picked her up and carried her out to the truck himself.

This was much easier on everyone.

Charlie nodded at him. "Why don't you help Zack finish up with the window, and I'll help Emma. We'll be downstairs in a few minutes."

He hesitated. It made sense that Charlie would assist her, but something in his chest felt constricted, like he wanted to be the one to help her.

Like he wanted to be her hero.

That thought was enough to have him turning away, crossing the room, and heading down the stairs.

He knew he wasn't the guy to be anyone's hero.

· · ·

Emma startled awake. The sun shone through the window, creating a square of early morning light across the pillows. Across strange pillows.

She shook her head as the night before came back to her. The frantic call to Cash as Leroy's brothers tore up the farm, the feeling of finally being safe as he'd stormed into the room and picked her up in his arms, and the friendship given to her by Charlie and Zack as they brought her back to Charlie's farm and set her up in the guest room.

Charlie had brought her a cup of hot tea, a warm cloth to wash her face, and practically tucked her in. Cash had come in and dropped into the chair at the foot of the bed, kicking off his boots and stretching his long legs out across the corner of the mattress.

"I'll just sit here till you fall asleep," he'd said. She should have been frightened to have a man she barely knew in the same room with her, watching her as she tried to sleep. But she didn't. Somehow, Cash Walker made her feel safe.

And she slept. Really slept. Like she hadn't in a long time.

She turned her head and clutched the sheet tightly to her as she saw a man slumped in the chair. Then, when he didn't attack, she realized it was Cash—a crocheted afghan across his chest, his head bent forward and his eyes closed, still fast asleep.

Her chest tightened as she studied him. He was so dang good-looking. It almost hurt to look at him. A shock of black hair fell across his forehead, which would have given him a boyish look, if not for the shadow of dark whiskers across his chin.

His long lean legs splayed out in front of the chair, and she smiled at the small hole in the corner of his sock.

He must have felt her staring at him, because he stirred and his eyes fluttered open. A grin curved his lips. "Hey, darlin'."

Chapter Four

Darlin'.

How did one simple word send shivers of heat racing down her back? Emma didn't think anyone had ever called her darlin' with such simple ease before.

The sound of that one word rolling off Cash's tongue in his deep sleepy voice was enough to have her melting into the pillows beneath her. "Hey, yourself. You didn't have to sleep there all night."

"I think you need to quit telling me what I have and don't have to do." He gave her a wink. "I'm a big boy. I can make up my own mind, and I'll do what I please."

Lord have mercy. Thinking about him doing what he pleased to her had her skin heating, and she worried her blush would give away her thoughts.

His grin widened, but he didn't say anything more. Instead, he stood, the afghan falling to the floor as he stretched his arms to the ceiling.

Cash was tall, well over six feet, and his forearms rippled with tight muscles as he stretched. His T-shirt lifted slightly with the movement, and a thin band of bare skin and firm abs showed at his waist.

Holy hotness. This man made her pulse race and her palms sweat. It had been so long since she'd felt attracted to anyone. Certainly not to Leroy.

Although she had loved him once. When they were in high school, and he was so kind to her. He'd been cute back then, funny and sweet, and treated her like she was special. As the years passed and life didn't hand him the cards he felt he deserved, he'd turned hard and bitter, and all the traces of that sweet, funny guy disappeared.

As the abuse escalated, her tender feelings for him were replaced with fear and loathing. She dreaded the hour that he would walk in the door from work, never sure what mood to expect or how bad things would get that night. She did everything she could to appease him, to keep his temper even until he drank enough to pass out on the sofa, praying that he wouldn't make it to their bedroom.

The thought of his hot, sweaty body pressing against her, the stench of body odor and stale beer coming off his skin, had bile rising in her throat. No, she hadn't felt attraction to a man in a long time.

Cash sniffed the air. "Smells like Charlie's got the coffee on. You want to come out, or should I bring you a cup?"

She couldn't think of a time that Leroy had ever offered to bring her a cup of anything in bed. It felt nice. Nice to be a little pampered.

Although she had to quit comparing Cash to Leroy. The two men were nothing alike. And there was no reason to think Cash was interested in her in *that* way anyway.

Which was for the best. She didn't need to be getting involved with someone new right now. She needed to find herself first. Before she found herself in the arms of another man.

Cash had introduced her yesterday as his friend. And that felt like a pretty good place to be. She needed to stop thinking about his muscled chest and the way his dark hair curled against the nape of his neck. Take his offer of friendship and be thankful for it.

"I'll come out."

He shrugged. "Suit yourself." He turned toward the door and, despite her inner declarations only moments before of thinking of Cash as a friend, she couldn't help but admire his butt as he ambled from the room, the denim covering it stretching with each move of his long legs.

A small bathroom was attached to the guest room, and she took a few minutes to freshen up. Thankful Charlie had helped her pack a few toiletries, she washed her face, brushed her teeth, and combed out her hair. She'd packed a few clothes and pulled on a fresh pair of jeans and a light blue cotton T-shirt. It was a small thing, but getting dressed felt as if she were donning her armor to face Charlie and Cash, the people who had invited her into their lives, instead of appearing for breakfast in only her nightgown.

Stepping out of the guest room, she was surprised to see the kitchen full of people.

Zack stood at the kitchen table, bent over the shoulders of a blond teenage girl, an array of schoolbooks spread out in front of her.

Charlie looked up from the stove where she was dishing up a plate of scrambled eggs to Cash. "Hey there, Emma. How'd you sleep?"

"Fine. I mean good. Thank you." Heat burned her cheeks. She had no idea all of these people would be here. And they all had to know why she was there—because she was too afraid to stay by herself. "I'll be out of your hair in a few minutes."

"Nonsense. You haven't even had breakfast." Charlie pointed to the table. "Have a seat. I'll bring you some eggs.

This is Sophie, Zack's daughter."

She pulled out a chair and sat across from the teenager who looked up and smiled openly at her. "Hi, Emma. Sorry about all the books. I have a test this morning, and my dad's been quizzing me."

The girl's smile was contagious, and Emma liked her immediately. She let out a breath and tried to relax the tension in her shoulders. "I hate tests. What subject?"

Sophie rolled her blue eyes. She wore purple rectangular-shaped glasses, and wispy bangs covered her forehead. "Me, too. Especially history tests. I love learning about all the stuff that happened in the past, but I hate memorizing all the random dates."

Cash set a cup of coffee in front of Emma and handed her a plate full of eggs and crispy strips of bacon. Her mouth watered at the scent of the food, and she found herself hungry, really hungry, for the first time in a long time. "Thanks. This looks delicious."

She picked up the fork and dug in, content to listen to the conversations and laughter of the other people in the room. It was obvious from the way they ribbed each other that Zack and Cash had been good friends for a long time, and Charlie and Sophie had an apparent affection for each other.

Charlie filled the cups around the table, leaning over Sophie's shoulder and pressing a hand against Zack's arm as she passed by.

Cash sprawled in a chair next to Sophie, nibbling on a piece of bacon. He pulled over one of the schoolbooks and quizzed her on the pages. The teenager fluctuated between serious studying and teasing laughter, cheering as she got the answers right and stealing a piece off the end of Cash's bacon.

They were a family.

An odd assortment of people who were connected by the apparent love and affection they had for one another.

Tears prickled at the back of Emma's eyes. She wasn't jealous exactly, but this was the kind of easy family atmosphere she'd always wished for.

And this was a new role that Emma hadn't seen Cash in. He was comfortable with this girl, almost like a second father to her.

He caught her looking at them, and a proud grin crossed his face. "Sophie's my goddaughter, and she's been pestering me since she was old enough to talk."

The teenager laughed and nudged his chair. "Oh stop it. You know you love me."

He dipped his chin in agreement. "I do love you, kid. But I've got to get to work." He passed the schoolbook to Emma. "Can you finish quizzing her? Just that last section—she's got the rest."

Emma took the book, still amazed at the fondness Cash had for this girl and the easy way he'd just told her he loved her.

It seemed there was more to Cash Walker than just a flirty bad boy. He was proving to be kind of sweet. Who knew?

He pushed back his chair, leaned over to kiss the top of Sophie's head, then took his cup to the sink and thanked Charlie for breakfast. Before heading out the door, he lifted a black cowboy hat from the coatrack and set it on his head, then turned back to Emma. "I'll be out in the barn most of the morning, if you want to come out and check on the new lambs. You know you're in charge of naming them."

"Me? Why?"

"It's a Tucked Away tradition. If you take part in bringing them into this world, you get the honor of naming them." He jerked a thumb at Charlie. "This one is the reason we have a half-grown cow in the barn named Rodney. Who names a cow Rodney?"

"You *have* to do it," Sophie told her. "It's a tradition."

Emma laughed. "Okay. I guess I'll do it then—since it's a tradition. I'll come out in a little bit and try to come up with some suitable lamb names."

"Good."

Zack pushed back from his chair as the door slammed behind Cash. "I've got to get going, too. Sophie, finish up that last set of questions, then I gotta get you to school."

Emma quizzed Sophie on the last set of questions, trying not to watch as Zack cornered Charlie in the kitchen, wrapping his arms around her middle and bending his head to lay a kiss on her neck.

"You got them all right. You're gonna ace this test," Emma said as she closed the book and passed it to Sophie.

The teenager shoved it and the other books into her backpack. "Thanks Emma. I appreciate the help."

She started as something furry brushed by her ankle. Looking down, her heart burst at the precious ball of gray fur that lay cuddled against her foot. "There's a kitten on the floor."

Sophie laughed, stepping around the table and picking up the little gray cat. "This is Percy. Isn't he adorable? Doyle and Jane Austen are around here somewhere, too. Charlie named them. You can tell she's a writer." She cuddled the kitten then set it in Emma's arms.

The little kitten climbed up her chest, sniffing at her chin, its tiny tongue scratchy as it licked her cheek. It was adorable—so cute it almost made her heart hurt. "It's so sweet."

Sophie laughed. "Yeah, kittens are the best. They make everything better." She waved and headed for the front door, her last comment leaving Emma wondering if even Sophie knew about the trouble with her ex and his brothers.

Zack followed his daughter from the house, and Charlie set the coffeepot on the table as she sunk into the chair across from Emma. The other two kittens tumbled across the floor, and Charlie picked them up and snuggled them in her lap. "Kittens do make everything better."

"They certainly help." She laughed as the kitten playfully pawed at her neck.

"Listen, Emma. We don't really know each other that well, and I wouldn't presume to know what you're going through, but I do know what it's like to start over. When I came to Tucked Away earlier this summer, I was flat broke and felt like my life was hopeless. I'd been lied to, cheated on, and stolen from. I barely had a penny to my name and didn't really feel like I had a friend in the world."

She didn't know what to say—or how to respond. Charlie Ryan seemed like she had it all together. She was a successful writer, had a great guy, lived on this beautiful farm, and was gorgeous, too. How could she possibly know what Emma was going through?

But something in Charlie's voice, in her expression, told her that maybe she did know a little.

"I know what it's like to feel alone and out of place. I was fortunate to have found Sophie and Cherry—well, they kind of found me. And finding Zack has changed my life, and my heart, forever."

"They do seem pretty great."

"They are. They all are. Even Cash." She grinned. "They all reached out to me in friendship, and having them around has completely changed my life. Having even one friend can make a huge difference. I guess my point is that I would like to be *your* friend."

Tears filled Emma's eyes. It had been so long since anyone had wanted to be her friend. At first, she'd tried to hold on to the few friends she'd made in high school, but once they moved to Great Falls, it was harder, and Leroy discouraged her from spending time with anyone but him.

Then, after the abuse started, she was embarrassed to go

out, ashamed and worried that someone would find out. It was easier to stay in, take care of their home, and read books about other women having adventures and romance.

She swallowed back the emotion filling her throat. "Thank you. I appreciate that."

"I mean it. And I'd like you to stay here until your dad gets back."

"Oh no, I couldn't."

"Yes, you can. I have an empty guest room just sitting there, and I cook enough to feed an army every night anyway. It would be fun to have you here. I mean it."

"But I don't even know how long my dad is going to be gone. It could be a week or more."

"Then we'd better go get you some more clothes." Charlie reached across the table and put her hand on top of Emma's. "I'm still new here, too. And still figuring out this whole Montana life. I'm not as outgoing as Cherry or as affectionate as Sophie, but I could use another friend, too."

Emotion swelled in her chest, and she squeezed Charlie's hand. "I guess you've got yourself a houseguest then, and a new friend." She smiled, and her next words came out as a whisper. "Thank you."

"It's settled then." Charlie let go of her hand and picked up the kittens in her lap. "As my new friend, I will tell you a secret. You know how Sophie told you the names of these furballs are Doyle, Jane, and Percy?"

"Yes."

"Well, I *am* a writer, and I love word play and symbolism, and those are names of famous writers, but each of them also has a double meaning. These kittens were born soon after I arrived in Montana, and I was tasked with naming them. I really wanted to do them justice, so I thought a lot about it and wanted names that would be good, but would also have special meaning to me and what was happening in my life at the time. You know how I told you that my life was a mess and I was starting over here?"

Emma nodded again, intrigued by the story and by being let in on a secret.

Charlie held up the white kitten. "This one I named Jane—for Jane Austen, obviously—but mainly because I love the book, Emma, and felt like I was totally 'clueless' when I got here." She paused, obviously waiting to see if Emma got the connection.

She grinned. "I love that book, too. And I know that the movie *Clueless* was loosely based on the book. Very smart."

Charlie smiled and held up the black kitten. "This one is named Doyle for Sir Arthur Conan Doyle because I love Sherlock Holmes and I felt like my life was a total mystery, and I had no idea what was about to happen."

"I can certainly relate to that." Emma cuddled the gray kitten to her chin. "How about this one? What's the significance of Percy?"

Charlie grinned. "That one is named for Percy Shelley, the famous poet who was also married to Mary Shelley. She's the one who wrote Frankenstein, which I thought was totally fitting because I felt like my life was this crazy monster made up of all these miscellaneous parts that I was just waiting to bring to life. And it has another meaning that I think you will appreciate."

"I already love these meanings and totally understand the feelings behind them."

"I figured that you would. I know they're kind of silly, and not everyone would get them. That's why the meanings behind their names have been my secret. But I wanted you to know. Especially about Percy, because that cat already thinks you're special. He doesn't usually let anyone cuddle him for long, but he's totally comfortable with you."

She looked down at the kitten who was now asleep in her

arms. His whiskers twitched, and his body let off a soft purr of contentment.

"That kitten's name is short for the one thing that I knew I would need to get me through the hard times and that I want you to remember, too. Percy is short for *perseverance*. Perseverance is the steady and continued action over a long period of time, despite difficulties or setbacks."

Emma's throat tightened over the sentiment, over the feeling that she struggled with every day. All she could do was nod at Charlie, afraid that if she spoke, she would burst out crying.

The other woman gave her a smile of encouragement. "I know you can do this. Even when it feels hard and you feel like giving up, you can do this. You're stronger than you think you are. And you *can* persevere."

"Thank you," she whispered, holding back the tears that threatened to spill down her cheeks. She took a deep breath. "Thank you. You're right. I am strong. And I can do this."

"That's the spirit." Charlie gave the kittens one last cuddle then set them on the floor. "And now I have to get to work. Lots of words to write."

Emma took a sip of coffee, composing herself, then smiled at her new friend. "I've read your books, you know."

"Oh, so you're the one."

Emma laughed. "Stop it. They're really good. Isn't there a new one coming out soon?"

"Yes, in a few weeks. As a matter of fact, I have to call my editor today to finish up some details with the release. I should probably do that now." She gestured to the kitchen. "Make yourself at home. I'll put together some sandwiches for lunch. Until then, I'll be chained to my desk pouring forth a new novel."

Emma cuddled the little gray kitten to her chest, unsure of how to accept all of these blessings. Her heart was full and her chest was tight with the overflowing emotions.

Yesterday she'd woken up alone and scared, terrified of what her future held. Today she woke up with a new job, new friends, and what felt like a new start. She was still scared, but she wasn't alone anymore.

Chapter Five

The fall sunlight filtered into the barn as Cash stood at the workbench trying to replace a hinge on the gate that Tommy Lee had broken through the day before. That dang bull was too strong for his own good.

The fence post lay across the tidy workbench, and Cash was thankful to have a place to work again. Earlier that summer, the barn had been burned to the ground through an act of arson. Charlie had felt disheartened over losing the old barn, but had her faith restored when half the town showed up for an old-fashioned barn raising and had the new barn constructed in a few weeks. One of the great things about a small town.

Normally, the fresh smell of cedar and the new clean surfaces made Cash happy as he worked. But this morning his mind was filled with other things. Things like a pretty brunette and the two asshats who had terrorized her the night before.

He was torn between thinking about protecting her and thinking about killing them. On one hand, all he wanted to do was take her under his wing, shelter her from the Purvis brothers' storm. But his other hand was balled into a fist, and it itched to slam into the faces of Earl and Junior.

Somebody needed to teach those guys a lesson. He'd called the sheriff the night before but didn't feel like that was enough. Not that Taylor couldn't handle it, but he felt so helpless not being able to do anything himself.

Anything besides watch over her and keep it from happening again. His back cramped from sleeping in the chair next to her last night. But he would do it again in a minute.

What was it about this woman that made him so crazy? He thought his heart would stop the night before when he'd found her curled in the corner of her bedroom, her eyes wide with terror. She'd reminded him of a frightened rabbit, holding perfectly still, hoping the predator wouldn't see it.

Pulling her into his arms had seemed so natural, and she fit perfectly against him. He didn't want to let her go. All he wanted was to keep her safe.

Well, that wasn't *all* he wanted.

He hadn't been thinking of her safety this morning when he'd awoke in the chair at the foot of her bed.

She'd looked so sexy lying there, her long hair tousled and spread out on the pillow around her. Her brown eyes were sleepy and unguarded, and he saw the shades of desire in them.

He knew how a woman looked when she wanted him, and Emma's gaze was filled with that look. And everything in him wanted to pull back the blankets and slip into bed next to her. Wanted to take her in his arms and slide her body beneath his. Wanted to lay his lips against her slender neck and inhale her sweet scent.

Hell, he wanted to do more than lay his lips on her neck. He wanted to explore her whole damn body—with his lips, his fingers, his hands. He wanted to learn the things she liked, the things that made her sigh and moan, and the things that took her breath away.

And he probably could have. Could have climbed into bed with her and taken her. But he didn't want to do that with her—didn't want to *take* her. He had a feeling she'd had enough of that in her life.

She needed someone gentle and sweet and loving—all characteristics that he saw in himself as sorely lacking.

But maybe it would be different with Emma, maybe *he* could be different. Maybe she could be the one to lift the darkness that lurked inside of him.

When he first woke up and saw her smiling at him, something inside him tumbled, and he was afraid it might have been his heart.

He smiled back, not yet awake and in his right mind. Instead, he was in those early morning moments—when all was right in the world and everything seemed possible, even a relationship with a beautiful woman—when his body, and his heart, reacted out of instinct. The smile took over his face before he could stop it, and he knew the slow burn of want filled his gaze.

She'd sat up in bed, and the sheets had fallen to reveal her in the sleeveless white nightgown. At first she'd seemed a vision to him, an angel in chaste white eyelet, then his gaze had fallen on her slender bare arms and the evidence of Leroy's abuse.

Seeing the scars from past injuries had fury building in Cash's gut, and he wanted to tear the man limb from limb. Him and his brothers.

And that fury, that blind anger inside of him, is how he knew that he wouldn't be sliding into bed next to Emma, wouldn't be kissing her or holding her, not this morning or *any* morning.

That same anger filled him now, mixed with a feeling of helplessness, wanting to fix Emma's problems, desperately wanting to be her hero, but knowing that was a role he would never fill.

Trying to get his focus back on the hinge, he stabbed at the top bolt and twisted hard with the screwdriver. The head had been stripped, and the screwdriver slipped across the hinge, scraping across his hand and leaving a long scratch.

"Shit." He flung the screwdriver across the room and grabbed the back of his hand, pressing down on the scratch — the damn thing hurt like a bitch.

"Holy heck. What did that screwdriver ever do to you?" Emma stood in the doorway of the barn. The offensive tool lay at her feet, and Cash was thankful she hadn't been in range when he'd thrown the thing.

She leaned down to pick up the screwdriver and carried it back to him.

He held out his cut hand to take it, responding with a scowl on his face. "Nothing. Sorry."

She reached for his hand. "Oh no. You're hurt. Are you all right?"

He pulled his hand back, hating how good it felt to have her hold it. "It's nothing. I'm fine."

"You're not fine. You're bleeding." She stepped into the small bathroom next to the workbench, and he heard the water hit the sink as she turned on the faucet. Emerging a few seconds later with a wet towel, she crossed back to him, picked up his hand, and pressed the cloth against the cut.

He grudgingly let her wash his hand, trying not to admit to himself how much he enjoyed the gentle caress of her hand. Trying to keep his eyes — and his mind — on his hand, his body still responded to the nearness of her. His breath quickened, and suddenly the barn seemed warmer than it had a minute before.

"You should probably put a Band-Aid on that. And maybe some antibiotic ointment, so it doesn't get infected.

Do you want me to go back to the house and try to find you some?"

"No, thanks. I'll take care of it when I come in for lunch. It's not that bad." He liked the way her eyes were filled with concern for him. It wasn't even that bad of a cut. He'd had a lot worse. But he didn't seem to mind the way she worried over it. Worried over him.

She was so nice. Dang—she really did remind him of an angel—the way her hands fluttered around his, the sweet curve of her cheek, the perfect pout of her pink lips.

She might seem angelic, but the sinful thoughts he was suddenly having about her mouth surely made him the devil.

He looked around the barn—anywhere but at her lips—searching for a distraction—anything to get his mind off her. "Did you want to see the baby lambs?"

She nodded. "Oh, yes. That's why I came out here. I thought I should spend a little time with them if I'm going to be responsible for naming them."

"They're pretty cute little buggers." He led her over to the corral. The ewe stood against the front fence wall munching on some hay, and the lambs stuck close to her side.

"Oh my gosh, they're so sweet," Emma said. "Can I pet one?"

"Sure." He leaned over the fence, picked one up, and cradled it in his arms. "They're both males."

She stepped closer, leaning against him as she stroked the fuzzy head of the lamb. "He's so cute and fuzzy. I love him."

The smell of her freshly washed hair wafted around him, and darts of heat shot through him as he imagined running his hands through the thick strands. "Got any ideas for a name?" He was getting plenty of ideas, but none of them had to do with naming the baby lamb.

"I'm working on it. They're both so little, and I know what it means to feel small and scared, so I want to give them names of strength, names that just stand for being tough. I don't want to rush this. It seems like an important decision."

Yes. It did. Not the naming of the lambs—he could care less what she named them. But spending time with her, filling his mind with thoughts of her, wanting to fill his hands with her—that seemed important, and not a decision to take lightly.

Actually, not a decision he should be making at all.

His resolve was much stronger when she wasn't standing next to him, the side of her hip touching his as she bent over the stall to cuddle the lamb. "You start your new job tomorrow. You excited?"

"Yes and no. I mean I'm excited about the job. But I'm nervous."

"What are you nervous about? I thought you said you'd already been waitressing in Great Falls."

"Yeah, but that was with strangers, people I didn't know. This is back in my hometown, where everybody knows me. And Leroy."

He nodded. "One of the perks of living in a small town. Everybody knows your business."

"Or at least they think they do. Nobody really knows what your life is like until they've walked a mile in your shoes." She turned away, absently running a finger across a fresh scar on her arm as she mumbled, "Walked a mile in your shoes or had your arm sliced open by your drunken husband and a broken beer bottle."

"But you got away," he said, trying to keep his fury in check as he watched her touch a scar on her arm. "You're not walking in those shoes or living that life anymore. That took guts, Emma. I admire you. Starting over is hard. It takes a lot of courage and bravery to do what you're doing."

"You're right. Starting over is hard." She stroked the top of the lamb's furry head, focusing on the fluffy down instead of looking at him. "But you're wrong about me. I'm not brave at all. I'm scared of everything."

"You are—" He started to speak then stopped and let out a sigh. "Okay, I hear you. I won't try to convince you that you are something you don't believe. Maybe you don't feel brave, and I get that you're scared. But when you feel like that—when you feel frightened or nervous—try to *imagine* what you would feel like if you weren't scared. Imagine what it would feel like to *be* brave and then just pretend that you are."

She looked up at him, searching his eyes as if she were trying to determine if he was serious or teasing her. "Pretend that I'm brave?" she whispered, and the doubt in her voice almost tore his heart in two.

He nodded, trying to convey his sincerity. "Just act like it and eventually you'll find that you really do feel it. You can do it. Hell, half the people you know are pretending to be something they're not. We've all fabricated feelings or actions that weren't really true. Like when you're having a crappy day and someone asks you if you're okay—and you're absolutely not—you still smile and say you're fine. Or when you're at church on Sunday, and one of the old ladies asks you if you're enjoying the pie she made as it's souring your tongue with its dry crust and awful flavor, but you swallow and smile and say it's delicious."

She grinned up at him, and he felt like he'd hung the moon. "So, all I have to do is eat the terrible pie and smile and say I'm fine. And act like I'm brave."

"That's it. Easy, huh?" He set the lamb down in the corral and turned back to her.

She looked up at him, her face inches from his, her eyes full of uncertainty, as if questioning his sincerity. Her breath was warm and tickled his throat when she spoke. "Do you ever pretend? Or try to be brave when you're not?"

He pretended all the time. He was pretending right now.

Acting like he only wanted to be her friend when he really wanted to kiss her, to touch her, to lay her down in the hay and slowly peel off her clothes. He tried not to look at her lips, tried not to think about her luscious mouth. Tried not to think about pulling her into his arms and kissing her until they were gasping and out of breath and she was clinging to him in desire.

As if drawn by an imaginary magnet, he tipped his head, his lips a whisper away from hers. His breath caught in his throat, and his body yearned to press against hers. Her gaze stayed fixed on his as her lips parted in anticipation.

He wanted to crush her mouth, to taste and devour her, but he couldn't. Just as natural instinct told him how to approach a skittish horse, he knew he'd need to be soft and gentle with Emma. He could do that.

Screw all that business of not getting involved with her. He wanted her. Wanted to kiss her so badly he could taste it. Wanted to kiss her beyond all reason, beyond good sense.

Closer. His head screaming at him to stop, but his heart and his body ignoring it, crying out with their own desires of want and need. He'd been thinking about her and now here she was—warm and in the flesh and so close to being in his arms.

His hands itched to slide up her arms, to caress her skin, to plunge into her hair. He ached to pull her to him, to slide her body under his, to touch and explore.

Closer still. So slow. So sweet. His lips barely brushing hers in the faintest of whispers. Her breath sucking in at the barest degree of touch. Her lips trembling.

Be brave, Emma. I won't hurt you.

He froze. His lips scarcely touching hers. Because he would. He would hurt her. Eventually. He always did. The darkness inside of him always won out, and he eventually ended up hurting them all. Not physically, but by his stubborn refusal to commit to a relationship, to not settle down with or give anyone a chance to really be with him. He hurt them by walking away, not giving anything of himself—anything real.

But he didn't want to hurt her. Couldn't bear to think of causing her any more pain. She'd had enough. Been through enough. The last thing she needed was him.

"Hey, Cash. You out here?" A deep male voice called into the barn.

Cash pulled away, and Emma shrank back, her cheeks tinging with pink as she ducked her head and looked away from him.

He touched her arm, a light press of reassurance, before stepping back and waving to the man standing in the doorway. "Hey, Taylor. Come on over. We're checking on the new lambs.

"You still on duty?" Cash asked, gesturing to Taylor's uniform and gold star as he ambled into the barn.

"Yeah, I wanted to stop by on my way home and make sure Emma's doing okay."

Cash introduced him as he approached the corral. "Sheriff Taylor Johnson, you remember Emma Purvis?"

She smiled up at Taylor. "It's nice to see you again. And I'm back to being Emma Frank now. I'd rather not be associated with my ex anymore."

"Smart choice," Taylor said as he leaned against the worktable, crossing his long legs at the ankles. "Unfortunately, it's your ex that's brought me out here this morning. I heard his brothers have been giving you a little trouble."

"I called him and told him what happened last night," Cash said.

"I've just been out to their place to have a little chat with them, and they claim they weren't anywhere near your dad's place last night. Said they were at home watching TV and drinking beer. Right now, they're each other's alibi and, without some kind of evidence, it's gonna be hard to prove they were out there."

"But I saw them," Cash said. "They almost ran me off the road with that piece of shit blue car Earl drives. Doesn't that count as evidence?"

"It's your word against theirs. And did you actually see one of them or just see their car?"

"They were driving too fast to see much of anything, but I know it was Earl's car."

Taylor shrugged. "Well, I did what I could. I gave 'em a warning and told them to steer clear of you, Emma. They seem to think they still have a relationship with you. So the next time you see them, you need to flat out tell them to leave you alone. That you don't want them around anymore and to stay away from you."

She nodded. "Okay, I'll try."

"That will help. Then at least I can use that if they bother you again. But for now, I warned them to keep away from you. That's about all I can do."

Cash ground his teeth, tightening his hands into fists. "You're kidding me. That's all you can do? Give them a warning? So, they just get away with terrorizing her?"

"I know you're upset. But unless they actually physically touch her or threaten her, there's not much else I can do."

"Well, they're not gonna get close enough to her to touch or threaten her. I'm not letting them anywhere near her. They try to mess with her and they're gonna end up messing with me."

"Simmer down. I know this is upsetting. But we know about the problem now, and we're keeping an eye on them."

"That's not good enough."

Taylor shook his head. "I'm sorry. My hands are tied."

"Thank you," Emma said, finally speaking up. "I appreciate that you tried. I've been dealing with my idiotic brothers-in-law for years now. I can handle it."

"But you shouldn't have to," Cash said.

She sighed. "It's just my life."

The resignation in her voice tore him up. He hated that she felt like she had to live with this. And he hated that he felt so helpless. If Taylor wasn't going to do anything about them, he'd take care of them himself.

"I know what you're thinking, Cash," Taylor said. "We've been friends since we were kids, and I recognize that look in your eyes. It's not gonna help anything for you to go out there and do something stupid."

"I don't know what you mean."

"Don't bullshit me, buddy. If you go out to their place and try to talk to them, or worse, they'll just say you were trespassing, and knowing those yahoos, they'd take a shot at you. Just let it lie for now."

His mouth formed a tight thin line as he pressed his lips together.

"I mean it. It will only cause more trouble if you go out there and threaten them. Tell me you won't go out to their place."

He shrugged. "Fine, I won't go out to their place."

But that didn't mean he couldn't give them a piece of his mind if he just *happened* to run into them in town.

Chapter Six

The next day, Emma was up with the sun, nervous about her first day. She'd spent the night at Tucked Away again and woke to find the little gray kitten, Percy, curled against her side and the smell of coffee in the air.

And filled with a feeling of hope. She'd held on to that hope, showering and dressing in the pink waitress dress that Cherry had dropped off the night before.

They had all been together again last night—Cash, Zack, Sophie, Charlie, and her—sitting around the table enjoying the evening meal. She'd filled her stomach with spaghetti and garlic bread and had loved listening to the farm talk and the easy banter among the friends. She interjected a little, but was really content to listen and just be part of their world.

Cherry had dropped by around seven, just as Zack and Sophie were leaving for the night. Cash had left earlier to complete the night's chores, and she and Charlie had just finished cleaning the kitchen.

Sophie had taken one look at the dress and declared that she had the perfect necklace for it. She'd told Emma she'd bring it with her in the morning and that she just *had* to wear it. Emma had chuckled at the teenager's enthusiasm and promised she would wear whatever Sophie brought her.

After they'd left, Charlie had poured the three women each a glass of wine, and they had sat around talking for another hour. It had been so long since Emma had visited with friends, she wanted to weep at the sheer loveliness of the scene.

It had been a good night, and Emma had gone to bed with a full belly, a head buzzing with wine, and a feeling of being safe for the first time in a long time. She'd drifted off to sleep thinking about the moment in the barn when Cash had almost kissed her. The way his lips had barely brushed hers, filling her with hunger and a need for more.

It was a terrible idea, getting involved with him, getting involved with anyone, really. She knew that. She needed to focus on herself and get her own life back on track. The last thing she needed was to get entangled in a fling with a bad-boy cowboy.

Because that's what it would be to him. A fling. A momentary distraction. She knew his reputation. He didn't *do* relationships.

So she'd told herself she wouldn't get involved. But she could still enjoy thinking about him. Thinking about kissing him and dreaming of being held in his arms. Thinking about him wouldn't hurt anything.

The only problem was that she was spending way too much time thinking about him. Thinking about what it would be like to be with him, in his arms, or better yet, in his bed.

Pushing him out of her mind, she focused on finishing getting ready. She slipped her feet into the pair of white tennis shoes she'd worn for her last waitressing job. She would probably need new ones, but would have to wait until she got an actual paycheck before she considered a new pair of shoes.

She took a look at herself in the full-length mirror hanging on the back of the bedroom door. Not having Cherry's curves, the dress hung loosely on her, but the color was good and accented her skin tone.

Sophie had dropped by with a necklace for her on the way to school. It was a short strand of multicolored glass beads. The bubbled beads varied in shades of purple, teal, and pink, and the teenager had been right that it went perfectly with the waitress uniform.

Emma smiled as she touched the fun piece of jewelry. She didn't care what the necklace looked like—she would have worn a circle of macaroni around her neck if Sophie had brought her one. She loved the teenager's enthusiasm and that Sophie cared enough about her to pick something out and bring it by so she would feel pretty on her first day.

In that respect, she'd taken a little extra time getting ready this morning, pulling her hair up into a high ponytail and brushing on a little eyeshadow and a trace of mascara. She hadn't worn eye makeup in a long time, but had thrown some in when she and Charlie had stopped by the house to get her a few more things the day before.

Leroy had hated it when she'd worn any makeup, said it made her look like a slut, and it wasn't worth spending the money on stuff that you just washed off every night.

Yeah, much better to spend their money on beer that he drank and pissed away every night. Anger and resentment filled her as she thought about Leroy, and that was the last thing she needed as she started her new job. Instead, she took a deep breath, calming her nerves, and told herself she could do this.

Twenty minutes later, she parked her car in the alley behind the diner, not wanting to take up a spot in front of the café, and approached the glass door of Cherry's Diner.

The breakfast rush hadn't started yet, but she could see a

few customers already at the tables and the counter.

Her heart pounded against her chest, and she could feel her hands beginning to shake. Squeezing her fingers into fists, she remembered Cash's words from the day before.

Imagine what it would feel like to be brave and then just pretend that you are.

If she really were brave, she wouldn't care what the town of Broken Falls thought about her, she would only be concerned with doing a good job for Cherry and helping her business to do well. If she really were brave, she would plaster on a smile and walk into the diner like she knew what she was doing and had every right to be there.

Imagine you are brave then pretend that you are.

She took a deep breath, put a smile on her face, and opened the front door.

Five hours later, she'd forgotten all about her fears, too caught up in the job and taking care of customers to be concerned with being brave or fearless.

When she'd first gotten there, Cherry had spent twenty minutes filling her in on where to find everything, how the cash register worked, and how to prepare orders for Stan.

Then the morning crowd had filled in, and she'd been off and running. She knew how to keep coffee and soda cups full and had enough waitressing experience to keep the orders straight and the customers happy.

Cherry had left mid-morning to take care of Sam. She had another waitress, a teenage girl named Sara who'd graduated the year before, who came in as she was leaving, so Emma never felt like she had to take care of the restaurant all on her own.

Her feet were killing her, but she was actually having fun. And she'd collected a nice pocketful of tip money already. A few people had mentioned her ex, and a few had asked invasive questions trying to get at the juicy gossip of her and

Leroy's split, but most had been kind and simply welcomed her back to town.

She felt good as she raced around the counter and passed another order to Stan. He had been a great help that morning, showing her around the kitchen and teaching her the order lingo he preferred. He made her laugh, and his kind and gentle nature had her feeling completely at ease around him.

She glanced around the diner, noting that the lunch rush was finally tapering off, as she topped off a cup of coffee for a customer at the counter. She looked up as the front door of the diner opened, a smile ready on her face to welcome the new customers.

Her heart leaped to her throat as she recognized the tall, dark-haired cowboy who walked in and flashed her a panty-melting grin. He ambled up to the counter, greeting a few townsfolk as he passed them, but his smile was just for her as he straddled a stool in front of her. "Hey darlin', you look awful pretty today."

Her cheeks warmed at the compliment. Had he noticed the light makeup or that she'd taken the extra time with her hair? Or did he say that to all the girls? After working all morning, she likely looked a mess. Most of the mascara had probably faded, and she reached to tuck the loose strands of hair back into her ponytail. "Thanks," she mumbled.

He grinned, apparently unfazed by her messy hairdo. "How's your first day going?"

Her mouth was dry, and she swallowed, trying to think of something clever to say. "Good," she croaked, which wasn't clever in the least. She cleared her throat. "Really good. It's going really well. I'm having fun."

"Glad to hear it."

She held up the pot she was still holding. "You want some coffee?"

"Nah, but I wouldn't mind a glass of iced tea, when you've

got the time. Charlie needed something in town, so we thought we'd come in for lunch, see how your first day was going. She had to grab something at the drugstore, then she'll be over."

"Wow. That was really nice. You guys didn't have to do that."

"I know. But we wanted to."

Why did every word out of his mouth sound sexy and sinful? He could have been talking about the weather, and the drawl of his voice would still send shivers of heat up her spine.

"I'll get you that iced tea." Her hands shook as she scooped ice into a red tumbler and filled it with tea. She'd been doing so well, but this man made her all kinds of nervous. It didn't help that his chin was covered in a sexy smudge of dark whiskers and his aftershave smelled amazing.

She couldn't believe he and Charlie had taken the time to come into town just to support her on her first day at work. Who did that?

Friends. Friends did that.

And Charlie was really beginning to feel like a friend. So was Cash. She reminded herself of the way he'd introduced her a few days before as his friend. But friends didn't kiss each other.

Although she and Cash hadn't really kissed, either. They almost had, but almost didn't count.

Just thinking about the "almost kiss" had her cheeks warming again, and she was glad to see Charlie walking into the diner as she set the glass of tea in front of him.

Emma smiled warmly at the other woman as she approached the counter and slid onto the stool next to Cash. "Hey, Charlie."

"Hey, yourself. How's it going?"

"Good."

"*Really* good," he said, giving her a wink as he teased her.

Oh boy. Tingles of nerves fluttered in her stomach.

"I'll take a glass of that when you get a chance," Charlie said, pointing to Cash's tea. She waved through the window to the cook. "Hey Stan, can you make me a cheeseburger and fries, with the works? I've been writing all morning, and I'm starving."

"Make it two," Cash said.

Emma filled another glass with tea, and the three of them made small talk for a few more minutes, then Stan hollered as he set two heaping pink plates of food onto the window. "Order up."

Charlie waved her hand. "Go take care of your customers. Don't mind us. We're just here for the support and for Stan's delicious fries."

"Right on, baby," Stan called from the kitchen. "My fries do rock."

"We'll grab a table and get out of your way." Cash picked up their glasses, and they moved to a booth against the wall.

Emma took care of the remaining customers, bustling around, bringing Charlie and Cash their burgers, and keeping the tables cleared. She and Sara split the bulk of the work, the teenager easygoing and friendly and patient with Emma's questions and mistakes.

So far, this job was going great. She was getting more comfortable, had nice coworkers, and she felt good about the work she was doing. She only hoped it would last.

• • •

Cash finished the last bite of his burger and pushed his plate away. "Damn, that was good."

"The burger or the woman you've been watching the last half an hour?" Charlie asked.

"What are you talking about?"

"Oh, come on. I've been watching you, and you haven't taken your eyes off Emma the whole time we've been sitting here. You like her."

Charlie had only come into his life a few months ago, but they'd had an instant rapport and always got along well. And they spent a lot of time together working the farm and living in the same place. He didn't let a lot of people in, but he cared about Charlie, and she already knew him better than most people did.

Which was why there was no use trying to hide his obvious feelings for Emma from her. She'd just wheedle the truth out of him anyway. "Of course I like her. She's sweet."

Charlie cocked an eyebrow at him and waited for him to go on.

"All right. I like her, okay. I have this strange urge to take care of her. Protect her."

"That's because you're not as tough as you act. Zack told me that you've always been one to take in the wounded and hurt animals."

He sighed. "I know. And maybe that's all this is. Maybe I just feel bad for her."

Charlie laughed. "If you just felt bad for her, you wouldn't have been watching her the past hour like you wanted to lap her up. And you wouldn't have been checking out her butt every time she walked by."

He grinned. "Yeah, probably not. She is a pretty little thing. She reminds me of a skittish mare—all full of spirit and grace, but timid and scared when you try to approach her."

"I can see that. She does seem to frighten easily. I find myself being careful with her, too."

"But I don't just want to take care of her. She gets under my skin, like an itch I can't quite scratch, and I can't stop thinking about her."

"You've got it bad, mister."

He sighed. "Yeah, probably. But it doesn't matter."

"Why not?"

"Because she's barely divorced from a violent man who brutalized and degraded her for years."

"And?"

"So she doesn't need the likes of me in her life. You know I'm terrible at relationships. I run from commitment like it's a house on fire and end up hurting every woman who's tried to get me to settle down. I'm not about to do that to Emma."

He didn't talk about the dark past that haunted his relationships or say that Emma didn't need another man who had violence in his blood.

"Maybe she *is* different," Charlie said. "Maybe she's the one who could break your streak of terrible relationships. You don't have to hurt her."

"No, but I will. I always do. And she deserves better. She's a sweet person with a big heart. She needs a nice guy. Someone who will treat her well and make her feel like a princess."

"You're nice. Why can't that be you?"

He narrowed his eyes at her.

"What? You *are* nice. When you want to be. I've seen you let down your guard with Sophie and do incredibly sweet things for her. And you're totally patient and kind to every animal on our farm. Except for Clyde. But that old goat takes the patience of a saint."

"That's true. But she needs more than just a guy who's good with animals and nice to his goddaughter." He glanced over, watching as Stan explained something on the cash register to Emma. She seemed relaxed as she smiled at the cook.

A spark of jealousy lit in his gut as Stan wrapped an arm around Emma's shoulder. He tamped it down as an idea came to him. "She needs a good guy. Someone who doesn't have a mean bone in his body. Someone like Stan."

"Stan?"

"Yeah, Stan. The guy's good-looking and always freaking happy. He's the most easygoing person I know. I've never seen him get mad or even raise his voice. He would be great for Emma, just what she needs."

"Hmm." Before Charlie could say anything more, Stan approached the table, four plates of pie in his hands, and Emma on his heels.

Stan set the pie on the table and slid into the seat next to Cash. "Hey, dude. We decided we needed a break after working so hard, and thought we could all use some pie. We brought a piece of each." He gestured to the plates, a different flavor on each one.

"We've got apple, pecan, chocolate silk, and lemon meringue." Emma named the flavors as she set a full pot of coffee and four cups on the table and squeezed into the booth next to Charlie.

Cash offered her a charming grin. "I've never been known to turn down a piece of pie. Especially when the pie looks this good."

A smile tugged at the corner of Emma's lips, but she looked at her hands as she filled their cups with coffee.

Charlie rolled her eyes at his flirty comment but didn't say anything about it as she pulled a plate toward her. "I'll take the apple."

"What do you want, Emma?" he asked and got a charge out of the way a pink tinge covered her cheeks.

She shrugged. "I'm not picky. I'll take whatever no one else wants."

Of course she would.

He reached out an arm to block Stan as he reached for a plate. He looked Emma in the eye. "No, you've been working hard. You deserve to have the kind you like the best. Take what you want, Emma."

She stared back at him, as if gaining courage from his gaze, then nodded in agreement. "Okay, I'll take the pecan. It's always been my favorite."

His head tilted, and he offered her a smile of encouragement. "Then it's yours." He pulled his arm away and let Stan take the chocolate silk.

Cash picked up his fork and stabbed at the flaky crust of the remaining piece of lemon meringue pie. "Cherry does make the best pie."

"I couldn't make a pie if someone offered me a million dollars," Charlie said.

Emma laughed. "Me either."

"I'm a terrible baker. Sophie's been trying to teach me how all summer."

"I do all right with cakes and cookies, but I've never been able to get the hang of pies."

"It's never too late to learn something new."

"No, you're right," Emma said. "I've already learned a ton of new things today. Like how to make a cherry soda and how to run the cash register."

"Well, you're *working* on learning how to run the register," Stan teased. "I wouldn't say you've mastered that one yet."

She laughed. "True. You'll probably have to teach me that control-Y key thing another hundred times."

Cash watched the easy way she joked with Stan. The easygoing guy would be a good match for Emma. He could teach her to make a pie while they listened to reggae music and made tie-dye T-shirts.

The thought of Emma with another guy had acid churning in his gut, but it didn't matter. What mattered was what was good for Emma. And he knew that he wouldn't be.

But Stan could be.

He pressed the tines of his fork against the remaining crumbs on his plate as he thought about how to get Emma and the cook together.

Fortunately, he didn't have to.

Charlie did it for him. "Listen, Emma, it's Friday, which means I don't cook, and Zack takes us all out for pizza. You should come with us."

Emma glanced at him, and it was almost like he could hear her telling herself to be brave, to try new things. "Um, yeah, sure. I'll come along."

Good for her.

Charlie pointed her fork. "You guys in for pizza tonight? Zack's buying."

Stan nodded. "Heck, yeah. I'm always up for a free meal. The usual? Six-thirty at The Pizza Shack?"

"Yep. Cherry and Taylor are meeting us there and bringing Sam." She raised an eyebrow at him. "Cash? You in for the usual? Pizza at six-thirty?"

This was as good a chance as any. A way to get Emma and Stan together. And without him around, she'd be more likely to spend time with the only other single guy in the group. "Nah, I can't make it tonight. I've got other plans."

He hated the pained look of disappointment that passed across Emma's face. But she'd only know more disappointment if she let herself get involved with him. Stan was a much better choice.

Charlie stared at him with skepticism. "What other plans? We all do pizza together every Friday night at The Shack. Those *are* your plans."

He shrugged. "Not tonight."

"Well, I'll be there," Stan said. "But now I've gotta get back to work. See you tonight." He slid out of the booth and headed back to the kitchen.

"Yeah, me too," Emma said. "But I'm excited for pizza later."

"It'll be fun," Charlie said.

"I'll bring you your check." Emma stood and brushed down the skirt of her dress then smiled proudly at them. "But the pie is on Stan and me. Our treat."

Cash couldn't help but smile back, she was so pleased with being able to treat them. But he didn't care for the way she said "Stan and me."

What the hell was wrong with him? One minute he's pushing her toward the guy, the next he's jealous that she would use his name in connection with hers. *Get a grip, man.*

He shook his head at Emma. "You don't need to do that."

"I know. But I want to. It's the least I can do. For the way you both have helped me and all."

"It's no trouble."

"Then quit arguing with me, and let me buy the dang pie." She grinned as she teased him, then turned to follow Stan into the kitchen.

Charlie chuckled. "She has a point. It's just pie."

"I know," he grumbled. "But it's her first day. And I don't think she has a lot of money. She doesn't need to be spending it on buying us dessert."

"If you're so concerned about her, maybe you should come to pizza tonight." Charlie cocked an eyebrow at him. "Oh wait, I forgot, you've got those big 'plans' for tonight. What were those plans again?"

"You know I *do* have a life. I could have plans."

She narrowed her eyes at him. "I think your 'other plans' are bullshit. I think the only thing you're planning is how to get Emma and Stan together."

Busted.

He shrugged. "So what if I am? It seems like she already likes him. From what I've seen, she doesn't warm up to people easily. But she's comfortable around him, and that says a lot."

"I think you're reading too much into it. It's easy to be comfortable around someone you consider a friend. It's being around the one you really like that can make you feel uncomfortable. Like all nervous and jittery and butterflies in your stomach kind of feelings, ya know?"

Oh, yes. He knew all about those kind of feelings.

"Kind of like the way she acts around you." Charlie waited a beat. "And the way you act around her." She laughed as he playfully nudged her foot under the table. "Just sayin.'"

Her laughter turned to an expression of alarm as her gaze flicked to the front door of the café.

He turned, and his hands balled into fists as he watched Earl and Junior Purvis saunter across the diner and drop onto the stools at the counter.

Chapter Seven

"What the hell are they doing here?" Cash asked, already scooting out of the booth.

Charlie put a warning hand on his arm. "Simmer down, cowboy. This is a public place. Maybe they're just here for a burger."

"Like hell they are."

"I know Taylor went out to see them yesterday and told them to steer clear of Emma. Maybe they don't even know she works here."

"Oh, they know." He spoke through gritted teeth as waves of anger rolled through him, but he heeded Charlie's advice and stayed at the table. For the moment.

"Well, I know that you going over there and picking a fight with them isn't going to help anything."

"It'll help me. Slamming my fist into Earl's smug little face will help me a lot."

Charlie lowered her voice. "It won't help Emma."

Shit. She had a point.

He eased back against the booth, still keeping his eye on

the two brothers as Sara, the teenage waitress, handed them menus and poured them each a cup of coffee.

He glanced at Charlie. "Are *you* all right? Have you seen Earl since—you know—that thing this summer?"

"That thing where he assaulted and tried to rape Sophie and me?"

"Yeah, that thing." Thinking about Earl Purvis laying a hand on either Charlie or his goddaughter only added fuel to the already furious fire that was burning inside him.

"No, this is the first time I've seen him. He really is a slimy guy. Look at his jeans. He's got a big grease stain on his leg."

Cash wasn't looking at his attire. He was watching the arrogant expression on his face as he slowly pushed the full coffee cup off the side of the counter. It crashed to the floor, coffee and broken china spraying across the linoleum.

Emma came hurrying through the doors from the kitchen, but stopped in her tracks as she saw Earl and Junior sitting at the counter. The lighthearted smile that had been on her face fell, replaced with an expression of fear.

"Wait." Charlie put a warning hand on his arm.

He shook it off as he slid from the booth and crossed the diner.

Like hell he would. Wait for what? For them to do something else to Emma?

Not on his watch.

"Hey there, sis. Sorry about the cup. It slipped," Earl was saying as Cash walked up behind him.

"Mine, too," Junior said as he pushed his cup off the other side of the counter then cackled in laughter.

Emma stood frozen in place, her eyes wide in fright, her mouth set in an expression of dread.

"You better pick that up, Emma. You don't want to get in trouble at your new job."

Emma pulled over a trash can then stooped to pick up

the broken glass.

Earl's mouth formed an evil grin as he tipped his glass over. Water and ice cubes spilled across the counter and splashed onto her shoulder and hands before hitting the floor where she worked.

"I think that you need to pick that up then apologize to the lady." Cash's voice was steely and hard, as he tried to suppress his rage and stay calm.

It wouldn't do anyone any good if he lost it and let the beast inside of him loose. Least of all Emma.

He'd lost control before, and it hadn't turned out well.

"Yeah, who's gonna make me?" Earl twisted on his stool, his cocky grin falling from his face as he looked up, way up, at Cash. Obviously ignoring Cash's stern expression, he turned back to Emma who was still picking up the pieces of china off the floor. "Who the hell is this guy? You got a new boyfriend already? You sure do move fast, sister."

"I'm not your sister," Emma said quietly as she picked up another chunk of the broken cup. Water dripped to the floor next to her from Earl's spilled glass.

"Leave it alone, Emma," Cash said. "Earl's going to pick that up himself."

"Like hell I am." Earl turned back to Cash, a vulgar sneer on his face. "Who do you think you are—telling her what to do anyway? You trying to be her new boyfriend? You boss her around in the sack too? You probably have to. She probably lies there like a dead fish—I bet she's a terrible lay."

He didn't stop to think, his body just reacted. Reacted to the insult to Emma, to the rage boiling inside of him. He grabbed Earl's arm and pulled it tight up behind him, dragging him from his seat and pushing him to his knees. "I told you to pick up the broken glass and apologize to the lady."

"Holy shit. You're hurting me, asshole." Earl pushed against his hand. He was a big guy, strong from working on the farm, but his strength was no match against the anger-fueled Cash.

"Hey, get your hands off my brother," Junior said, but stayed in his seat, his weak threat meaningless.

"Pick it up," he said through gritted teeth. He applied more pressure to Earl's arm.

The other man grunted in pain. "Fine. Whatever." He picked up the last two pieces of glass and tossed them in the trash can.

He let Earl stand up, but kept a firm grip on his arm. He squeezed it a little tighter. "Now, apologize."

Earl sneered at Emma, his tone holding an undisguised threat. "I'm sorry, sis. Just like you're gonna be when you don't have your new boyfriend around."

His fury boiled over, and he let go of Earl's arm, hauling back his fist to throw a punch into the other man's face.

A strong hand clamped down on his arm, and Taylor's voice spoke from behind him. "Calm down, friend. What seems to be the trouble here?"

Earl jerked a thumb at Cash. "This guy is assaulting me, that's what going on. Practically broke my arm."

"Really?" Taylor asked. "It doesn't look like he's even touching you. What'd you do to provoke him?"

Betrayal and embarrassment crossed Earl's face as he must have realized he wasn't going to get any sympathy from the sheriff. "I didn't do shit. I slipped and spilled my coffee, and the cup broke. It was an accident." He stared at Emma, a warning look in his eyes. "And accidents happen, don't they, Emma?"

What the hell? Was this guy really threatening Emma? Right in front of them?

Cash felt Charlie put a hand on his arm. He knew he couldn't punch the guy out right in front of the sheriff. Even if Taylor was his friend, he'd still have to uphold the law and take him in for assault. Although a day spent in jail might be worth it if he could get in one good punch and knock out a couple of Earl's tobacco-stained teeth.

"I thought I told you boys to steer clear of Emma. Didn't we just have that conversation yesterday?"

"We didn't even know she worked here. We just came in to get us some lunch. Is that a crime? You gonna arrest me for ordering a burger?"

"I think right now I'm just going to ask you to leave." Taylor's tone was firm.

"You can't do that. This is a public place. We haven't even ordered yet."

"We're out of burgers," Stan said. He'd come from the kitchen and stood next to Emma, a supportive hand on her arm.

"Then I'll order something else."

"We're out of that, too," Stan said. "We're out of whatever you order."

Earl's gaze flicked to Stan's hand on Emma's arm. "What the hell is this? You boning this guy too, sis?"

Cash felt a growl build in his throat as his hands balled into fists.

"Who I am or am not *boning* is none of your business," Emma said in a small tight voice. The room quieted in shock at her statement. In the fact that she said anything at all.

Stunned, he looked over at her in surprise, then nodded his encouragement.

Good for her. She needed to stand up to these jerks. *Keep going.*

She straightened her back, standing taller, as if she took strength from his encouragement. "And I told you I'm not your sister. I am no longer married to your brother, and I don't want anything more to do with your family. I don't want to see you again. I want you to stay away from me, and leave me the hell alone."

Speechless, Earl looked at her in slack-jawed surprise. "Who do you think you are? You can't talk to me like that. And you don't just get to throw our brother away, like he's a piece of trash."

"Yes, I do. Because that's how he's treated me for the past ten years."

"You heard the lady," Taylor said. "She said she wanted you to leave her alone."

Earl turned to the sheriff, an ugly sneer on his face. "I don't see a lady."

Holy crap. He couldn't believe it. This guy didn't know when to quit. He was like a wild animal trapped in a corner, baring his teeth and lashing out. A wild animal that needed a muzzle and a cage.

"It's time to go, Earl," Taylor said, taking a step back but resting his hand on his gun as he gave Earl and his brother space to leave.

"You going to make me, Sheriff?"

"If he doesn't, I will," Cherry said, stepping out of the kitchen. She must have come in the back door. "This is my place of business, and I have the right to refuse service to anyone in this establishment. And I'm refusing service to you *and* your brother. Now get the hell out of my restaurant. And don't come back."

He must have known he was beat, because Earl grudgingly got off the stool and nudged his brother. "Let's go, Junior. Suddenly I lost my appetite. And I heard the food in this place sucks anyway." He glared at Emma. "See ya around, sis."

Taylor followed the Purvis brothers out of the restaurant, which was a good thing, because if Taylor hadn't been there, he probably would've followed them out and beat them black and blue on the sidewalk.

Cherry turned to Emma. "I'm so sorry I wasn't here. Are

you okay?"

Cash could tell she was shaken. Actually, everyone could tell because her face was pale, her hands trembled, and she looked like she might faint. He took a step forward, planning to—he didn't know what—catch her if she fell, maybe. Or maybe sweep her up into his arms and carry her out of there.

He didn't have a chance to do either of those things, though. Instead, Stan stepped closer and put his arm around Emma's waist. It tore a hole in his gut to watch her lean her head onto his shoulder. It should be him—*his* arm wrapped around her and *his* shoulder she was leaning on.

Damn. He couldn't remember the last time he'd actually felt jealous. But he knew the feeling, and envy was rearing her ugly green head.

He stepped back, let Stan take the lead. This was the perfect opportunity for Emma to see what a great guy Stan is. Besides, this was what he wanted. *Right?*

Cherry spoke loudly to the few remaining customers in the diner. "Nothing to see here, folks. Everything's going to be fine."

He knew that it wouldn't take long for the rumors to start flying about the Purvis brothers being in town and causing a ruckus over Emma in the restaurant.

"I think your shift is about over. Why don't you get your purse, and we'll take you back to Tucked Away," Charlie said to Emma.

"You don't have to," she answered. "I've got my car."

"You're not in any shape to be driving. Just leave it here, and I'll bring you back into town later when we come back for pizza."

"Okay."

Cherry grabbed her purse from the back and handed it to Emma, who followed Cash and Charlie out of the diner. His truck was parked at the curb, and he opened the door and helped Emma into the cab. Charlie slid onto the bench seat after her, and he closed the door.

Climbing into the driver's seat, he buckled his seat belt and tried not to think about the way Emma's leg rested alongside his or the way her bare arm brushed his as they bumped along the road out of town.

She let out a heavy sigh and relaxed against his side, leaned her head slightly onto his shoulder.

"You okay, darlin'?" he asked, sneaking a quick glance at her.

She sat up and took a deep breath. "Yeah, I am. I'm really okay. I think I might even be pretty good. That's the first time I've ever stood up to those guys. I'm afraid I usually just kind of let them walk all over me, because I don't want to cause a scene or make a fuss."

He chuckled. "I'd say you made a pretty good fuss this afternoon."

She grinned. "I did, didn't I? And nothing terrible happened. In fact, I feel like something good actually happened. I certainly feel pretty good about myself, instead of the way I normally feel. Which is awful and that I acted like a coward."

He patted her leg. Damn it, he couldn't help himself. He just wanted to touch her, to reassure her. And surely a *friend* could tap another friend on the leg. "You should feel good. You did great. You said all the things that Taylor told you to tell them. I'd even venture so far as to say you acted *brave*. Just like you thought you could."

She smiled up at him. "I did act brave. I remembered what you told me all day today, but especially with Earl and Junior. I imagined that I was brave, then I acted like I was."

"And it worked," he said, smiling back. "I'm proud of you."

"I'm proud of me, too."

He could hear the pride in her voice, and he liked that he had a small hand in helping to put it there.

Tucked Away was only a few miles out of town, and he pulled the truck into the driveway and parked in front of the house.

Rounding the front of the truck, he opened the door and helped Charlie and Emma out. "I've got to see to a few chores this afternoon. But I'll check in with you all later."

Charlie tucked her arm under Emma's and gave him an encouraging nod before they headed up the porch steps. "Thanks. I've got this. But you let us know if your 'plans' fall through, and you can join us for that pizza."

"Yeah, I'll be sure to do that," he said to their retreating backs.

But he knew he wouldn't.

...

"Thanks again for the inviting me to have pizza with you all. It was really fun. And the pizza was delicious," Emma said as she and Charlie stopped on the sidewalk in front of the diner later that night.

It was close to nine, and the streets of the small town were deserted and quiet.

Cherry's family had left earlier to put Sam to bed, Stan had given Sophie and her friend a ride to the movie theater, and Zack had offered to pay the bill and bring the truck around while Charlie walked Emma back to her car.

"I'm glad you came with us. And I wanted to tell you that Sophie is sleeping at her friend's house tonight, so I was thinking of spending the night over at Zack's. If you're comfortable staying alone tonight—not that you're really alone—Cash is right across the yard."

She wasn't sure if the thought of him being so close made

her feel better or made her even more uncomfortable. "I can go home tonight. I don't want to wear out my welcome."

"Don't be silly. I want you to still stay at the farm. I'll feel better knowing you're there, especially after this afternoon. Besides, it would help me, because you could feed the kittens and keep an eye on them tonight, and I won't have to bother Cash."

"Yeah, since he had those *plans* and all." Emma hated the curl of envy that filled her stomach as she wondered if his plans involved another woman. "Okay, I'll stay. Helping out with the kittens is the least I can do. You've been so great to me."

Zack pulled up and rolled down the passenger window of the truck. "You sure you don't want to ride back with us, Emma? We could easily drop you at Tucked Away."

"I'm sure. I've got my car." She gestured to the alley behind the diner where she'd left her car that morning. "Thanks again for the pizza."

Charlie opened the door and climbed into the truck. "We'll watch you to make sure you get to your car okay."

There was no use arguing with them, so she nodded and started down the darkened alley. It was a small town, and there was no one around, but the dim shadows still felt a little creepy, and her heart rate sped up as she quickly walked to her car.

Pretend to be brave.

Reaching her car, she hurriedly fit the key into the lock then turned to wave good-bye. "Thanks. I'm good."

Zack gave the horn a little toot before pulling away. She unlocked the door as the noise of his engine faded.

An ominous chill raced down her spine as the slight sound of a whisper-click came from the dark alcove on the other side of her car.

A flicker of flame sparked in the gloom, illuminating Earl

Purvis's face as he lit a cigarette.

He drew a sharp inhale of tobacco then stepped out of the shadows. "You havin' yourself a pretty good night there, sister?"

Chapter Eight

Emma clutched the car door, her heart pounding hard against her chest as she fought the panic that was building there. "What are you doing here? I told you to stay away from me."

Earl ambled around the back of the car. "Yeah, I got to thinking about that, and it didn't sit very well with me. We're still family, Emma, and I feel like it's my duty to watch out for you while my brother is wasting away in a jail cell."

He didn't add that she was the one who put him there, but she knew he was thinking it. Correction—*he* put himself there. She had to keep reminding herself of that fact. But it wouldn't do any good to argue the point with Earl.

"I don't want or need you to watch out for me."

He sidled closer, now only a foot away, and close enough for her to smell the booze oozing from his every pore. "See now, I think that you do. It appears that you've taken up with the wrong sort of crowd. In particular, Cash Walker. That guy's bad news. He's got himself a reputation around town as a bit of a ladies' man, and I don't think that's the kind of guy I want sniffing around my sister-in-law."

An image of Cash's grin flicked through her mind, giving her courage, even as every part of her wanted to flee in fright.

She pulled open the door—her trembling hands slick with sweat—afraid she might drop the keys she still had clutched in her fingers.

All she wanted to do was slide into the driver's seat, but she was terrified to turn her back to him. She knew all too well the consequences of turning your back on a pissed-off man. "Who I've taken up with is not your concern. I told you to stay away from me."

"I am staying away from you." His voice was sticky sweet as he moved to the other side of the car door and held it open for her. "I'm not even touching you. I'm just making sure you get in your car all right. There ain't nothing wrong with that."

But there was something wrong with it. Something in the sinister look in his eye that told her he had something else up his sleeve.

Trying not to let him see her fear, she slowed her breathing as she turned with him, her back now against her seat. All she had to do was sit down and pull the door shut. And then snap the lock down.

It sounded easy, but she knew it wouldn't be. Earl was like a snake, crafty in his meanness, and she never knew when he would strike. All of the Purvis brothers knocked one another around, and she'd seen Earl's anger flare at the slightest provocation.

She needed to be quick, but careful not to set him off, cautious enough to keep the snake from striking.

The dark edges of the alley faded away as all of her senses focused on the danger surrounding her.

"I'll be fine now. Thank you." She slid into the seat and pulled the door toward her.

Almost there, inches away. So close.

Earl's hand grabbed the door, yanking it back and out of

her grasp. He leaned his face into the gap above the door, his tobacco and booze-scented breath wafting toward her with his menacing words. "You be careful driving home now, sister. I wouldn't want you to have an accident."

He slammed the door shut, and she jumped in her seat. Jamming the keys toward the ignition, she fumbled and dropped them to the floor. She could hear Earl laughing as he stood outside the window, but she didn't care.

All she cared about was starting the car and getting the hell out of this alley. She wiped her hand on the leg of her jeans, then groped the floor for her keys.

Finding them, she shuffled through for the car key, then shoved it into the ignition.

Please start.

She had a sudden new terror that Earl had somehow disabled her car, and he was just waiting for her to realize it. Waiting for her to get back out and that's when he would assault her. Or worse.

No. She couldn't go there. She'd heard stories about her brother-in-law, some of them from him, and she knew he could be brutal and violent toward women. She couldn't think about that. Instead she prayed.

And her prayers were answered. She almost wept with relief as the engine caught and started. She threw the car into gear and pressed on the gas. Gravel spit behind her as the tires spun then gained purchase and the car flew out of the alley.

Her knuckles were white as she gripped the wheel and tried not to cry.

I'm okay. I did it. I was brave, and I got away.

Taking a deep breath, she tried to slow her heart rate as she worked to convince herself she was okay. She snapped on her seat belt and hit the lock button on the door. Not that he would be running down the road after her, but locking the door somehow made her feel safer.

She made the turn out of town and onto the highway toward the farm as a strong sense of foreboding suddenly surrounded her.

If Earl didn't attack her, then why was he there? What did he want? She knew he wasn't really concerned about her welfare, but something had him waiting for her in that dark alley.

There had to be more going on here. They'd been in the pizza place for hours. Had Earl been waiting all that time for her? For what reason?

The speedometer was inching close to fifty-five, and she applied the brakes as she approached the curve in the road.

Except nothing happened.

Instead of the normal pressure of the brake pedal, her foot went straight to the floor. She pumped the brakes, but again, nothing happened.

Fighting the panic forming in her chest, she tried to stay calm and think. She downshifted into second gear, but that only slowed the car a little.

The curve came up fast, and she pulled on the wheel, twisting her whole body into managing the curve in the road. Her shoulders wrenched as the car fought her, skidding on the pavement.

Her gaze flicked over the highway, looking for a way to slow down. Anything to reduce the speed without causing the car to spin or roll.

She ordered herself to stay calm as everything in her fought to spin out of control. Thankfully there weren't any other cars on the highway.

A guardrail lined the side of the road up ahead, and she steered the car toward it.

She hit the gravel of the shoulder too quickly, and the car jolted as the passenger side collided with the railing. The seat belt bit into her shoulder as it locked, and the eerie scream of metal filled the air as her car slid along the steel barrier.

The railing wasn't long enough, and the car was still going too fast as it leaped forward when the barrier ended. She grabbed for the parking brake, pulling it back to slow the car.

She must have pulled too hard, because the car went into a skid, spinning in a circle and crossing the road.

Everything had been happening too fast, until this minute, when time slowed down, and she felt like the car was spinning in slow motion.

A motion that she had no control of.

Hitting the gravel of the other shoulder, she screamed as the car continued to skid. It hit thin air as it flew off the side of the road and slid into the ditch.

Emma's body slammed against the seat belt, and her teeth clacked together as her head shot forward and hit the steering wheel.

But at least the car had stopped. And no one had been hurt. No one but her.

Adrenaline was flowing through her as she frantically looked around at the damage. She couldn't tell the extent of her injuries, but she had a smear of blood on her arm, and the front half of the dashboard had crumpled forward, pinning her legs.

She was trapped. Reaching into her front pocket, she slid out her cell phone. Her list of contacts was pitifully small, but it didn't matter, there was only one person she wanted to call.

• • •

Cash paced the floor of the bunkhouse cabin, wishing Buckshot, the other ranch hand, were home in the cabin next door.

Nearing seventy, Buckshot had worked on Tucked Away for most of his adult life, and Cash had always suspected his heart belonged more to Gigi Tucker than to the land itself. He'd never married but was close to his sister's family and was spending the month visiting them in Colorado.

He could sure use Buck right about now. Sharing a beer or a game of checkers would take his mind off a certain brunette whose shy smile had his palms sweating like a high school kid with a crush.

He peered out the front window at the still-empty driveway in front of the house. Why weren't they back yet?

His gaze flicked to the clock above the mantel. It was after nine.

How the hell long did it take to eat some pizza?

His big "other plans" for the evening included fixing the fence gate and eating a bologna sandwich while he barely watched an old crime series on television.

Some plans.

He'd been listening for Charlie's and Emma's cars to pull into the driveway, figuring he might amble over and see how things went. Or not.

Yeah, probably not. Best to let sleeping dogs lie and not stir up anything more with Emma. If things had gone well with Stan tonight, she didn't need him around messing up her good thoughts of him.

But now he was starting to worry.

He was just being stupid. Acting like an old mother hen.

They could have decided to go see a show, or maybe they went back to Zack's or out to the lake. They sure didn't have to check in with him. He was nobody's father. And he didn't want to be.

His cell phone rang, and he practically dove for it where it sat on the coffee table. Expecting it to be Charlie, he was surprised to see Emma's name come up on the screen—he'd programmed it in after she'd called him the last time.

But why would she be calling him now?

He had a bad feeling something was wrong as he tapped the phone and held it up to his ear. "Emma?"

"Cash? I need help." Her voice was soft and weak, breathless as she spoke. "I've been in an accident."

He was already out the front door and running for his truck. "I'm on my way. Where are you?"

"In the ditch. I was heading back to Tucked Away. I spun out and went off the other side of the highway, right after the big curve, but before the Haring farm."

"Okay, I'll be there in two minutes. Are you all right?"

"Um, I'm not sure. My legs are pinned under the dash, and I hit my head, and there's some blood."

Oh Lord, please let her be all right.

His foot pressed the gas pedal as he pushed his truck to eighty miles an hour. He slowed as he passed the Haring farm, scanning the ditch for signs of her car.

There. He spotted the red glow of her taillights as they stuck out of the ditch.

The car was face down, practically standing on end. "I see you, Emma. I'm gonna hang up, but I'll be right there. Just hang on, darlin'."

He screeched to a stop, opening the door and racing toward the car. His boots skidded in the soft dirt as he slid down the embankment next to the car. "I'm here, Em. Hold on."

Reaching up, he awkwardly pulled the handle, releasing the door, and jumping out of the way as it fell open toward him. The window had broken, and chunks of glass scattered across the ground.

Emma was leaning forward, held in place by her seat belt. She turned her head and let out a cry of relief as she reached out her hand. "I'm so glad you're here."

"I'm gonna get you out of there." He took her hand, squeezed it in his, then leaned into the car, trying to assess the damage. Tipping her head toward him, he could see a small cut above her eye, but it didn't look too serious. At least he hoped not. She also had blood smeared on her arm and across her lap. "Where are you hurt?"

"I hit my head and scraped my arm, but otherwise I think I'm okay."

"Can you move your legs? What if you've got a back injury? I don't want to risk hurting you more. I think we should call an ambulance."

"No. I can't afford an ambulance or another hospital bill. I'm not that hurt. I can wiggle my toes and feel my legs, I just can't get them out from under the dash."

"I'm not worried about how much it will cost. I'm worried about you. What if you have a concussion?"

"I appreciate your concern, but I'm fine, just a little banged up. I know what a concussion feels like, and if I have any problems I'll go to the doctor tomorrow, but I don't need an ambulance right now. I just need you to get me out of this damn car."

"All right, for now. But if I have even one cause for concern that you might be concussed, I'm taking you in to the doctor. Deal?"

"Fine. It's a deal. Now, please just get me out of here."

The front of the car was crumpled in, and her legs were trapped under the mangled dashboard. He ran his hand along one of her calves, then the other, trying to see if her legs were actually caught on something. They didn't appear to be.

Stepping into the open frame where the car window used to be, he reached an arm across her middle and searched for the seat belt release. "Can you brace your arms against the dash? I'm gonna try to catch you, but once I push the button, I don't want you to fall forward and bust your head on the steering wheel."

She held out her arms and locked them on the dashboard.

"Ready?"

She nodded, and he pressed the button. The belt loosened, and her body slumped forward onto his outstretched arm. He slowly pulled her toward him, easing her legs out from under the dash. "Easy there. I've got you."

He took a step back, drawing her all the way out of the wrecked vehicle, and pulled her into his arms as he sunk onto the grass. "You're okay now."

She trembled in his arms as she buried her face in his neck.

"What happened?"

"I don't know. I came up to the corner, and suddenly I had no brakes. Like nothing. The pedal went right to the floor."

"Have you been having problems with your car?"

She shook her head and took a deep breath. "No more than usual. I mean, it's an old car, it has plenty of problems. But no problems with the brakes. I just had them replaced last spring."

A sinking feeling struck him. "You don't think…?" Surely this was going too far for them. This was too low. Even for those redneck bastards. "Do you think Earl and Junior had something to do with this?"

"I don't know. Earl was waiting for me in the alley, after we got back from having pizza."

"What? Why?"

"I don't know. He said he just wanted to check on me."

"Check on you, my ass." Anger bubbled up in him, and he took a deep breath, trying to control it. Trying to focus on Emma instead of tearing out of there to find the Purvis brothers and rip 'em a couple of new ones. "Why didn't you call me?"

"Why would I?"

He hated that question and hated to think about the answer.

Why would she call him? He didn't have any claim on her. Just because he felt this insane urge to protect her didn't mean she wanted to be protected by him.

He shrugged. "Because I'm your friend."

"Well, I'm not used to having a lot of those." She looked down and rubbed at the smudge of dried blood on her arm. "Actually I'm not really used to having any at all."

"Well, you've got one now. You have more than one. If you don't want to call me, call Charlie or Zack or Cherry or Taylor. I'll make sure you have all of their numbers. Call any of us, and we'll be there for you."

"I appreciate that. But honestly, I didn't have time to call anyone. It all happened so fast. I walked up to my car, and he just appeared. All I wanted to do was get out of there."

"I get that." He reached up and pushed back her bangs to get a better look at the cut on her forehead. "I don't think this is gonna need stitches, but I still think we should run you up to the emergency room and have them check you out."

She shook her head. "No. I told you, no hospital. I've been in the emergency room too many times in my life already. I'm just banged up a little. Nothing a good soak in the bathtub won't help." She stretched out her arms. "Besides, nothing feels broken."

He hated that she'd been hurt so many times that she could recognize what a broken bone felt like. "All right, I'll trust your judgment. But let's get back to the house and get you cleaned up." He shifted her off his lap and helped her to stand, then stood up beside her and held out a steadying arm. "You okay? Can you walk?"

She nodded. "I can manage. But what am I gonna do about my car?"

"Nothing. We'll leave it here, and I'll call Bud at the auto shop tomorrow and have him come out and get it. He's gonna need the tow truck to haul it out of the ditch anyway." He peered into the damaged car. "You want me to grab anything out of it? You got anything of value in there?"

"I don't really have anything of value, period," she mumbled as she shook her head at the car. "And there's nothing in the car. I didn't even bring my purse tonight. I just stuck my stuff in my pockets."

"Okay." He slipped an arm around her waist to help her navigate up the embankment of the ditch then got her settled in the truck.

The drive back to the farm only took a few minutes. He parked in front of the porch and helped her up the stairs and into the house.

He pulled out a kitchen chair and eased her onto it. "I'll get a warm washcloth and some ice, and we'll get you cleaned up. You want me to get you something—some water or a cup of hot tea?"

Geez, he sounded like an old granny fussing over her and offering to bring her a cup of tea. But he couldn't help himself. He hated to see her hurt and just wanted to do something—anything—to help her feel better.

"I'm okay. Really, you don't need to make a fuss over me."

"I know I don't have to. I want to." He turned around before she could argue and stepped into the kitchen. He gathered a washcloth and a small bag of ice, ran some warm water into a bowl, then poured a cool glass of water for her.

He carried everything over to the table, balancing it all in his arms, then pulled up a chair across from her. Scooting closer, he fit his legs on either side of hers, then tried to ignore the heat that built in his gut from being so close to her and having her legs rest against his.

She smiled up at him as she took a sip of the water. "Thank you. This is good."

Wetting the cloth in the warm water, he tipped up her chin and gently washed the blood from her forehead. He pulled back as she cringed in pain. "Sorry, I don't want to hurt you." He never wanted to hurt her.

"It's okay. I'm actually pretty tough."

He had a feeling she *was* pretty tough, and it pained him to know the reason why she had to be so tough.

"It doesn't look too deep," he said, examining the cut. "A Band-Aid and a little antibiotic ointment oughta fix you right up."

"Oh, good. I've heard a nice big bandage across your forehead is what all the girls are wearing right now."

He narrowed his eyes at her. "Are you trying to make a fashion statement?"

She chuckled. "No. I wouldn't know a fashion statement from a fashion question."

"Cute." He smiled at her, trying to ignore the fact that her face was so close to his, so close that he could easily lean forward and kiss her.

Instead, he rinsed the cloth and picked up her hand to clean the scratch on her arm. Her hand was cool and fit perfectly into his. "You don't need to be like all the other girls out there anyway. It's okay to be different. It makes you more—I don't know—special, I guess."

A tinge of pink colored her cheeks at the compliment.

He reached for the bowl, accidentally bumping it, and it tipped forward, spilling a little water onto the table.

What the heck was wrong with him? Why was he so nervous?

He could usually charm the pants off any woman. Why was this one totally throwing him off his game?

Because she wasn't just any woman, and this wasn't just some game. She was important. She mattered to him. Whether she agreed or not, she *was* special.

At least, she was special to him.

And right now she was hurt and bruised up, and all he

could think about was touching her smooth skin and the way her lips would feel against his.

Get a grip, man.

She yawned, her mouth forming a perfect *O*, and he could see the fatigue in her eyes. "Sorry," she said, shaking her head.

"Don't be. You've got to be exhausted. You want me to start the water for a bath for you?" *Then climb into the tub with you and soap up your smooth skin?*

Thoughts like that were definitely *not* in the "get a grip" column.

"No, I think I just want to crawl into bed and go to sleep." She stood up then gripped the table as she swayed on her feet.

"Easy there," he said, reaching for her arm. "I've got you." He picked her up, cradling her against his chest, and carried her into the guest room.

Not bothering to turn on the light, he crossed the room and laid her down on the bed. The moon gave off just enough light to see by, and his face was inches from hers.

He paused, his arm still cradling her, searching her eyes, looking for a sign. Any hint that she wanted him, too—wanted him to kiss her, to touch her, to lie down with her.

She blinked up at him, tucking her bottom lip under her top teeth, and he almost came undone.

"Emma," was all he could say, his voice coming out in a gruff whisper.

Chapter Nine

What the hell am I doing?

He knew he shouldn't. She'd just been in a car accident, for cripe's sake.

But he couldn't stop himself. Logic and reason seemed to have deserted him and had been replaced by the heady scent of her perfume and the absolute rightness of holding her in his arms.

He eased his face closer, and she didn't move to stop him, didn't push him away. He wanted her so much, wanted to pull her against him, wanted to taste her sweet lips, and explore the contours of her body.

Aw hell, he wanted her naked and whimpering and calling out his name.

But he didn't want to scare her, didn't want to move too fast. He leaned a little closer, anticipating the feel of her soft lips, as he slid his arm out from under her legs and braced his hand on the pillow next to her head.

What he wasn't anticipating was the next moment of pain when a paw full of tiny claws bit into his skin as a kitten pounced on his hand.

He reared back, letting go of Emma and shaking out his fingers. "Holy crap."

Emma broke into laughter, reaching for the tiny kitten that must have been asleep on the pillows. She snuggled it against her face. "Oh Percy, you silly kitty."

The moment was lost, but hearing Emma laugh and giggle was worth it. She seemed so happy cuddling the animal, her usual shyness gone.

He jammed his hands in his front pockets. "I guess I should go. Let you get your rest."

"Stay." Her voice was soft, barely a whisper—but he heard it—heard it, and his heart did a little flip in his chest.

He turned to take a step toward the chair at the end of the bed, but she reached out and grabbed his hand.

She slid over in the bed, making room for him, and tugged on his hand. "Can you just lie down with me for a few minutes? Would that be okay?"

He didn't say anything. Instead, he pulled off his boots and lay down next to her. The old bed creaked with his weight. He turned on his side to face her and propped his head up on his fist.

She curled on her side facing him and plopped the kitten between them. "The other kittens could care less about me, but this one seems to really like me."

"I know the feeling," he said, not looking at her, instead focusing his attention on playing with the little cat. Best to change the subject. "You must be wiped out. You've had a crazy day today."

"Crazy, yes. But it was also a good day."

He gave her a skeptical glance. "A *good* day? How do you figure? Your creep ex-brothers-in-law showed up at your new job to bully you, and you ended your night in a ditch after crashing your car. How could that possibly be considered a good day?"

She smiled. "Because I *had* a new job for those idiots to show up to, and I wrecked my car after spending a night in town out for pizza with new friends. And my day didn't end with a car crash." She paused, looking down at the kitten, then shyly peered up at him. "It's ending with being here with you."

Butterflies filled his gut, the kind of butterflies he hadn't felt since he was in high school and one of the popular girls flirted with him. Because that's how he felt now—with his hands sweating and his stomach churning—just like a kid in high school who had a crush on a girl.

And she'd just given him the sign he'd needed. The cue that told him she wanted him, too.

She reached out and touched his hand, sending darts of heat shooting up his spine, and he scooted closer.

"Thank you for being such a good friend to me."

The spinning butterflies dive-bombed his gut and lay in a heap. He paused mid-scoot.

She was giving him a cue all right, and the cue was to back off. Retreat back into the friend zone.

He nodded, not trusting his voice, his cool completely blown.

"Can I ask you a favor?"

"Sure, anything," he said.

"I feel kind of foolish even asking."

"What is it?"

She looked down at the kitten, her voice quiet. "Would you stay here for a while? With me? Just until I fall asleep?"

A vise grip clamped down on his heart, and he knew he was sunk.

He would do anything for her. Even if it meant he would never kiss her or touch her skin. Being her friend was enough. "I'd be glad to."

She picked up the kitten and rolled over, then scooted

back until she was spooning him. He tried not to groan as she nestled her backside into his groin.

She fit neatly against him, and the smell of her hair filled his senses.

"Thank you," she whispered.

He gently rested his hand on her hip. "You're welcome, darlin'. And this isn't foolish at all."

The only foolish part had been him thinking there was something between them. That she wanted him as much as he wanted her.

For now, he was content to just lie beside her, her body snuggled against his, and let her sleep.

• • •

The front door slammed, and Emma struggled awake as she heard someone calling her name.

The weight of a man's arm fell across her waist, and she had a moment of panic that Leroy was back.

But this man's arm did not belong to Leroy. It belonged to Cash, who had evidently spent the whole night nestled against her.

She breathed in, savoring the moment, the feel of his lean muscled body pressed against hers, the feeling of being safe and protected and truly cared for.

The moment was short-lived as Charlie burst into the bedroom. "Emma, oh my gosh, are you okay?"

Cash startled awake next to her. "What's going on?" he grumbled, his voice still full of sleep.

"That's what I'd like to know," Charlie said.

Oh no. Is she mad about finding Cash and me snuggled up in her guest bed?

Did Charlie assume they'd taken advantage of her hospitality and had a wild night of sex while she was away?

But she didn't seem to be upset by anything to do with Cash. Instead, her concern was solely for Emma, as she rushed to her bedside and peered at her bandaged head. "Are you okay? Zack just brought me home, and we saw your car in the ditch. What happened?"

"That's a good question," Cash said as he sat up in bed and stretched his arms. "It seems that Emma's brakes failed, and I have a pretty good idea of who was behind their failure."

"What? Someone tampered with your brakes?" Charlie asked. "And you think it was Earl and Junior?"

"We don't know anything for sure," Emma said.

"We know that Earl was waiting to ambush Emma in that alley last night when she walked to her car."

"Wait—we watched you walk to your car. We didn't see Earl."

"He was hiding in the shadows," Emma explained. "He didn't come out until after you'd driven off."

"Oh my gosh, Emma. We never would have left you if we'd known. I feel terrible. I should have driven home with you."

"Then you would have been in the car wreck with me." She rested a hand on her new friend's arm. "You couldn't have known."

"So, are you okay? I can see the bandage on your head, but are you hurt otherwise? Did you go to the hospital? Why didn't you call us?"

"Geez, slow down, woman," Cash said. "She called me, and I went to pick her up. We didn't see the need to go to the hospital, and there was no point in calling you and getting you all upset when there was nothing you could do."

Emma flashed him a thankful smile. He said it all so simply and kept her from having to explain why she didn't want to go to the emergency room.

Charlie threw her arms around her in a hug. "I'm just so glad you're okay. Let me do something now, though. I can make breakfast. At least let me feed you. Then you can take a bath and lie around in your pajamas all day."

"No, I can't." Emma glanced at the clock on the bedside table. "I've got to get in the shower and get to work. Cherry's expecting me."

"What? You can't go to work after this."

"Of course I can." Emma stretched her arms and could feel the tenseness and ache in her muscles from the crash and from sleeping in her clothes all night. But she'd certainly been through worse and had to function the next day. "I'm fine—nothing that a hot shower and a couple of ibuprofen won't fix. I really like this job, and I don't want to lose it. Besides, Cherry is counting on me to show up, and I don't want to let her down."

Charlie nodded. "Okay, I get that. You're much tougher than I am. Why don't you hop in the shower, and I'll make some bacon and eggs."

Cash was already bent over the side of the bed, pulling on his boots. "I need to start my morning chores, but text me when breakfast is on, and I'll come in and eat."

"Sure. Give me twenty minutes," Charlie told him.

"That'll be good." He was just going to leave, without any mention of him spending the night in her bed.

Not that anything had happened, but he *had* slept there all night. And really, what was there to say? Thank you? *I wish you would have kissed me?*

He stopped at the door of the bedroom. "I'll give Bud a call to tow your car in this morning, and I can drive you into town after breakfast."

"I can do it," Charlie said. "I have to run in to the grocery store this morning anyway. Can you pick her up though?"

They were discussing her like she wasn't even in the room. "You guys know I'm sitting right here."

"We see you," Cash said. "We also know that your car

is in a ditch, and you need a ride to and from work, so we're figuring it out."

"I appreciate that, but I just don't want anyone to make a fuss over me."

"This isn't a fuss," Charlie said, flashing her a smile. "This is just life. And this is what friends do, we take care of one another. You're just not used to having others do things for you. But we've made you part of our family now, so you'll have to get used to it."

Emma's heart felt like it would burst with happiness. Everything in her life was changing so fast, but having friends and being part of a "family" was something she felt like she *could* actually get used to.

Especially if Cash were one of those friends.

• • •

Cash leaned against the side of his truck as he watched Emma through the window of Cherry's Diner. She was just finishing up her shift, and she smiled and waved at the remaining customers on her way out. Cherry's son, Sam, ran across the diner and gave her a hug.

She looked happy. And beautiful.

Her hair was pulled up in a high ponytail, and her smile was open and genuine instead of shy and guarded. And thanks to Charlie's cooking, she'd put on a little weight and now filled out her waitress uniform in all the right places, the pink fabric hugging the curves of her hips.

Pushing open the door, a bright smile beamed from her face as she hurried toward him. His heart beat fast against his chest knowing that smile was for him. And knowing that he had a matching goofy grin on his own face.

"Hey, beautiful," he said as he opened the truck door for her.

"Hey, yourself," she said, a shy grin crossing her face as she climbed up into the cab.

He let himself take one glance at her curvy little butt before he looked away then shut the door.

Yeah, the extra weight looked good on her. Really good.

"How was work?" he asked, sliding into the driver's seat and starting the engine.

"Great. I had a really good day." The hem of her uniform dress had ridden up her thighs, giving him a perfect view of her shapely legs.

He tried to keep his mind off sliding his hands along her legs and under her skirt as he pulled out onto the street and headed for the farm. "Did Charlie tell you that she has to leave for New York tonight? Her editor needed a face-to-face, and I think she said she set up a couple of book signings for when she's there."

"Yes, she told me at breakfast. What an exciting life she leads, being a famous author and getting to jet off to New York for a few days."

"She didn't seem too excited about it. I think the country has gotten into her soul, and now she doesn't enjoy the bustle and craziness of the city as much. But she'll get to see her folks, and she always enjoys the book signings and meeting her readers."

"She asked me to stay and keep an eye on the house while she's gone. I know she probably doesn't really need me to stay there, but it's nice of her to be concerned about me. And I enjoy staying at Tucked Away and being around all of you."

"We like being around you, too." He probably enjoyed having her around too much.

Maybe he wouldn't think about her so much if he didn't have to look at her every day over the breakfast table. "And speaking of being concerned about you, did you have any trouble with the Purvis brothers today? Did they come in to bother you?"

She shook her head. "Nope, I didn't see them all day."

"Taylor told me that he went out and had another talk with them—told them about your accident and that the sheriff's department was looking into the cause. Hopefully he put the fear of God into them, and they'll leave you alone now."

"That would be great."

She was pretty great. And he was feeling great sitting next to her. Too great. He needed to dial it back. "So, how is Stan doing?"

"Stan? The cook at the diner? He's fine, I guess. He's a funny guy, he keeps all of us laughing throughout the day."

"I never got to ask if you had a good time hanging out with him while you all had pizza the other night." He tried to keep the jealous note out of his voice, but he was failing miserably. He sounded like a dope.

Emma turned to him, one of her eyebrows raised, and he knew she was on to him. "I had a great time at pizza the other night hanging out with *everyone*. I wasn't there *just* with Stan."

"But he seems like a pretty good guy. He's nice, and like you said, he's funny and all. I was just thinkin' he might be a good candidate for you to consider dating." Yeah, that was smooth, real smooth.

She burst out laughing. "First of all, I'm flattered that you've put so much thought into who would be a good 'candidate' for me to consider, but my dating life is not a presidential campaign. Stan and I are just friends. I'm not interested in dating him at all. My interests lie elsewhere at the moment. But I sure appreciate your concern."

Her tone held a teasing note, and he couldn't tell if she meant her "interests" were in her job and getting back on her feet or in another man. Even though he'd been pushing for Stan, the thought of her interested in another man had his gut churning with envy.

Time to change the subject. Before he said something really stupid.

"I saw you through the window," he said. "It looks to me like you're enjoying the job and feeling more comfortable."

"I am. I only have to give myself the 'pretend you are brave' pep talk a few times a day now, instead of every ten minutes."

He chuckled. "Emma, I think you have scads more courage than you give yourself credit for. But you obviously don't see yourself that way. Tell me what being brave means to you. Like name me three things that you feel you can't do because you're not brave enough."

She let out a heavy sigh. "I can name you twenty. I'm scared of everything. Of trying new things and going into new situations."

"Twenty might be a little hard to tackle, but we can try three. Don't overthink it. What are the first three things that pop into your head that you wish you had the courage to do?"

She sat up taller in the seat. "Okay, I wish I had the courage to be able to defend myself and stand up to Leroy and his brothers and not feel like a scared little mouse whenever they are around."

"Okay, what else. What's something that you've been scared to try?"

"Um, I've always wanted to learn how to ride a horse, but the idea of trying scares me to death."

"What? You grew up on a farm, and you never learned to ride?"

She shrugged. "I was so timid and shy as a girl. I was more interested in sewing and crafts and had my nose in a book most of the time."

Those were the things he remembered most about her from high school. That she'd been shy, a little plain, and kept mostly to herself. She'd been the perfect target for a guy like Leroy. All he'd had to do was show her a little attention, and she would have fallen for him, not knowing that there were other types of guys out there. Good guys.

"Okay, what else? Name one more thing you'd like to try or learn to do. It doesn't have to be rocket science; pick something simple that you feel like you can accomplish."

"All right. This might sound silly, but I'd like to learn how to bake a pie. I've been sampling Cherry's pies every day, and I keep wishing I could figure out how to make a pie myself."

"Good. Excellent. That's an attainable goal, and you have some great experts who can help you. Cherry could teach you. Or Sophie. Charlie's grandmother, Gigi, taught Sophie how to cook from the time she could pull a stool up to the counter. She's a talented little chef."

"Okay. I'll try to ask one of them for help. But asking for help would be a fourth thing to add to my list, 'cause I'm not very brave at doing that either."

"Well, I'll make that task easier. I can help with the first two things, and you don't even have to ask me. I'm just offering." He turned into the driveway of the farm. "We have a real sweet old mare that I could use to teach you to ride. We've even put little kids on her. The weather's supposed to be great this weekend. How about if we plan a horseback ride for Saturday? I can take you out in the afternoon after you're finished working at the diner."

She nodded. "Okay. I'd like that. I think. My palms start to sweat just thinking about it, but I want to try. And if a little kid can ride this horse, I should be able to as well."

"Good girl." He put the truck in park and turned off the engine. "And as for the first thing, I think I can help with that, too."

She gave him a skeptical glance. "You're going to help me be less scared of Leroy and his brothers? How do you propose to do that?"

"By teaching you a few moves to defend yourself. And by empowering you with some self-defense techniques that might help boost your confidence when you're around them."

"Why would you know self-defense techniques? You don't seem like you're afraid of anything."

If she only knew. He was afraid right now. Afraid of a woman who probably weighed a hundred pounds soaking wet. Scared to death that he was in over his head and already had his heart invested in a game that he had no chance of winning.

"Remember, this is a small town and one of my best friends is the sheriff. He and Zack and I are all volunteer firemen, and Taylor had us trained as relief deputies, in case of an emergency or if we need to stand in to help with special events like the big rodeo we have in the summer. I know just enough to be dangerous." He offered her a devilish grin and loved the way her cheeks tinged with color.

"I think that's actually a pretty good idea. I don't know if it will really help, like if I could really stand up to them physically when they are actually in front of me, but it can't hurt to have a couple of tips under my belt." She smiled up at him. "When do we start?"

"How about tonight? Come on out to the barn after supper, and I can show you some basic stuff."

"Sounds good. I think Charlie is making spaghetti for supper."

"One of my favorites. I need to finish up some chores, but tell her that I'll be in after a bit."

• • •

Emma crossed the driveway to the barn later that night. Cash had told her to wear comfortable clothes, so she'd put on a

T-shirt, black yoga pants, and a pair of sneakers. She carried a lightweight sweater in case the night got cool.

Poking her head into the barn, she saw Cash standing at the workbench and paused to admire the view. He had on a pair of sweats and tennis shoes, and a snug-fitting black T-shirt, the sleeves hugging the finely toned muscles of his biceps.

He was magnificent. He reminded her of one of the stallions that galloped down the fence line of the pasture, or one of the new colts that he spent his time working with to break. His flirty manner was smooth, but his wild streak was still apparent, and he had a bit of a rough edge to him.

Which is probably what made him so irresistible to so many women.

Including her.

With the way her body was heating up just looking at him, she sure wasn't going to need that sweater she held.

He turned around and gave her one of his wicked grins, and everything inside her melted into a puddle.

"Was that Zack's truck I heard?" he asked.

"Yeah, he just picked up Charlie to take her to the airport. She said to call if you need anything."

"I'm sure we can handle things on our own for a few days." He rubbed his hands together. "You ready to get tough?"

No, she wasn't ready. She wasn't tough, and she didn't know how to even begin to pretend to be. All she wanted to do right now was forget this silly idea, run back into the house, and hide under the cover of the blankets on her bed.

"I see you backing up," Cash said. "Come on in here. I'm not gonna bite you."

Oh Lord. Now why did he have to say that? Thoughts of him biting her, nipping at her skin, filled her mind, and her skin heated, making her even more frightened and desperate to run.

Pretend to be brave.

She forced herself to take a step forward. Then another, and another, until she stood in front of him. "I'm ready."

He took her sweater and laid it on the workbench then pointed to the floor of the barn where he'd created a makeshift mat by layering clumps of hay and covering them with an old quilt. "Step on up here, and we can start with the basics."

He held out his hand, and she took it, letting him lead her onto the improvised mat. Facing her, he bent forward in a combative stance. "Now an assailant is gonna come at you one of two ways. They'll either come toward you head on or sneak up on you from behind."

She nodded. "Okay."

"If they're facing you, you have a few choices. Keep in mind, your main goal is to get away, and hopefully to keep them from chasing after you. You can always go for the tried and true method of kneeing them in the nuts, but it's more effective to thrust the sole of your foot out and try to kick them in the kneecap. The kneecap is harder to protect than the groin or the face, and this will often incapacitate them, giving you a chance to run."

She practiced the move, thrusting her foot out but stopping short of actually connecting with his knee. He showed her how to position her hand to shove her palm up and into an assailant's face to break his nose.

He reached out and grabbed her wrists, and she automatically tried to pull away. "Now, if someone has a hold of your wrists, don't try to pull away like that, instead, rotate your wrists until your thumbs line up with where their thumbs meet their fingers, so usually your palms are face down, then jerk back by sharply bending your arm at the elbow."

She tried it, twisting her hands and jerking her arms back and was surprised at its effectiveness.

"Good job," he said. "Now keep in mind, your head is often one of your best weapons. Not just to think, but a good hard head-butt to the solar plexus can knock the wind out of someone. Just make sure you're looking at the ground when you ram your head into their gut."

She laughed and tipped her head down in preparation to ram him. "This seems like a trick Clyde would use."

"That old goat would take a nip out of you first. Which is an option, too. Use whatever you have at your disposal. Bite them, scratch them, kick them, whatever will inflict pain. And don't forget to scream. A good battle cry can work in more ways than one. It can sometimes knock your attacker off-balance, giving you a chance to run, it signals for help, and it can also summon up your courage as you unleash that bottled-up fear and scream. Try it."

"Try what?"

"Try to give a good scream."

"Right now?"

"Sure. It's a common fear that you won't be able to scream when you need to, so it's good to practice a few times just so you can know it feels."

She gave a halfhearted stage scream.

He shook his head. "That was weak. You can do better."

"I feel silly."

"Don't feel silly. Feel angry. Imagine if someone were trying to attack you and you needed help." He gestured to the few animals in the barn. "No one's around to even hear you, except me and a few critters, and we won't care. Really do it. I want to hear you scream."

Okay, that might have come out wrong. He did want to hear her scream, but only if she was in his bed and screaming his name. Several times.

Geez, focus buddy.

He shrugged at the raised eyebrow she was giving him. "You know what I mean."

She offered him a chuckle. "Okay, here goes." After

taking a deep breath, she opened her mouth and tried another scream, this one a tad louder than the last.

"Louder," he yelled, encouraging her with his own volume.

She screamed again.

"Louder."

Curling her hands into fists, she closed her eyes and tipped her face up to the cavernous ceiling of the barn, then let out a ferocious shriek.

He grinned as she offered him a shrug. "Good job. How did that feel?"

"Kind of good actually."

He liked the way her shoulders settled as she seemed to feel more at ease with him.

"So, you've shown me how to break a wrist hold and how to scream—and these are all great ideas, like if I were getting attacked in an alley by a stranger, but I know these guys. And Leroy was my husband. Was I supposed to break his nose?"

Cash narrowed his eyes at her, giving her a meaningful look. "He may have been your husband, but when he's abusing you, he's an assailant. And let me ask you this, has he ever broken *your* nose?"

She looked at the floor, staring at the errant strand of hay sticking out from under the quilt as she remembered a night that Leroy had put her in the emergency room. It was the first time he'd actually punched her in the face. She'd been so shocked by the violence and the pain of it, she couldn't breathe. Then the blood filled her throat and ran down the front of her face, and a look of fear crossed Leroy's face as he realized what he'd done.

After that he hadn't hit her in the nose again.

"Only once," she said softly, still avoiding his eyes. "I ended up at the hospital. So he didn't try it again. He still gave me a black eye once in a while, but he usually avoided hitting me in the face."

"And they say domestic abuse happens when the spouse is drunk or gets out of control." He shook his head in disgust. "Bullshit. An abuser *is* in control, calculating where to hit you so it will show the least damage, often hitting you just hard enough to inflict pain, but not hard enough to put you in the hospital. Abuse is all about control."

She tipped up her head, searching his eyes. "How do you know so much about it?"

"Because I lived it. I don't talk about it much, try to avoid thinking about it if I can. But I guess I want you to know that you're not alone. You're not the only one this has happened to. My dad was a man with tendencies much the same as your ex-husband. I know the fear and the pain of being hurt by someone who's supposed to love you. And the helplessness of watching someone abuse your mom and not being able to do a damn thing about it."

"I had no idea." Was this why he was so good to her? Why he went out of his way to protect her? Because he wanted to help someone now when he couldn't help his mom before? "I'm sorry."

He nodded, a quick bob of his head, his eyes conveying compassion but not pity. He didn't feel sorry for her, he empathized with where she'd been, and he understood her. "It was a long time ago. And the only reason I told you was so you'd know that I understand what you've been through. And that's part of why I want to help you. So you never have to feel that helpless again."

His face changed, his lips turning up into a devilish grin, as he gave her a wicked grin. "And 'cause you're pretty."

She laughed, the sound bursting from her before she could stop it. She knew he was only trying to lighten the mood, and it had worked. Slapping playfully at him, she teased him back. "You're kind of pretty yourself."

What the heck? It was a rare enough feeling to have a

man flirt with her. And did she just flirt back? She must be getting braver after all.

The grin stayed on his face, and he circled around her. "You ready for part two of your lesson?"

She swallowed. As long as he kept grinning at her like that, she thought she'd be ready for just about anything.

He moved quickly, coming up behind her and wrapping his arm tightly around her chest, pinning her against his torso.

Okay, she hadn't been ready for that.

A quick jolt of fear ran through her as she fought against him. But her movements were ineffectual. She was helpless against his strength.

"Most attackers rely on the element of surprise, and they don't want you to see their faces. You're more vulnerable in this position, especially if your assailant is stronger, which he usually will be. It takes me little effort to hold you here."

She struggled against him. "I can't even move."

"Okay, so what can you do? What do you have at your disposal? Remember I told you to bite, scratch, or kick them. Stomp your foot down on their instep, bite down on their hand or scratch at their arm. If you can reach back, try to pull on their ear or poke them in the eye. Shove your head back to break their nose. Or use your elbows to jab into their gut. All you need is for them to loosen their hold just enough to allow you to turn and attack or to get free and run."

She practiced getting the feel for jabbing him with her elbow and kicking back at his instep or his knees.

"Think about your surroundings. What do you have around you that you can use as a weapon? Jab him with your keys, spray hairspray at him, throw dirt in his face, hit him with anything heavy that might be around you. Look around us now. What could you use as a weapon?"

She looked around the barn and pointed out several items. "The pitchfork, the shovel, any of the tools on your workbench."

"Good. Those are all great ideas. Think out of the box, too. Slapping someone with the leather straps of that bridle would hurt, even throwing grain at someone's face could cause some of it to get in their eyes, giving you that split second to get away."

"Okay, I just hope that I have a shovel or a bucket of grain handy if Earl or Junior come after me."

He took her by the shoulders, looking down into her eyes. "Emma, you are stronger than you think. You've got this. You don't have to be afraid of them. You are a survivor, which makes you a fighter. You don't have to be big to be scrappy."

She wanted to believe him. She felt stronger. He made her feel confident in herself. Made her feel like she mattered.

Like she mattered to him.

He grabbed her wrists again, holding them loosely in his. "Try again. Show me how you'd break free."

She rotated her wrists, jerked her elbows back, and broke free. Then she playfully poked him in the chest. "Take that."

The corners of his lips turned up in a naughty grin. "Oh, so now you want to play." He made a grab for her, and she shrieked and turned to run. He grabbed her around the waist, lifting her off her feet and spinning her around.

Laughing, she squirmed against him, wiggling free and turning to face him. She held up her hands, palms flat, in a mock karate stance. "Don't make me karate chop you."

He gave her a wicked grin, and her heart raced inside of her chest. "I'm shaking in my boots."

"You're not wearing any boots." Her thoughts went to him not wearing anything, remembering a few days ago when she'd caught sight of him working in the corral with a new colt. The day had been hot, and he'd been shirtless, wearing only jeans and a pair of boots, his muscles tense and flexing as he went through the paces with the horse.

He ducked his head, bending forward and grabbed her

around the waist, as she pummeled his back with karate chops.

"Hi-ya," she cried with each playful blow.

Laughing, she took a step backward and stumbled on her own feet, falling onto the mat, and Cash fell on top of her. The weight of him felt so good, but it only lasted a second as he flipped over, rolling her on top of him.

She lay on his chest, her arms braced on either side of his head, her laughter ending as she looked down into his face. His gorgeous face. With his ice-blue eyes and chiseled jaw, he was beyond handsome.

And she wanted him. Wanted to kiss him, to touch him.

He'd spent the last hour convincing her she was worthy, a fighter, brave.

Was she brave enough to take what she wanted right now? To lean down and press her lips to his? To finally taste him?

Pretend you are brave.

Everything in her fought to run, to hide, her body flooding with fear as her heart pounded against her chest. She inhaled a sharp breath, fighting back a tinge of nausea as butterflies swooped and churned in her stomach.

But she also felt the heat of desire and passion filling her, spreading to parts of her that she'd thought were dead and lifeless. Parts of her that were straddled against his waist, and currently informing her that parts of him were certainly not lifeless or dead.

Screw it. This is what being brave was all about. Throwing caution to the wind and going for what you want. Putting your fears aside and living.

Without giving herself another second for her resolve to weaken, she leaned forward and pressed her lips to his.

No subtle whisper of touch, instead she kissed him full-on, crushing his lips in an onslaught of passion.

Chapter Ten

Emma's heart raced. What the hell was she doing?

She'd just leaned in to kiss the man who had filled her dreams for the past several nights. The man who was so handsome that it sometimes hurt just to look at him. The man whose grin could send butterflies storming through her chest.

And he was kissing her back.

His lips were soft, and his mouth tasted like spearmint gum. His strong arms wrapped around her, pulling her against him, his hands sliding along her back.

A moan of hunger escaped her lips as she felt his hand slide under her T-shirt and grip her waist. The touch of his callused fingers against her bare skin sent shivers of heat down her spine.

His other hand slid across her shoulders and into her hair, pulling out the elastic band and freeing her hair to fall in a cascade around them. Every place that he touched felt like fire burning her skin with the heat of passion.

Then he pulled back, gasping for breath, as he put the slightest pressure against her shoulder.

Oh my gosh. What have I done?

That slight pressure, the tiniest bit of pulling away was like a mammoth sign of rejection, and her insecurities came slamming back with the force of a giant blow.

What a fool she was. He was Cash Walker. He could have any woman he wanted. And he was probably used to women throwing themselves at him.

She scrambled off him, the scratchy hay digging into her palms. "I'm sorry. I'm so sorry," she mumbled.

He'd made it clear that he only wanted to be her friend.

She must have misread the signals—the flirting, the playful teasing.

Cash was known to be a huge flirt. That didn't mean he actually liked her.

She'd just thrown herself at him—practically jumped him. *He must think I'm an idiot. And a fool.*

Pulling her shirt down as she stood, she pivoted and ran from the barn.

"Emma, wait."

She heard him call her name, but she was already out the door, running for the house, a sob building in her throat.

• • •

The first drops of rain fell on his shoulders as Cash climbed the front porch steps to Charlie's house the next night. He paused, turning to search the night sky, analyzing the clouds and hoping for a big storm. A heavy soaking tonight would sure help the fall crops.

Thunder rumbled a few miles away, dark clouds filling the sky and echoing in his chest. Last night still weighed heavily on him.

He'd found her forgotten sweater in the barn, and he now laid it across the back of one of the rockers.

It was probably the coward's way to do it, but he wasn't quite ready to face her yet.

He'd tried to talk to her the night before, knocking on the door and calling her name. But she hadn't answered. Hadn't answered his knock, or his call, or even his text. So he figured he would just give her some space.

But he wished she would at least let him explain.

She'd taken him by surprise, leaning down and kissing him like that. He hadn't had time to think about his actions, he just reacted.

He'd been thinking about her for so long, imagining what it would be like to kiss her, to feel her body, to touch her. When she'd kissed him, he couldn't help himself. God help him, he kissed her back, drew her to him, steeped himself in the scent of her skin.

Trying to regain his wits, and his breath, he'd pulled back.

Unfortunately, he thought Emma must have taken that as a sign of rejection. That was the only thing he could figure that would make her take off and refuse to talk to him.

He *wasn't* rejecting her. He was just taking a second to breathe.

But she evidently didn't see it that way.

Damn it. He never should have let it get this far. Should have never let them get in the position where this could happen. It was his own damn fault.

She'd been doing so well, too. He could see her confidence building as she learned the simple self-defense techniques.

Then in one moment, he destroyed it all. The hurt in her eyes was unmistakable. He knew it would happen. Knew it all along. Knew that he would end up hurting her. One way or another.

But now what the hell should he do? Keep trying? Trying to talk to her—to explain? Or should he just leave her alone? Let her lick her wounds then just forget about him.

He wished he knew the answer. But men had been battling the mysteries of women for thousands of years, and he wasn't going to solve anything tonight.

He turned to leave, then heard a loud crash and a woman's voice cry out.

Emma.

He grabbed the screen door, yanking it open, and stormed into the house.

Emma stood in the kitchen, a mess of dough on the counter, and a shattered mixing bowl at her feet. Her face and shirt were covered in flour, and tears welled in her eyes.

He stopped short of the mess. "You okay? Are you hurt?"

She didn't say anything, just shook her head, her face filled with despair.

"It's all right, darlin'. No use crying over spilled dough, or whatever it is that you were makin' here." He tried to tease her into smiling, but it didn't work.

"I broke Charlie's mixing bowl," she said quietly as she sunk to the floor. "She told me her grandmother gave it to her."

"Don't worry about it. Her grandmother gave her everything in this kitchen. And Gigi broke plenty of dishes during her years in this kitchen. Let me get this bowl so you don't cut yourself." He picked up the broken pieces, carried them to the trash bin, then brought back the small brush and dustpan set that hung under the sink.

"What are you working on here?" he asked.

She looked up at him, one lone tear slipping from her eye and rolling down her cheek. "I was trying to bake a pie."

Oh, dang. He couldn't have felt worse for her if someone had actually ripped his heart from his chest and tore it in two. "Well, shoot. I thought you were gonna ask Cherry or Sophie to teach you."

"Sophie had a fall break at school, so she went to New

York with Charlie, and I didn't want to bother Cherry. I wanted to figure it out by myself. To actually do it on my own."

"Okay, I get that." He knew that feeling all too well. He'd tried, and failed at, many things because he was too stubborn or pigheaded to ask for help. Bending down, he reached out and wiped the tear from her cheek. It had left a heartbreaking trail through her flour-covered cheek. "Would you let me teach you?"

She looked up at him, a questioning look in her eyes. "You? You know how to make a pie?"

He offered her a devilish grin. "Heck yeah, I do. I used to help my mom in the kitchen all the time, and she taught me how to cook a lot of things. I can bake the hell out of a pie."

She laughed, then her face fell, and the tears welled again. "That almost makes me feel worse. Even you can make a pie, and all I can make is—" She looked around at the mess on the floor. "A big ball of glop."

He chuckled and held out a hand to her to help her up. "Everybody starts with glop. You don't climb onto a bike and just start riding it. You take it easy, you make mistakes, then all of a sudden, you get it."

She swiped at her face with the back of her hand, straightening her spine in resolve. "Okay, you're right. Yes, I would like it if you could teach me how to bake a pie."

A stupid grin covered his face as he waved her away. "Go change clothes while I clean up your glop, and we'll start over."

Five minutes later, she emerged from the guest room. She had on her black yoga pants, and a short sleeved button-up top. Lifting her arms, she pulled her hair up into a ponytail as she walked toward him. He swallowed at the slim band of her bare stomach that showed under the hem of her shirt.

She smiled at him, her face freshly washed, and he knew he would do anything for her—hang the moon, pluck the stars from the sky, teach her how to make a hundred pies. Anything to earn him that smile.

"I'm ready," she said.

He looked down at her and knew he wasn't. He wasn't ready at all.

"Let's do it." He tamped down his feelings, instead choosing to concentrate on the task. Grabbing one of Gigi's aprons, he dropped it over her head and turned her away from him to tie the strings around her waist. "First things first. You can't make a pie without starting with the essentials."

She pulled her hair out from under the top strap, displaying her slender neck, and his hands fumbled as he worked to tie a simple bow. So much for concentrating on the task.

How was he supposed to think straight when his hands were around her waist, and he had a great view of her perfect round butt?

Turning around, she smoothed the simple white apron down her front and gave him a teasing grin. "What about you? Aren't you going to wear one?"

"Of course." He grabbed the frilliest apron, a bright pink one with ruffled trim and a herd of dancing cows holding mixing bowls on the front, and pulled it over his head. Who cared about his pride when wearing a funny apron could illicit a sudden burst of laughter from her?

She was still laughing as he led her over to the sink where they washed their hands then crossed to the freshly cleaned counter.

A cluster of the ingredients and measuring cups covered the back part of the counter, and he pointed to the bag of pecans and bottle of corn syrup. "I remember the other day that you said pecan was your favorite, so I assume from the fixings you've got set out here that we're making a pecan pie."

She nodded. "I found the bag of nuts in the pantry, and that's what got me started on this idea. You don't think Charlie will be upset that I'm using this stuff, do you?"

"Heck, no. She'd love it. She was a terrible cook when she first got here. About all she could make was scrambled eggs and grilled cheese sandwiches. Sophie taught her almost everything she knows. She'd be happy to have you use these things. Really."

"Okay. I found a recipe on the back of the bag of pecans. That's the one I was using."

"That's fine for the filling. We just might add a couple of tweaks to it. But we'll do my mom's recipe for the crust. It's similar to the one Charlie's grandma Gigi used."

"Works for me. What do we do first?"

"So, the key to making a great crust is to make sure your ingredients are really cold. And to use real butter or shortening. Gigi always used oleo, but my mom liked real butter, so we'll stick with that." He pointed to the partially melted butter and the bottle of vegetable oil. "I'm sure these two things were the main culprits in creating your glop."

She shrugged, a guilty look on her face. "My baking skills have always run to boxed cake mixes and chocolate chip cookies, and you always soften the butter for those. And I couldn't find any solid shortening so I figured this would do in a pinch."

"The only thing we're going to pinch is the edges of the crust. You can't skimp on the right ingredients. And the colder the better. I'm sure Charlie has a couple of sticks of real butter already in the freezer just for piecrusts."

Opening the freezer, he grabbed two from the door. "I'll show you a trick my mom taught me. You can use a cheese grater to grate the frozen butter. Then it mixes with your dry ingredients slick as can be."

He quickly grated the butter, filling a mixing bowl with cheery yellow shreds. He pushed another empty bowl toward her. "You can measure the flour and salt, then I'll dump in the butter. My mom always added a teaspoon of sugar." He filled a measuring cup with ice water as she dumped in the ingredients.

"I always thought you were supposed to use lukewarm water."

"Not for crust. You always want everything really cold. You want to use warm water when you're baking bread."

"You know how to bake bread, too?"

He offered her one of his most charming grins. "Darlin', I know how to do a lot of things."

Her cheeks tinged pink as she reached for the sugar. "So anyway, about this pie. How much sugar did you say I should use?"

Chuckling, he handed her the measuring spoons. "A good full teaspoon should do." He held up his hands as she sprinkled the sugar over the flour. "Ready to get messy?"

Dumping the butter into the bowl, he used his hands to mix it together. "Get your hands in here. This dough isn't gonna mix itself."

She laughed and stuck her hands in next to his, making a face as she squeezed the dough between her fingers. "Oh, it is cold. And gooey."

He chuckled and drizzled a teaspoon of the ice water onto the dough, earning a shriek from her as he sprinkled the last cold drops onto her hand.

Sticking his hands back in the bowl, they formed the dough into a ball, the familiar butterflies building each time their fingers touched. "You don't want to overwork the dough. And it's okay to leave little chunks of butter in there; it just adds to the flakiness of the crust."

Sprinkling flour across the counter, he instructed her to dump the ball out, then covered a rolling pin with flour as well before handing it to her. "Now gently roll it out into a circle."

She pressed down on the dough, creating a gulley in the

middle. "Like this?"

"Here, I'll show you." He stepped behind her and wrapped his arms around her sides, trapping her in a loose embrace. He covered her hands with his and guided the rolling pin along the dough. Darts of heat shot up his spine as he leaned forward, pressing his body against hers.

The smell of her hair almost drove him insane, and he held back from dipping down and nuzzling her neck with his lips.

He felt her catch her breath as he spoke, the whisper of his breath tickling her skin. "You want to take your time with this part. Take it slow and easy. You don't want to mess with it too much or the crust won't be as good. Like you don't want to do the old playdough back and forth movement—piecrust doesn't like that. Roll from the center outward in one easy stroke."

Oh Lord, did he really just say "one easy stroke"? His mind drifted from the crust into a sinful place with her naked and straddling him as she took several easy strokes, and he fought back a groan.

She leaned forward, pressing on the rolling pin, and her backside rubbed against his groin in a torturous shift of movement.

Shit. With the way things were starting to swell, his thoughts weren't going to stay hidden for long.

"So, tell me about your mom."

Huh? His mom? Okay. At least changing gears to a new subject would quell any other thoughts of her in his bed, and would certainly stop the bulge developing in his suddenly too-tight Wranglers. "What do you want to know?"

She shrugged. "Anything. Everything. What is she like? This woman who taught her son how to bake a pie."

"She's great. You would actually love her. And not just because she's fun and easy to get along with. But because you've lived through a lot of the same things."

Emma nodded, and her ponytail bobbed. Her hair tickled his neck as he leaned over her shoulder. "Were you always close?" she asked.

"Yeah. I didn't have any brothers or sisters, so it was always my mom and I against *him*. My dad would come home around suppertime, and if I was in the kitchen with her, he'd usually leave her alone. I picked up the basics, and my mom taught me a lot of stuff. He knew I helped her, which was good, so if something wasn't cooked right, or he didn't like it, I could take the blame instead of her."

Her hands stilled on the rolling pin, and her voice was soft as she asked, "Did he hurt you, too?"

"Yeah, he did. He wasn't my real dad. My real dad was a bull rider and was killed when a bull kicked him in the head during a rodeo."

"I'm sorry. I understand what that's like. My mom died when I was eight. Cancer."

No wonder she was so shy and kept to herself. He knew Clyde Frank was a widower, but had never really thought about the implications of that where Emma was concerned.

"That's worse. I was still a baby when I lost my dad, so I didn't really know him. My stepdad married my mom when I was around five, so he was the only dad I ever really knew. And in the beginning he was good to us, ya know?"

"Yes, they always start out that way."

"He seemed so nice and fun. I'd never had any real male attention before, and he used to play catch with me and take me to baseball games. Even after, you know, he started beating us, he was always so sorry. He brought us gifts and took us out to eat and was that fun, nice guy again."

He leaned his head against the side of hers, caught up in the memories. "It almost made it worth it. I mean the bruises healed, and it was like it was worth getting them to have that good guy back for a while—to have his attention and have him treat us so kindly."

She didn't turn, didn't look at him, like it was almost easier to talk about the hard stuff if she just kept her eyes on their hands. "Leroy used to be so good to me afterward, bringing me flowers and offering to take me on dates. It didn't seem so bad at first, 'cause he was always so sorry, and then he'd be so sweet."

"It's like they're two different people. I always felt like I had two dads, the good one, and the other one. At least in the beginning. Then the drinking got worse, and it's like the good one simply disappeared."

She didn't say anything, simply nodded instead.

"My dad was a gambler, always looking for the easy score, the one that was really gonna make him rich this time. He gambled away most of his paychecks and any savings we might have had. The more he lost, the more he drank, and the more he took out his desperation and anger on us."

She squeezed his hand, still not responding, just letting him talk.

He cleared his throat. "Anyway. I don't know why I just told you all that stuff. You asked me about my mom, not my life story. My mom's name is Kathleen, but everyone calls her Kitty. You'll really like her. She's coming to town in a few weeks for the Fall Festival so you'll get to meet her then."

"I'd like that."

"I'd like to get this pie in the oven. You have this way of distracting me." He gave her a nudging tease. "The trick is to fold it in half, then fold it in half again, then lay it in your pie pan and gently unfold it. It's okay to have this extra crust around the sides, just tuck it under and crimp the edges like this." He showed her how to transfer the crust and pinch the edges. "Now for the filling."

He grabbed another mixing bowl. "I'll melt the butter

and chop the pecans while you measure out the other stuff."

"Okay, I can handle this part." They worked in companionable silence, measuring and dumping ingredients into the bowl.

"Now, not everyone does this, but my mom always sprinkled about a half a teaspoon of cinnamon into her pecan pie. She said it gave it a kick and made hers seem just a little unique. She also used the darker variety of corn syrup to intensify the flavor." He sprinkled cinnamon into the bowl then drizzled the dark syrup over the other ingredients.

"Good tips. I would have just followed the recipe on the back of the bag."

He handed her a mixing spoon. "You can take it from here."

The radio was on and tuned to a country station, and Emma hummed along to a Carrie Underwood song as she stirred the sticky filling then poured it into the prepared piecrust.

Cash set one of Gigi's ancient pie shields on top of the rim of the crust. "This will keep the edges from getting too brown." He held open the door of the already preheated oven, and Emma slid the pie onto the center rack.

"Now we set the timer for forty-five minutes and clean up this mess." He filled the sink with hot water and squirted in some dish soap. "I'll wash if you dry."

"Deal." She brought over the dishes and dumped them into the water then found a clean dish towel. Standing near him, she leaned her hip against the counter, watching his hands as she waited for the first dish. "Thank you for telling me. You know—about you and your mom."

He kept his gaze on the soapy water as he washed the mixing bowl. "I don't know exactly what you went through, but I get how hard it is to live with a man like that. It took a hell of a lot of guts to leave him for good."

"Everyone always talks about why women stay so long. And why they don't just leave. It's so hard to make them understand. Leroy wasn't always like that. He used to be funny and was actually pretty good to me. Things seemed to get worse for us after Leroy lost his job. And like you said, the drinking got worse, and when he was drunk he lost control. And those times started happening more and more often till I couldn't even remember that sweet guy. I dreaded the minute he would walk in the door, not knowing if it would be a good night and I could keep him calm or if it would be bad."

"It probably felt like you could keep him calm, but it didn't really matter what you did. My mom and I used to do that, too. Like if we could just make the perfect dinner and talk about just the right stuff, he would be okay and not drink so much that night and get mad. But it didn't really matter what we did. Or what you did. It was out of your control, Emma. And none of it was your fault."

She took the bowl and ran the towel along the edge, catching the drops of water as she dried it. "I get that now. But I didn't think like that then. All I thought about was doing whatever I could to keep him from getting mad and taking it out on me."

His heart broke for her and the things she must have gone through. It was so hard for other people to understand what it's like. Unless they'd been through it themselves. People always think *why didn't she just leave*? But it wasn't that simple.

"I know I should have left sooner than I did, but I was afraid. I had nothing. I had no one to turn to. I mean I had my dad, but he'd already done enough. I'd gone to him before, but then I went back to Leroy. I was ashamed and embarrassed. And I didn't have any friends." Her voice lowered to a whisper. "Not like I do now."

He turned to her, took the towel, and dried his hands.

"We *are* your friends, Em. All of us. You can count on us. We'll be here for you. *I'll* be here for you."

She looked at the floor. "I believe you. That's why I'm so ashamed of what happened last night. I know you just want to be my friend, and I overstepped those bounds. I'm horrified that I threw myself at you when you've made it clear several times that you don't think of me that way."

What the hell was she talking about? Was that the reason she ran out on him? Not because she thought he was rejecting her, but because she didn't think he wanted her at all?

He reached out and touched her chin, tipping her face up to look at him. "You're wrong, Emma. I do think about you that way. I think about you *every* way, every day, all the time. Thoughts of you haunt my dreams, and I spend a good part of my day wondering what you're doing, how you're feeling, and if you're okay."

His gaze drifted to her mouth. "I also spend a fair amount of time thinking about your lips and about kissing you."

"You do?" She tugged the corner of her bottom lip under her front teeth, and it made him want to kiss her now, to suck her lip in between his. To taste her.

"Then why don't you? Why haven't you?" she asked, her voice soft.

"Because I do care about you. I care *too much* about you. And you don't need to get involved with a guy like me. You deserve so much better."

"But I like you."

"Why? Why the hell would you want to get mixed up with someone like me?"

She searched his gaze as if trying to determine if he was seriously asking her that. "Why wouldn't I? You're kindhearted, you're thoughtful, you treat me with care and like you want to protect me. Plus you're so cute, and you have all these muscles." Her lips tipped into a teasing grin. "And you have a great butt."

He chuckled, a soft laugh. "I could say the same of you."

"Then what's the problem? I don't understand. I thought it was because, you know, you're used to women who are prettier, and curvier, and way more fun than I am. I was sure it was because I wasn't enough."

She was breaking his heart, shattering it into tiny pieces.

How could she think she wasn't enough? "You're *more* than enough. You're…" He paused, searching for the right word. "Special, I guess. Those other women are fun, but that's all they are. You're more than that to me. You matter."

Reaching up, she laid a hand on his cheek. "You matter to me, too. You're the only one who really makes me feel safe."

He closed his eyes and pressed his hand on top of hers, savoring her touch for a moment before he pulled her hand away.

Opening his eyes, he stared into hers, bracing his arms on either side of her against the counter, his voice now gruff with emotion. "But I can't keep you safe. If you get involved with me, I can't protect you from the thing that will surely hurt you—could possibly destroy you. And that's me. I can't risk hurting you, and I would never forgive myself if I did."

"I don't understand. Why would you think that? You've only been good to me. And I'm the one taking the risk. So what if it's a chance I'm willing to take? Because I don't think you *will* hurt me. You know what it's like to live with a monster; that doesn't make you one." She inched forward, straddling his leg as she pressed against him.

He sighed, a heavy sound full of the torture he felt. He wanted to believe her. Wanted to see himself through her eyes.

He also wanted to take her in his arms and kiss her senseless, peel off her clothes, and have his way with her right here on the kitchen floor.

But that would be a selfish move on his part. Selfish and stupid and only thinking of his own desperate need for her.

He bent his forehead down, leaning it against hers. "Emma, I have a lot of darkness in my past. A lot of stuff that I'm not proud of. You're just getting out of that darkness. You have so much to look forward to. A future. Actual happiness. I don't want to be the one to keep you in the darkness. Not when you deserve to be in the light."

"My heart is hammering in my chest, and I can barely breathe. But being here with you, standing so close and praying that you'll kiss me, this feels like I *am* in the light."

His breath caught in his throat, his defenses cracking, as she gazed up at him with such tender emotion, and such raw desire. He knew he should step back, collect his wits, at least *try* to come to his senses.

But he couldn't. His good sense had deserted him, leaving him with only his sense of want and need.

He didn't care if it was selfish or senseless. He wanted her, and he wanted her now. His good conscience be damned, he knew he was about to do something stupid.

Never taking his gaze from hers, he lifted her onto the counter, pressed between her open legs, then reached up and took her face between his palms. He rubbed his thumb gently along her bottom lip. "Lord help me, I can't resist you."

Chapter Eleven

Emma couldn't move, could barely breathe, her whole body frozen in anticipation of this kiss. And holy mother, what a kiss it was.

His lips crushed hers, his mouth devouring hers. One of his palms held her cheek, while the other slid around her neck, his fingers tangling in her hair as he cupped her head.

Each nerve in her body came alive, anticipating his every touch. Her body trembled, and she clung to his arms, gripping his muscled biceps as shivers of desire coursed through her.

He moaned against her lips, a low throaty rumble, and it was one of the sexiest things Emma had ever heard. How could kissing *her* elicit such a response from him?

She could feel the tremble in his fingers as he skimmed his hand down her throat and over her shoulder.

Wanting more, she parted her lips, allowing his tongue to press through, to taste, to sample, to consume her mouth. He tasted like the brown sugar and vanilla he'd snuck a bite of as they'd mixed the filling for the pie, and she couldn't get enough of him.

He pulled back, taking her breath with him, and looked down at her. "You need to tell me right now if you want me to stop."

"For the love of God, please don't stop." She kissed him again, then pulled slightly back, her words coming between ragged breaths. "Don't ever stop."

He swept her into his arms and carried her to the bedroom, setting her carefully down on the bed. Yanking the apron over his head, he threw it behind him, then leaned down and tugged off his boots. Climbing onto the bed, he straddled her legs, rising above her. Heat spread through her body as she anticipated his next move.

In one quick movement, he yanked off his shirt, and Emma's mouth went dry at the sight of his muscled chest.

An intricate tattoo covered his broad shoulder and spilled onto the edge of his chest. She reached up and lightly touched the drawing.

The center of the image was an old wooden cross, with an American flag hanging off one side, the edges of the flag crossing over onto his chest. A cowboy hat hung off the other side of the cross, and a band of barbed wire circled his bicep under the picture.

Her fingers drifted over the inked illustration. "I didn't know you had a tattoo."

He shrugged. "I did it years ago. I designed it because I feel like it's the combination of the three things that define me—God, country, and being a cowboy."

"I think it's crazy sexy," she whispered.

Before she had a chance to turn away in embarrassment of her bold statement, he reached for her chin, holding her gaze with his own piercing stare. "I think *you're* crazy sexy."

Oh my.

Her heart raced as his hands slid down through her hair and untied the apron from around her neck, pulling the strings seductively along her skin, then reached under her back and loosened the bow tied there.

The straps of the apron slid across her hips, whispering against the fabric of her pants, as seductive as any striptease. He tossed the apron to the floor and lay down on the bed next to her.

Skimming his fingers across her cheek, his gaze traveled over her face. "You are so damn beautiful."

She shook her head. "No, I'm not."

He put his finger to her mouth, shushing her, and she sucked in her breath at the feel of his callused finger against the tender skin of her lips. "You are beautiful to me."

His hand traveled across her cheek, then slid down as his fingers sunk into her hair. Holding her head, he leaned in, his breath warm on her neck as he pressed his lips against her throat.

Barely floating over her skin, he laid a trail of soft teasing kisses up her neck and to the sweet tender spot below her ear. His voice was husky as he whispered, "I want to touch you. I've been dying to touch you." He barely nipped her earlobe with his teeth. "Will you let me touch you, Emma?"

She couldn't breathe, couldn't move, the sound of her name on his lips asking permission was almost more than she could bear. Unable to speak, she only nodded her head, her body already aching in eagerness for his touch.

Sliding his hand out from under her hair, he traced the line of her throat, skimming his fingers inside her collar, along her shoulder, and under the strap of her bra. Leaning down, he kissed the center of her chest, then pulled his hand free and slowly released the top button of her shirt.

He looked into her eyes, seeking permission, and she nodded again, not trusting her voice.

Undoing one button at a time, his movement slow and seductive, he followed each opened button with a soft kiss against her newly revealed skin, until her entire shirt was open, and she lay exposed to him. Turning his hand over, he skimmed the back of his fingers across the tops of her uncovered breasts.

She sucked in her breath, arching up, aching for his touch. She was embarrassed by her simple white bra, but Cash didn't seem to mind it. And she had a feeling she wouldn't be wearing it much longer anyway.

But he wasn't there just yet. He was still torturing her as he kissed her ribs, her sides, her stomach, the stubble of his five o'clock shadow grazing against the skin above her waistband.

Hooking his fingers in the top edge of her pants, he slid them down her legs, bending her knees and pulling them free.

He rolled over, this time spreading her legs and kneeling between them. It didn't matter that he was still fully dressed. Having his muscled thighs press against the soft insides of her legs was delicious torment.

His gaze was wild, but his hands were calm, gentle, as they skimmed down the outside of her arms, across her ribs, and teased the top edge of her bikini panties along her belly.

He took her hands and pulled her up, just far enough to peel off her shirt. His hands circled her back, seeking the clasp of her bra.

"I need you naked. I need to see you," he said, his voice hoarse with emotion.

Her shirt hit the floor followed by her white bra, and she lay back—vulnerable and exposed—as he gazed down at her, a look of carnal hunger in his eyes.

And that's what this was—a carnal yearning—sexual need in its purest form. Her body obeying its primal craving for this man.

Her body wanted him, but her head warned her to wait, to protect herself, to conceal her scars.

Her hands automatically reached up to cover herself.

What would he think of her if he saw the evidence of what the years of abuse had done to her body.

"Don't. You don't need to cover yourself. I can take it." It was as if he read her mind, as if he knew her fears.

He gently touched her hands, pulling them away, and her heart beat hard against her chest, as his gaze traveled over her, taking in each blemish, each trace of damage, each wound.

She watched his eyes, waiting for the look of horror or disgust. But instead of shock or judgement, all she saw was acceptance.

He traced the thin white line of scar tissue crossing her hip where Leroy had shoved her into the kitchen table, then he leaned down and softly kissed it. He kissed the small puckers of skin on her shoulder where Leroy had burned her with a cigarette.

Kissing each scar, he acknowledged and accepted her pain, what she'd been through.

"Don't ever be ashamed of your scars," he said. "They aren't marks of shame; they're evidence of your survival. Each one is a testament to the bravery and strength that it took to survive."

His words filled her, taking her shame and humiliation and offering them grace, turning them into confidence and self-assurance.

She fell in love with him in that single moment.

She'd felt it coming, had been tumbling and stumbling toward it, but that moment sealed it. Whether it was smart or not, whether it made sense or not, even if they hadn't known each other all that long—none of that mattered—she was head over heels in love with Cash Walker.

He ran the back of his fingers down her neck and skimmed the inside of her breast.

The look in his eyes was full of tenderness and adoration, and his voice was choked with emotion. "Not one of those scars matters to me. They're just marks on your skin. I care about what's in here, and I know that your heart is good and sweet, and that's what makes you so beautiful to me."

Yep. In love. All the way. No turning back.

Cash was the one.

Her heart felt like it would burst with the intensity of love she felt for this man. She couldn't speak, afraid that if she tried, she would ruin this moment or start crying. And this moment was perfect. One she would remember for her whole life.

And Cash wasn't through with her yet. He dipped his head, kissed her softly then brushed his thumb across the bottom of her lip. "Let me show you what it's like to be treated the way you deserve to be treated. To be cherished. To be cared for."

She held her breath, waiting for him to say "to be loved." He didn't, but she could still feel it. She knew he cared about her. Not the same way she felt for him. She couldn't imagine anyone feeling for her what she felt for him. But she knew his feelings were real.

His words were so raw, so full of emotion, so different from the normal flirty tough cowboy that he portrayed to everyone else. And that was enough. Enough for her.

"Tell me what you like," he said, his voice husky as his gaze roamed over her body.

Heat rushed to her cheeks. She didn't *know* what she liked.

Things with Leroy had always been a frantic rush of him getting in and out, only concerned with his own needs and never hers. It was often a sweaty, awkward fumbling that she bore in hopes that it would be over soon. He'd never taken the time to pursue her needs, never taken the time to even look at her the way Cash devoured her now with his intense gaze.

She shrugged, self-conscious again. "I don't know. I mean,

I'm not sure. Leroy never—I mean—he never asked me about stuff like that."

His look darkened at the mention of Leroy's name. "But surely other men did—" He stopped, a stunned look on his face. "Weren't there other men, before you got married?"

She shook her head, her eyes cast down, embarrassed. "No, he's the only man I've ever been with. Until now, I mean."

He touched her cheek tenderly. "I didn't know. Are you sure you want to do this? Do you need more time? I can wait."

"I can't. I want this." She took his hand from her cheek and entwined his fingers with hers. "I want you."

He leaned forward, dropping a soft kiss in the spot on her neck just beneath her ear and sending another shiver of pleasure racing through her. "I want you, too," he practically growled. "I want you so bad."

"I've waited years for a man to want me like that, to touch me the way you do. I don't want to stop. Please don't stop. I want to feel what's it's supposed to be like. To be wanted like that."

He leaned back, eyeing her with a look of indecision, then a teasing grin tugged at the corners of his lips. "I guess when you put it like that, there's no way I can refuse. And at least I know the bar's been set pretty low."

She laughed, and the tension left her shoulders.

This was what sex was supposed to be like. Not the way it was with Leroy and not the way it was portrayed in the movies where everything was perfectly choreographed. This was real.

And evidently *real* sex was messy and clumsy, but full of fun and laughter mixed with steam and passion.

Yes, this was what she wanted. This man, making her insides go soft and swirly as he teased her body with his mouth and hands, while he still made her laugh and quieted her unease and self-consciousness.

His eyes were dark and intense, but his touch was soft. His hands were rough and reverent as they slid down her legs. He lifted her leg, bending it at the knee, and laid a kiss inside the arch of her foot.

Holy crazy hotness. The feel of his whiskered chin scraping her sole sent rushes of desire tearing through her, not to mention that she lay exposed and open before him.

His fingers circled her ankle then slowly traced up her leg. She shivered at the exquisite anguish as he teased and tickled her skin. Bending forward, he lay a kiss on the inside of her thigh.

Sucking in her breath, she waited, waited to see where his lips would touch next. A moan escaped her as his whiskers grazed the tender crease of her thigh. She'd never experienced a feeling like this—the way her body reacted with a desire that verged on pain.

Everything else fell away—her scars, her past with Leroy, her insecurities—they were all replaced with this experience with Cash. With these breathless moments filled with passion and anticipation.

She savored each feeling, each new sensation, as the flame built inside her, creating a fire of need and wanton fervor.

His lips kissed and teased, getting closer to her feminine core, and she thought she might explode if his mouth got any closer and actually touched her *there*.

On the other hand, she might explode if he *didn't*.

Speaking of his other hand—it was doing delicious things as he searched out her warm center, exploring, rubbing, bringing her closer to the edge with each stroke.

"Damn, woman, I don't know what you're doing to me, but I can't wait any more. I need to feel you." He stood up, hurriedly working his jeans over his hips, stopping to yank his wallet from his pocket before dropping them to the floor. He pulled a foil-wrapped condom from its folds before tossing the wallet onto his jeans, then covered himself and settled back between her legs.

His weight on top of her felt wonderful, his muscled arms cradling her against him as he pressed into her. She sighed as his strong fingers ran down her back and dug into her hip.

It had been so long. And it had never been like this. This was all new—the sensations foreign and even a little frightening. But she didn't want him to stop.

She caught her breath—a quick gasp at the sweet intensity of the stretching fullness that bordered between pleasure and pain. Then the slow rhythm of movement as he rocked against her, her core pulsing with need for him.

Glancing up at him, she saw his jaw tighten, as if he were trying to cling to some form of control. And losing.

His motion quickened, and threads of pleasure slid through her.

Her thoughts were jumbled, she couldn't think straight, couldn't think at all.

Could only feel. Feel the toned muscles under her fingers as she clutched his back. Feel the scrape of his teeth against her collarbone. Feel the sheets twisting beneath them.

Her body quivered with bliss as he carried her higher and higher, her toes curling as she teetered on the edge.

A sigh caught in her throat, her breath coming in short, tight gasps as his quickened movements sent her falling over, holding on to him as the flashes of heat coursed through her. Again. And again.

Then she was dissolving under him, melting into the bed, as he slumped on top of her, spent and sated.

She kissed his shoulder, his neck, his cheek, then he slid off her and drew her close to his side.

Trying to catch her breath, she curled in to him.

And. Couldn't. Stop. Smiling.

It was as if she had no control of her own facial muscles;

the grin overtook her face, and she couldn't stop. A tiny ripple of laughter bubbled up inside her.

He jostled her against him. "I don't know if laughter was the reaction I was going for."

Her grin practically split her face. "I'm just so dang happy. And that was really amazing."

He chuckled. "Okay, I'll take that reaction. Especially the amazing part."

"Cash Walker, I think you have ruined me for every other man."

He took her chin in his hand and tilted her face up to his. "Good. Because I plan to be the only man who makes you feel like this. The only man who's ever gonna be in your bed again. In fact, I don't think we should ever leave *this* bed. What do you have to say about that?"

"I say that sounds good to me." She gave him a sideways glance as she pulled her bottom lip under her teeth. "I just have one question for you though."

"What's that?"

"When can we do it again?"

Chapter Twelve

Cash draped an arm around the back of the bench seat in his truck and grinned as Emma scooted closer and slid under the crook of his elbow. "You have a good day?"

It was the next day, and he'd just picked her up from the diner. They'd planned to go horseback riding that afternoon, and Cash'd had Cherry put together a full picnic supper complete with fried chicken and strawberry lemonade. He was surprised at how antsy and excited he'd been all day as he'd waited for Emma to get off work.

"It was good, but long." She gave him a gentle nudge in the ribs. "I know it's only three o'clock, but I've been thinking about our—um, date, I guess—all day." He felt her shoulders tense. "Is it okay to call it a date?"

"Sure. You can call it whatever you want." He dropped his hand down to rub her neck, and he felt her shoulders relax as he said, "And I've been thinking about it, and you, all day today, too. I've got it all planned out. We can take the horses down through the back pasture and up into the hills behind the farm. There's a real pretty lake up there that I thought you might like to see. And I even had Cherry make us a picnic to take along. She brought it out while I was waiting for you."

"So that's what was in the basket. I saw her bring it out while I was hanging up my apron." She shook her head, her gaze fixed on her clasped hands in her lap. "I've never had anyone actually *plan* a whole date for me before."

"Well, then it's about damn time you did."

She turned her head to him, a beaming smile covering her face, and he would have planned a hundred dates, arranged for a hundred picnics—hell, he'd fry the chicken himself—if it earned him another grin like that one.

He pulled the truck into the driveway of the farm, and thirty minutes later, Emma had changed into jeans and boots, and Cash had packed up their supplies and saddled the horses.

He patted the neck of a golden-colored mare. "This is Ginger. She's a real sweetheart. She's been around forever. We let little kids ride her because she's so gentle. She's the horse that Charlie learned to ride on as well, and she was way more scared than you are."

She nodded and rubbed her sweaty hands on her jeans. "Okay."

"So stick your foot in here, then grab a hold of the saddle horn to help pull yourself up." He held out the stirrup. "You nervous?"

"Heck, yeah, I'm nervous." She fit her boot into the stirrup, grabbed the horn of the saddle, pulled herself up, swung her leg over, and dropped into the saddle. Offering him a brave grin, she said, "But I'm not scared."

Cash brushed his hand down her leg as she settled into the saddle. "You're going to do fine. I'll lead, and Ginger will pretty much follow along behind my horse."

"Pretty much?" Her voice was a little shaky, leading Cash to believe she might not feel as brave as she was acting.

"Trust your horse. Yeah, she's big. But she's solid. Even

when she's walking on rocky ground or trotting a little, to her, she's just walking. She's very surefooted so she won't fall down or anything." He showed her how to guide the horse using the reins then patted the horse's mane. "She's a good horse. She won't let you down."

Not like I might.

The thought struck him as he climbed atop his own horse, a dark brown gelding named Renegade. But he didn't want to think about that. Didn't want to contemplate all the reasons why getting involved with Emma was a bad idea.

Waking up beside her this morning sure hadn't been a bad idea. She'd looked like an angel with her hair spread across the pillow and her expression serene as she slept.

They'd sliced the pie the night before, scooped on dollops of vanilla ice cream, and eaten it naked in her bed.

He'd grinned that morning as he'd brushed an errant crumb off his pillow, remembering the way the vanilla ice cream had tasted as he'd licked drops of it off her bare skin.

The movement on the pillow had woken her. Her eyes fluttered open, and she must have liked seeing his grin, because she rewarded him with a smile and cuddled into his arms.

They'd made love again that morning, slow and sweet, and by the light of day, Cash could see the multitude of scars on her body. Scars that Leroy had given her. His gut churned with anger at the thought of Leroy hurting her, and he knew if he ever ran into him again, he just might kill the son of a bitch.

Pushing those thoughts from his mind, he focused on the ride ahead and making sure that Emma was okay on the horse behind him.

He gave his horse a nudge in the side and clicked his tongue, and the animal plodded forward. Ren had been his horse for the past ten years, and they had an understanding.

Turning in the saddle, he checked on Emma. "Just give

her a little kick in the sides with the heel of your boot, and she'll start walking."

Emma prodded the horse with her heels and gripped the reins, her face showing a slight bit of alarm as the horse lumbered forward.

He chuckled. "You okay?"

She gave a nod. "Yep, I'm okay."

He turned around and guided Renegade through the pasture and up toward the wooded area behind the farm. The path through the fields was easy, and he wanted her to have that time to get comfortable before it got a little rougher as they entered the trees.

"You still doing all right back there?" he called over his shoulder.

"I'm doing fine. Ginger is just following behind your horse. I don't really even have to do anything besides sit here. I'm having fun, actually."

"Good. It's gonna get a little rocky through this next part, but just hold on. I promise it will be worth the wait."

Twenty minutes later, the woods opened on a clearing, a sparkling blue lake in its center. He heard Emma's gasp and grinned. "I told you so."

He led them over to a large cottonwood tree, climbed down from his horse, and helped Emma dismount.

She slid down and leaned against him as her knees started to buckle. He grabbed her before she fell. "Whoa there. You all right?"

Rubbing her legs, she looked up at him with a sheepish grin. "Yeah, I'm fine. My legs are just a little shaky. It's just been a while since I've used my horseback riding muscles."

"I thought you said you hadn't ridden a horse before."

"I haven't. But I used the muscles plenty last night." She arched an eyebrow at him, waiting for the meaning of her words to soak in.

"Oh, you mean—" He wiggled his eyebrows then chuckled at the pink tinge in her cheeks.

She laughed with him as he led the horses closer to the tree. Its trunk was massive, with snarled roots snaking out along the ground and thick branches strong enough for him to toss the reins around to hold their horses.

Even though it was early fall, the tree's branches were still thick with leaves, and they formed a canopy over the base of the tree. A slight breeze blew, and whispers of sound fluttered through the multicolored leaves that were just starting to change.

"It's beautiful," Emma said, her voice holding a tone of awe.

Cash slipped up behind her, sliding his arms around her waist and speaking into her ear. "You're beautiful."

She ducked her head, obviously embarrassed. "You don't need to say that, Cash. I know I'm not. I've always been plain. Even in school, I knew I was kind of like a dandelion in a bed of roses."

"What are you talking about?" He turned her around and tipped her chin up. "You're no dandelion. And you *are* beautiful to me. Being beautiful is about more than the way you wear your hair or how you look. It's the way you are on the inside. It's how you treat people and how you care for animals and old folks. Your beauty shines through when you smile at customers in the diner, when you laugh with Charlie, when you put a comforting arm around Sophie, and when you grin up at me in the moments after you've just called out my name and God's in the same breath."

A pink tinge colored her cheeks as she offered him a small laugh.

"I think we've already established that the person who made you feel less than beautiful was an asshole."

"True."

"But I don't see you as a rose, either." He turned her to point at a row of flowers growing beside a fallen log. "See those wildflowers growing there. Aren't they beautiful?"

She nodded.

"That's how I see you, darlin'. Like a wildflower. One that stands tall and grows where it's planted. Full of color and brightness. Wildflowers can bloom anywhere, on the side of the road, in a field or on a mountain, even next to a cow pie. Because they're strong and resilient. They use the resources they have available, and they make everything more beautiful just by their presence."

She inhaled sharply, and he worried that she might start to cry. "Dang, but your words can sometimes just make me weak in the knees."

"Then you better sit down and have you some of Cherry's fried chicken—best solution for weak knees." Cash pulled the supplies from the back of his saddle.

He'd brought a couple of blankets and laid one down among the roots of the tree, set the picnic basket on top of it, then plopped down next to it. He kept the other blanket folded and placed it next to him, patting the top for her to use as a seat.

Emma settled onto the blanket, exclaiming over the food that Cash pulled out of the basket. "Oh my gosh, that fried chicken smells amazing. It all looks wonderful."

Cherry had packed paper plates and disposable utensils, and they set about dishing up the food and pouring lemonade into two plastic cups. As they ate, they chatted easily about their day and the people in the town, and Emma told him a funny thing that had happened at the diner that day.

He'd heard from Charlie that morning, and he filled Emma in on how she and Sophie were doing in New York. "I guess they saw a play last night, I can't remember the name. I'm sure they'll tell you all about it when they get back. And I guess Sophie is in shopping heaven. She wants to go in every store."

Emma laughed. "I'm sure she does." She cleaned up their plates and packed everything but their drinks back into the picnic basket. Patting her stomach, she proclaimed, "I'm so full, I couldn't eat another bite."

"Then we'll have to save the pie that Cherry packed for later."

She groaned. "More pie. I'm gonna gain ten pounds hanging out with you."

"Good. Then you'll have more for me to hold on to." He made a playful grab for her butt, and she giggled and squirmed away.

He pushed himself back and leaned against the base of the tree. "Come on over here," he said, patting the space next to him.

She scooted across the blanket and settled under the crook of his arm. "Thank you for bringing me."

"It was my pleasure. How you feelin' about the horseback riding? You still scared or are you getting used to it a little?"

"I'm getting used to it. Granted, we're only walking, but I found myself calming down and really enjoying the ride." She toyed with the buttons on his shirt. "I feel like such a chicken about stuff. I hate to admit to you all the things I'm scared of."

"Why?"

"Because you don't seem to be afraid of anything."

He huffed. "You're wrong about that."

She looked up at him, narrowing her eyes as if to judge if he was being serious or not. "Tell me one thing you're scared of."

"You. I'm scared as hell of you." The words popped out before he could stop them. And now they were out, hanging in the air, and he couldn't take them back.

"Me?" she asked softly. "Why on earth would you be

afraid of me? I wouldn't ever hurt you."

He pulled her closer and rubbed his hand over her hip. "I know that, darlin'. But I'm afraid I'm going to hurt you. Like down-in-my-bones, gut-deep terrified of it."

"Why? Why would you even think that?"

He stroked his hand over her hair, his thumb brushing her cheek as he tucked a strand of it behind her ear. "I tried to tell you last night. There's darkness in my past. In me."

Looking him straight in the eye, she said, "Tell me. Tell me your darkest part."

He shook his head, the shame of it welling in his chest. "I can't."

"Last night, I bared myself to you, showed you my body, let you lay witness to my scars and the evidence of *my* darkness. I shared that with you."

"I know. But I've got scars you can't see."

"So do I. That's okay. It doesn't matter what you tell me, I'm not going anywhere. I lo—like you."

He wanted to believe her. Wanted to believe with all of his heart. "I like you, too, Em. I like you a lot. But my past ain't pretty. I'm afraid if I tell you—if you know the truth about me—you're not gonna want to have anything to do with me. And you sure as hell won't like me anymore."

"There is nothing that you could say that would change the way I feel about you." She laid her head on his chest. "Tell me."

Chapter Thirteen

Cash took a deep breath. "I don't know if I can. I've never spoken to anyone about it."

She picked up his hand and held it in hers. "You can. You can talk to me."

He'd been telling her all week how she should be brave and step outside of her comfort zone. Well, this was way the hell out of his zone. But she had shown courage this week. She'd pretended she was brave. He could do the same.

For her. She was that important. *This* was that important.

Clearing his throat, he worked to swallow back his fear. "You know I told you about my dad, my stepdad, and the way he treated my mom and me?"

She nodded against his chest.

"Well, it was bad. Real bad. And it went on for a long time. And a thing like that gets inside of you and starts to eat away at you. It makes you question who you are, what kind of person you are that you let that go on, that you don't try to run, or fight back. That you take it, again and again. And then this kind of hate starts to build inside you. Not the kind where you hate brussels sprouts or the color orange. But a bone-deep pure kind of hate. The kind of hate that then makes you question even your own faith. Like if you have that much hatred inside you, how could you be worthy of any kind of love that God would offer?"

"I know." She squeezed his hand. "I know that feeling."

"I know you do. But it was different for me, because I'm a man. Or I was supposed to be a man. I was supposed to be strong, and I felt like I was supposed to take care of my mom. And every time I failed at that responsibility, that ball of hate grew inside me. It grew until it was this nasty, steaming, churning, mass of rage, and I carried it around knowing that I was like a time bomb just waiting to go off and waiting for that rage to spew out of me like lava from a volcano.

"Then one night, it happened. My dad was on a terrible bender, and he came after my mom with a baseball bat. She hadn't even done anything. We'd just been sittin' on the couch watching television. We thought he'd gone to bed. Then all of a sudden, he came out of their room, yelling and swinging that bat, breaking stuff and knocking holes in the wall."

He could feel Emma tense against him and knew that she'd probably had similar experiences of her husband going off on an unprovoked rage.

"He took a swing at my mom, just swung that bat at her, and I swear to you that I heard the bone crack in her arm. She scrambled off the sofa, crawlin' across the floor, that broken arm just danglin' at her side. I stepped in front of her, but he pushed me out of the way, like I was nothing. But that night, as I fell to the floor, that ball of rage finally broke apart and came gushing out of me like vomit. I can remember tasting the bile in my throat as I decided I wasn't gonna take it anymore. That night was different. There was something in his eyes—some kind of demon—and I think he wanted to kill her.

"So, instead of backing down, I stood up to him. As afraid

of that rage as I was, it gave me courage—that, or made me stupid enough to think I had a chance against him. But you see, by this time, I was sixteen years old, and I was stronger than I realized, stronger than he realized, and that nasty old rage gave me a kind of strength that I didn't know I possessed. So when I got up and stepped in front of my mom again, he took a swing at me, and I caught that bat. I caught it and tore it from his filthy hands."

"It sounds to me like you were a hero, like you saved your mom."

"Don't ever call me a hero, Emma. I'm nobody's hero."

"But you stepped in and protected your mom. Even at your own risk. You did save her, right?"

The memories of that night swirled in his head, the images so vivid, he could almost smell the coppery scent of the blood.

"Yeah, I saved her. But I didn't just take the bat from him. If I would have just taken the bat and left it at that, I might have been a hero. But I didn't. So help me God, I didn't. I took that bat away and swung at him. I'll never forget the feeling of that wooden bat connecting with his body."

She gasped, then raised her head to look at him. "Did you…did you kill him?" Her eyes narrowed, her gaze penetrated his. "Because I wouldn't blame you if you did."

"No, I didn't kill him. I probably would have if I'd connected with his skull, but my aim wasn't that good, and I caught him across the shoulder. It was enough to knock him down though. He was stunned—like he couldn't believe I'd done it—hell, I couldn't believe I'd done it. Then he came back at me, swinging. Hard.

"But you see, I had all this rage brewing inside me, and so when he took a swing at me, I dropped the bat and started slugging back. Like a decade of anger and frustration poured out of me, and I couldn't control the fury in my fists. I hit him in the face and the stomach. I'm pretty sure I broke his nose 'cause there was blood, a lot of blood, but I didn't care. It was like the blood fueled my rage, and I just kept swinging. Then he was down on the floor and holding up his hands in surrender, and he stopped fighting—just lay down and started crying.

"My mom was crying, too, and pulling me away from him. He started apologizin' and telling us how sorry he was, but I didn't care. I wasn't listening. Not this time. I told him to leave, that we wanted him out and never wanted to see him again. He couldn't believe it—he begged my mom to give him another chance, but something changed for her that night, too, and she told him no, she wanted him out."

"Did he go? Did he actually leave?"

"Yeah, he did. I told him I was taking my mom to the emergency room and that he'd better be gone by the time we got back or we'd call the police and press charges against him. And he must have believed me, because by the time we got back from the hospital, he was gone."

"And that's it? I mean that's an awful story, and I'm sorry you had to go through that, but you stood up for yourself and your mother. Why would that make me think less of you?"

He took off his hat and set it on the ground next to them then ran a hand through his hair. "Because you're only hearing the part of the story that you want to hear. You're missing the part where I lost control and let loose my anger—the part where I was just like him."

"You're nothing like him."

"Don't you see? I acted *exactly* like him. I used my fists and my anger to beat him, to draw blood, to break his nose, and to drive him out of our house. I'd grown up watching him do it, and it was the only way I'd ever seen an adult man handle his problems. It must have seeped into my consciousness, got into my blood, my instincts, because when my back was against the wall, I came out swinging, thirsting for blood. Just. Like. Him."

She shook her head. "I don't believe it. I've seen you—"

"That's not the end of the story."

"Did he come back?"

"No, he didn't. He never came back. But what happened that night stayed with me. It changed me. I knew I had that rage, that beast inside me. And it terrified me. Made me afraid that if I let anyone get too close, they might glimpse the monster that was inside me."

"You don't know that."

"Yes, I do. Because it happened. Or it came close to happening. Because I did let someone in. I was a senior in high school, one of those angsty bad-boy rebels who acted tough and cool."

"But were actually hurting inside."

He shrugged. "Yeah, I guess. But I wasn't tough enough to withstand the attention of Gillian Carter. She was a cheerleader and the prettiest girl in school."

"I remember her."

He hated the way Emma's shoulders shrank in at his comment. "Or she was to a stupid eighteen-year-old kid who thought he was in love with her. But she wasn't in love with me. Hell, I don't know if she even liked me or if she was just using me to piss off her dad. It doesn't matter. The point is that she drew me in like a fish on a hook, spinning my head and my heart around so much that I didn't know which way was up. And I let her in. She told me I was her first, and I got caught up in the moment—thinking that actually meant something—and I told her how I felt."

"It does mean something," Emma said softly, reminding him that she had confessed the night before that he was only the second man she'd ever been with.

"Well, it might mean something to some, but not to her. I told her I loved her. That I wanted to marry her after graduation. I was serious about it. I'd even borrowed Zack's car and taken her to this park by her house for a picnic so I could ask her."

"And what did she say?"

"Nothing. She just laughed. Then she told me she didn't want a relationship with someone like me, that she'd only gone out with me because she thought I was cute and her friends had dared her to. She said that she'd heard Cash Walker didn't have feelings, that I was only interested in one thing, and wouldn't make things complicated."

He looked out over the lake, caught up in the memories. "I'd never felt so foolish—and worthless—in my life. She made me feel like an idiot. And I got mad. So help me, I lost my temper, and that monster inside of me reared its ugly head."

"Did you hit her?"

"No. Hell no. But I might as well have. I wanted to hit something. I was throwing our stuff in the car, and the trunk was open. I grabbed the tire iron and started beating the side of the car. I smashed a big dent in the back end and shattered the taillight. She took off and ran home. I ran after her, but when I got there, she slammed the front door in my face and never talked to me again. Zack took the blame for the damage to the car, told his dad that he'd backed into a tree, but I spent the summer paying him back for what I'd done."

"So you destroyed the car, but you didn't actually hurt her."

"Not physically, but you should have seen her face. It was in her eyes and the set of her mouth. She was afraid of me. Hell, I was afraid of myself. I was so mad. And I was ashamed which, looking back, probably fueled that anger. But the point is, she was *scared* of me. Scared that I would hurt her. And I never wanted another woman to look at me that way again. Ever.

"Which is why I don't get involved. Don't let myself get

close to anyone. Close enough that they could break my heart, or cause that deep of an emotion to boil up in me again. It's easier for me to keep things light, and not let my feelings enter into it. Not let anyone into my heart. Until you."

He looked down at her, and his heart swelled with the love and compassion he saw shining in her eyes.

"Thank you," she said.

"Thank you? What the hell are you thanking me for? For telling you that I'm an emotionally closed-off broken man?"

"For telling me your story." She reached up and caressed his cheek. "And we're all broken. We all have things in our past that form who we are now. I thought I was broken, thought my heart was so torn apart that it wouldn't ever work again, that I wouldn't ever be able to feel anything real again. And that I'd never be able to care for another man. But meeting you started my heart beating again. And even in the short time I've known you, my heart acts like it's been waiting for you all along."

Her words flowed through him, like a salve to his bruised and shaken soul. "I haven't cared enough about anyone since then to want to take the chance on—to risk letting myself get caught up with—to hazard giving them my heart."

"You can take a chance on me."

He looked into her eyes, and he believed her. He'd been alone for so long, and she was the first person he'd wanted to try having a relationship with. The first person who made his heart stand up and take notice.

Hell, it wasn't just his heart that took notice when she was around. Every part of him responded to the simple nearness of her.

Looking at her now, her eyes full of care and her lips slightly parted—rose-colored and full—and just waiting to be kissed.

"I already have." Leaning down, he took her mouth,

captured it in his, kissing her with all the passion and hunger that he felt for her. He'd bared his soul, and she hadn't gone running.

In fact, she'd snuggled closer and held out her own heart.

And he didn't want to hurt her. Ever.

If he took her heart, he vowed to protect it, to protect her, to never let her be hurt again.

A rumble of thunder rolled through the air, and raindrops fell on the blanket at their feet.

He pulled back, noticing for the first time the dark clouds that had rolled in.

Montana was known for its thunderstorms that snuck up without warning, swiftly turning the big blue sky dark and ominous. They didn't always last long, but they could be sudden and fierce.

"Shit. I should have been paying attention." He peered out from under the canopy of the tree. Thick gray clouds covered the sky, and he could see the long dark lines of rain casting down from the sky. "I think we're stuck waiting this one out, darlin'."

Pulling the folded blanket out from under her, she spread it over them and cuddled closer in his arms. She grinned up at him. "I love the rain. And I can't think of any other place I'd rather be."

Damn, but he did like this woman. He more than liked her. He could feel the tendrils of love creeping into his heart like the deep ivy vines that covered the side of the farmhouse.

She tipped his chin down and kissed him. Her hands swept up his cheeks and wound their way into his hair, holding his head while she deepened the kiss, her body curving against his.

Even with no words, with only the language of their entwined bodies and the urgency of her kiss, she conveyed a message. A message that told him that he was worth it, that he mattered, that she trusted him.

The skies broke loose and the showers poured down, filling the air with the scent of wet earth and fresh rain, and as the storm raged in the sky around them, it loosened the hold around his heart. Like the rain was washing away the past and giving them — giving him — a clean slate. A fresh start.

A fresh start with Emma.

He pulled her against him, his hands — as if they had minds of their own — finding their way under her shirt. He needed to touch her, to feel her skin.

He didn't think, didn't consider if this was a good idea or not — he'd spent enough time analyzing and scrutinizing his decision — this time he just reacted, did what felt right.

And right now, nothing felt more right than having her bare skin against his.

He fumbled with the snaps marching up the front of her shirt, popping each one loose and exposing her stomach and her pale pink bra.

Groaning, he dipped his head, laying a row of heated kisses along her shoulder and into the cleavage between her full breasts.

Reaching for the hem of his own shirt, he didn't bother with the buttons, instead he yanked both his button-up shirt and the T-shirt he wore under it over his head. All he could focus on was getting closer to her, connecting to her through their bodies, getting her skin against his.

She must have sensed his frenzy and felt it too, because her hands went to his belt buckle, wiggling it free then unzipping his jeans. Kissing his chest, his neck, the spot behind his ear.

His nerves went wild with want and hunger as he heard the soft sexy sounds she made, the quick gasp of breath, as he reached inside her bra to cup her breast and flick his thumb over the taut bud of her nipple.

A bolt of lightning shot through the sky, cutting through

the rain that continued to fall. The thunder sounded a minute later, the rumbling boom rolling through him, barely drowning out the noise of his own heartbeat as it hammered against his chest.

Unable to wait a second longer, the intensity of the storm escalating the force of their passion, he sat up, pushing back the blanket and pulling off his boots, then wriggling free of his jeans.

Turning to her, he saw she'd already wiggled out of her shirt and bra and tugged off her own boots. Laying her back against the blanket, he peeled her jeans and panties down her legs, leaving her naked and exposed.

His breath ragged and his heart beating in rapid anticipation, he pulled her under him, pressing his bare skin to hers. Ignoring the cool air, the heat coming off their bodies keeping them warm, he kissed her again, his tongue slipping between her lips.

She tasted like strawberries, and he sucked lightly on her tongue, eliciting another soft moan of arousal.

Dipping his head, he kissed her neck, her throat, the hollow between her breasts. Her pink-tipped nipples pebbled—either from the cool air or arousal—and he drew the nub of one into his mouth.

Her hands grasped handfuls of the blanket, and her back arched to meet him as he circled her nipple with his tongue then sucked it between his lips. The harsh gasp of breath he earned only spurred him on, and his hand grazed over her waist and across her belly.

He glanced up at her, noting how her eyes fluttered closed in ecstasy and the way she bit at her bottom lip. Her legs parted slightly, which he took as an invitation and slid his hand between them, finding her warm and so deliciously wet.

Darts of heat shot through him, ramping up his own desire, and he knew he had to taste her.

Scooting down, he laid a line of kisses along her stomach, her waist, his mouth seeking her sensitive folds. Licking and sucking, he brought her to the edge, loving the way her breath came in quick gasps, and she clasped handfuls of his hair.

Every moan, every pant, every time she squirmed with want enflamed his desire, his hunger for her.

The sky continued to storm around them, the flashes of lightning only escalating their passion.

Unable to take another second, he sat up, grabbing for his jeans and pulling his wallet free from the back pocket. He'd stocked it with a couple of extra condoms that morning, just in case the need for one arose.

And right now, he had a need. A desperate need as he jerked the foil packet free, dropping the wallet onto the blanket in his haste to open the packet and sheath himself with its contents.

She watched him, her lips moist and slightly parted, catching her breath as he took care of business. Kneeling between her legs, he glanced up, awaiting her permission.

"You okay?" he asked, praying she would say yes.

Nodding, her head moving in quick bobs, she panted out her answer. "Yes. Now. Please."

He slid into her, sighing as she surrounded him with a tight, delicious heat. Her legs wrapped around his waist, and everything else fell away. Everything except this woman, this moment in time, as they moved in rhythm with each other in a primal dance of ache and need, creating their own storm as the sky raged around them.

Drops of water fell through the leaves of the tree, dripping onto his back, but he barely noticed. All of his focus was on Emma, watching her face as he took her to the edge of desire, her soft sounds and the way she arched in to him.

Knowing he could illicit such emotion only fueled his own passion, and he thrust harder, increasing his tempo and speed until she was crying out his name and clutching his back.

Then he was gone, lost in the waves of pleasure rocking through him.

Spent, he fell to the blanket next to her and drew her into his arms. Pulling the other blanket up, he covered them, and she shivered against him.

The rain had finally started to let up, and the storm seemed to be dying down.

She cuddled against his side. "Holy cow. I don't think I've ever experienced a thunderstorm like that before."

"Oh, was it raining? I hadn't noticed." He chuckled and pulled her closer, kissing the top of her head. "I do believe you have worn me out." Closing his eyes, he relaxed against the base of the tree, sated and content. And happy.

"The poor horses. They're all wet."

"They don't mind. They stand out in the rain all the time. The saddles will be wet, though, so your jeans will probably be soaked clear through by the time we get back to the house."

"Maybe I won't bother putting them back on then," she teased.

He chuckled. "Now *that* I would like to see. It would be a whole new version of 'bare' back riding." Scanning the sky, he let out a sigh. "Speaking of riding, we should probably pack up and head back while the storm's let up."

She groaned. "Do we have to? I think I could stay here all night with you. Just like this."

A warm feeling of happiness filled him as she curled tighter against his side. A feeling that he could get used to if he wasn't careful. "I'd agree, if we had more fried chicken."

She laughed, then her body shivered.

"And if I had another blanket." He rubbed his hand briskly along her back. "Let's get you back and warmed up. We can save the pie until we get back to my cabin, then I can build a fire and work on getting you naked again."

Reaching for her clothes, she laughed again. "Pie, a fire, and you? You're not going to have to work very hard."

...

Thirty minutes later, they plodded into the barn. The rain had started again, and Emma was soaked and cold. She shivered as he helped her down from the horse.

"Head over to my cabin—the door's unlocked—and get out of those wet clothes."

"You trying to get me naked again already?" She tried to laugh but her teeth chattered instead.

He wrapped a dry blanket around her from a stack in the barn. "I'm *always* trying to get you naked. But right now, I'm also just trying to get you warm. I've got about ten or fifteen minutes of chores to do then I'll join you. I just need to get the horses put up and the animals fed."

"I can help you."

He smiled at her suggestion and leaned down to speak low into her ear. "Thanks, you're a sweetheart to offer, but I've got it. It won't take me long, and I'll go quicker if I'm imagining you waiting for me in a hot bath. I've got a big old bathtub, and if you get the water started, I'll be there in a few minutes."

His deep voice sent shivers down her spine that had nothing to do with her wet clothes. She dashed through the rain, crossing the yard, and let herself into his cabin.

The anticipation of being with him again had her nervous and jumpy, and she shivered again as she pulled off her wet boots and left them by the door.

The light above the sink was on, and she looked around the cabin. She was standing in one large room with a fireplace and living area on one side and a kitchen on the other. A large butcher-block island sat in the middle.

She could see two rooms off to the right, one the bedroom, and the other looked to be an office or study.

The room smelled like him—masculine. Like warm wood and an even hotter male—with undertones of pine and his aftershave.

The décor was western with lots of browns, burgundies, and blue, and she wondered if he'd done it himself. A large recliner sat next to a comfy looking sofa, an end table stacked with books standing between them. Peeking at the titles, it appeared that he enjoyed old westerns and modern spy thrillers. She smiled to see Charlie's latest book in the stack.

Despite a few stacks of paper and a pair of moccasin slippers next to the recliner, the room was tidy and neat. The kitchen was clean and, peeking into his bedroom, she could see his bed was made. Impressive.

His bedroom was big with heavy oak furniture and a king-sized bed. Sparks of heat shot through her as she imagined being naked in that bed with him. It felt strangely intimate walking through his bedroom, but she could see the corner of the bathtub through the door to the master bath.

The bathroom was good-sized and modern. A large glassed-in shower with multiple heads was in one corner, and the deep soaking tub was centered between it and an oak vanity. It was obvious the cabin had undergone renovations. Had he done them himself?

He continued to surprise her.

She hadn't expected the picnic supper and wouldn't have imagined—even in her wildest dreams—that they would end up making love under a tree in the rain.

The afternoon had been one of the best of her life, and her body quivered in expectation of what the night would hold.

Turning on the water in the tub, she squirted some of Cash's shower gel into the stream and masculine-scented bubbles formed on the water.

Peeling off her clothes, she imagined his hands on her as she stood naked next to the tub.

"Now that's a view I could get used to." Cash's deep voice came from behind her. "Nothing like walking into a room and finding a gorgeous naked woman standing in it."

Chapter Fourteen

A smile tugged at the corner of Emma's lips as gooseflesh pimpled her skin. She turned and caught her breath at the sight of Cash as he stood in the doorway of the room.

His jet black hair was wet from the rain and curled around his neck and ears. He'd pulled off his shirt and boots and wore only his jeans. The muscles of his chest and abs were toned and ripped and still tan from working outside in the summer.

He was so perfectly male and ridiculously hot.

The sexy grin he wore on his face would have melted the panties right off her. Except she wasn't wearing any.

She stood naked before him, bare and vulnerable, and it was both thrilling and terrifying at the same time.

He tugged off his jeans and underwear and crossed to her, wrapping his arms around her from behind and dipping his head to kiss her neck. The feel of his warm breath on her neck had her very core heating and clenching.

He must have been heating up, too. She could feel him go rigid and firm against her as his lips moved from her neck to her shoulder, and his hands reached up to caress her breasts.

She could die from the delicious torture of him touching her. Like seriously, die right here, right now. And she would die a happy woman.

But she'd rather not. She'd rather live, and feel, and experience every nuance of this incredible moment. Because for the first time in years, she finally felt like she was alive.

And she didn't want to miss anything.

She shivered against him, her body filled with tingling anticipation.

"Let's get in the tub and get you warmed up."

Even though her hair was damp and she was naked, she actually wasn't cold at all. In fact, she felt like she was burning from the inside out, on fire from his very touch.

How could she be cold when the hot cowboy standing beside her was generating so much heat?

He stepped into the bubbly water then sat down with his back to the tub's edge and held out his hand to invite her in. She followed him in, pausing to adjust to the temperature of the water as she leaned back against him.

Holy hot bubble bath. His muscled arms wrapped around her, the water swishing against the sides of the tub and filling the air with the scent of his shower gel, and she sighed at the incredible feeling of sitting between his legs with his arms around her.

"You okay?" he asked, his voice carrying a note of concern.

She hugged his arms to her chest. "I'm more than okay. I'm over-the-moon happy."

He chuckled, and she could feel the low rumble of his laugh on her back. Leaning forward, he nipped at her earlobe and spoke huskily into her ear. "And we haven't even gotten to the good part."

"All of this is the good part to me." She laid her head back into the crook of his neck and tipped her face up to look at him. "I've never been treated like this before."

"You mean treated to a bubble bath with a cowboy taking up most of the space?"

"No, not that. I mean I never have shared a bathtub with a man before, but that's not what I mean. I mean I *like* the bath, I LOVE the bath," she paused and set her hand on top of his, intertwining their fingers, "I mean, I've never been treated with this much care and attention before."

He squeezed her hand. "You deserve it."

"Why? What did I do to deserve it?"

"First of all, you're a woman. And all women deserve to be treated with care and attention and like they're something special. And because you are you. Emma, I wish you could see yourself through my eyes. I see a woman who cares about other people, who treats everyone with kindness and respect, who is strong and brave, and who is just discovering all those great things about herself."

His words filled her, like warm tea fills a cup, their meaning reaching her brim and making her feel toasty and cozy all over.

And loved. Whether he felt that for her or not, she felt loved and cherished. All of this was new to her, but she was quickly getting used to it.

Which should have scared her. But it didn't.

Because she didn't care if this lasted one day or the rest of her life, she'd felt it, and now she knew what it was like to be treated like a gift instead of a possession.

"Thank you," she whispered and tipped her head forward to lay a kiss against the side of his arm.

"Don't thank me. I'm the lucky one."

She rolled over, pressing her breasts against his chest as water splashed over the sides, and gave him a flirty grin. "Not yet, but you're about to be."

...

A few hours later, Emma rolled over in bed, her eyes heavy with sleep, her muscles liquid and loose, and reached for Cash. But the other side of the bed was empty.

The bathtub had been foreplay, their bodies wet and slick as Cash found inventive new ways to arouse and stir her. When the water got cold, he'd toweled her dry, then carried her into his room and laid her on his bed.

The rain had started in earnest again, and the scent of it came in on the breeze through the open window. The sound of the thunder rumbled, and lightning flashed outside, temporarily filling the room with bursts of light.

The music of the storm was like their soundtrack as they explored and discovered new things about each other and new ways to create their own tempest.

Cash knew just how to touch her, to tease her, to bring her to the brink of release and to send her crashing over. And he taught her to do the same for him. Although not quite as many times as her.

She smiled into the pillow just thinking about it. The soft flannel sheets on his bed were comfy against her naked skin, and even though her body was spent, wrung out, and exhausted, just thinking about the bathtub had sparks of desire flitting through her and awakening the same spots that she'd thought were worn out.

Sitting up in bed, searching for Cash, she could hear the sweet tones of a guitar playing. Wrapping the sheet around her, she climbed out of bed and peered into the living room.

Cash sat on the sofa, naked except for a pair of boxer briefs, playing the guitar and softly singing in a low deep voice.

The room was dark, except for the flickering of the firelight, and the song he played was soft and full of melancholy, too low for her to make out the words. A short glass with a quarter inch of amber liquid sat on the table next to him.

She couldn't have imagined a sexier scene.

And couldn't believe that she'd just been in bed, being touched and caressed by that ridiculously handsome man. She padded over to the sofa and sat down next to him.

His hands stilled on the guitar.

"Don't stop. I like it." She kept her voice quiet, not wanting to break the spell of the moment. "I didn't know you played."

"I don't play very well. But it relaxes me, eases my mind, and sometimes helps me sort out things that are troubling me."

"Do you have a lot of things troubling you right now?"

"I've always got something troublin' me, darlin'."

With a man like Cash, she figured that was probably true. But she didn't push it. The night had been perfect, and she didn't want to ruin it by bringing up more of his worries.

She just hoped those worries weren't about her.

"What were you playing when I came out? I heard the tail end of it and recognized it, but couldn't place it."

"Desperado." The corner of his lip tugged upward, and he gave her a discerning look. "I play a lot of southern rock, and I love the old Eagles songs. I had that one running through my head all day today, and I guess I needed to get it out."

Hmmm. She knew the song, knew the lyrics, and wondered how much of that song running through his head had to do with her and this thing they were starting. "I love that song. Will you play it for me?"

He picked up the glass, swirled the ice cubes, then swallowed the last of the amber liquid. Taking a deep breath, he closed his eyes and strummed the beginning chords of the song.

His voice was deep and strong, full of soul and feeling as he sang the lyrics.

She caught her breath at the sheer perfection of the

moment—the firelight, the rough timbre of his voice, sitting on the sofa naked except for a flannel sheet while listening to the sexiest man she'd ever known sing a song about walking through this world all alone.

The emotion of the song—and the man singing it—brought tears to her eyes.

He must have felt the emotion too, because his voice caught on the last line.

Caught up in the moment, she sang a few lines with him, her voice pure and rich.

He joined her on the last line, their voices harmonizing in a sweet melody as they sang the part about letting somebody love you before it's too late.

His fingers held on the strings, then he put the guitar on the table and turned to her. Reaching for her face, he ran the back of his fingers gently down her cheek, sending a thrill of heat racing along her back.

His gaze was intense as he stared into her eyes, and she could tell the emotion of the song was still haunting him.

His hand slid around her neck and pulled her head toward him. Leaning in, he kissed her—full on the mouth—his tongue slipping between her lips. She could taste the whiskey, mixed with the fervor of his passion.

Clutching his back, she clung to him, pouring herself into the kiss, trying to convey that if he would just let her in, he wouldn't have to be alone anymore.

He broke the kiss, pulling her tightly to him, as he buried his face in her neck. "Damn it, Emma. This scares the hell out of me. And I'm a pretty tough bastard. But you walked into my life and stole my breath and my heart in the same instant. I don't know what's gonna happen, I'm so damned scared that I'm gonna hurt you."

"I'm pretty tough, too. Tougher than you think."

He laughed against her neck then pulled back and gazed

into her face. "I know you are. You're probably tougher than me. Especially right now. I keep trying to get a grip on this thing, to hold back and keep my heart out of it. But I can't. So help me God, I can't."

"You don't have to."

Brushing her hair from her cheek, his hands were gentle, but his eyes were full of pain. "I don't know how to do this. I've kept my heart locked up for so long, I'm not sure if it even still works."

"It does." Her own heart sang at the vulnerability and passion in his words. She'd given up fighting her own feelings for him and just given in to the possibility that he could break her heart.

"I've fallen for you, darlin'. And fallen hard. Dammit if I know what to do with that, but I know I don't want to let you go."

"Then don't. Don't let me go. Hold on to me, and don't ever let me go."

Chapter Fifteen

The next two weeks flew by in a flurry of activity. Cash had the fall calving season to plan, Emma was working more at the diner, and Charlie and Sophie returned home from their trip to New York.

Charlie gave Cash a knowing look when he told her that Emma had been staying in the cabin with him.

His and Emma's days may have been moving quickly, but their nights were slow and sweet, tangled together in the sheets of his bed.

They usually had dinner together with Charlie, Sophie, and Zack, and sometimes stayed in the house to visit or help Sophie with a project. But the nights belonged to just the two of them, and they created their own little world.

A world of passion and tenderness, of discovery and pleasure, as they continued to learn more about each other and their needs and desires.

Cash walked around the farm with a stupid grin on his face half the day, and his heart raced every time he got a text or a call, in anticipation that it was from her. He felt like a kid in high school, with a terrible crush, and so help him, he kind of liked the feeling.

He looked forward to seeing her, to hearing from her, to taking her to work, and to picking her up at the end of her shift. He liked the way she scooted into the truck and sat next to him, her hand on his leg, as he drove and she told him about her day.

Emma had blossomed right before his eyes. He watched her changing and growing every day, gaining confidence in herself. Thanks to Charlie's cooking and the food at the diner, she was also gaining more weight, and he loved the new curvier shape to her hips.

She looked healthier. And happy.

"You look particularly smug today," he said, as she walked out of the diner. He was leaning against the bumper of his truck, waiting for her to finish her shift.

It was close to three on Thursday afternoon, and she wrapped her arms around his neck and kissed him on the mouth. "I got a raise."

"A raise? Already? Good for you."

A broad smile beamed across her face. "Cherry said I've been such a big help to her and that I've been doing such a good job that she offered me a raise. It's only a quarter an hour more, but hey, it's the first raise I've ever gotten."

His heart swelled with pride for her, but what he really loved was the way she was proud of herself. Proud of her own accomplishments.

"This calls for a celebration. How about we stop and get a bottle of wine to have for supper tonight?"

She laughed. "I think Charlie said Zack was grilling burgers for supper, and she was making macaroni and cheese. Doesn't sound like a wine kind of meal to me."

Alcohol had been a bad idea. Not that Emma didn't have a glass of wine with him sometimes, but he knew too much drinking still made her uncomfortable. "You're probably right. Forget the wine. Let's stop at the store and pick up root beer and ice cream and make root beer floats for everyone for dessert."

He was rewarded with a grin, and that was all the prize he needed. She was so simple to please, so happy with the smallest token he offered. Which only made him want to give her more—more affection, more attention, more words of affirmation.

He'd brought Charlie's dog, Joy, with him today, and the black-and-white border collie mix licked Emma's face as he opened the door, and she climbed into the cab of the truck. She squealed with laughter and hugged the dog to her chest.

Cash slid into the driver's seat and headed for the grocery store. He nodded at the dog who had laid her head in Emma's lap. "That dog sure does love you. I swear you have a gift for working with animals."

"It's funny you say that, because I was just talking to Charlie and Zack about that very thing this morning at breakfast."

"Oh, yeah?"

"Yeah. I guess I mentioned something about Charlie's career and how much I admired her, and she asked me what kind of career I wanted for myself."

"And what'd you say?" He felt like Emma had a whole world of opportunities open to her now, and he was happy to see her thinking about and making plans for her future.

"I said I didn't know. That I hadn't given it a ton of thought. And we started talking about different careers and what I thought I was good at. And honestly, I don't know what I'm good at, but I said that I really liked animals and they seem to take to me."

"I'll say. You're like the goat whisperer with Clyde, and I swear Rick and Daryl know your voice when you walk into the barn," he said, referring to the new lamb siblings that Emma had helped to birth and for whom she'd finally picked out names. "They run over to the fence and get all excited to see you. Although why you named them after a couple of guys who fight zombies in *The Walking Dead* is beyond me."

She laughed. "Because they get perceived as weak, so I wanted to give them tough names. And Rick and Daryl are the two toughest guys I could think of. And I get excited to see them, too. I get excited to be around all animals. Zack suggested that I look into becoming a vet tech. It would require some schooling, but I think it might be worth checking out. And Zack said that I could come in and help out at the clinic to see if it's something I'd be interested in. What do you think?"

"I think you're practically bouncing out of your seat with excitement just talking about it, so it seems like a great idea to me."

"No, not that. I mean, I am excited about it. But what I mean is, do you think I could do it? Like go back to school and all?"

He hated the way she doubted herself. "Of course I do. I think you can do anything you set your mind to. And it seems like a great field for you. You're kind and thoughtful and care about animals. You'd make both the pets and the pet owners feel at ease. Plus you're smart as a whip. If you want to do it, I say go for it."

A shy expression of pride crossed her face as a smile tugged at the corner of her lips. "Thank you. I appreciate you saying that. Do you think I could use your computer tonight to look into it?"

"Of course. And you don't have to ask. You can use anything of mine that you want." He squeezed her leg and gave her a wink filled with naughty innuendo.

A blue car passed them, reminding him of Earl's, and his

grin turned into a frown. "Speaking of smarts, you have any surprise visits from Dumb and Dumber today?"

She laughed. "Nope. I haven't seen either of them in a couple of weeks now. Taylor's warning to stay away from me must have helped."

Somehow Cash didn't think that Earl and Junior were much for heeding any of the sheriff's warnings, and he worried that the brothers were biding their time because they had another plan in mind. They didn't seem the type to give up easily, not when their pride, or their brother's pride, was at stake.

Like a couple of snakes in the grass, Cash was just waiting for them to strike.

He pulled into the parking lot of the grocery store and cut the engine. "You need anything else while we're here?"

"No, but I heard Charlie say she was almost out of milk this morning."

Opening the door, he stepped out. "You coming in?"

She leaned back against the seat and let out a sigh. "Nah, I've been on my feet all day. I'm happy to sit here a few minutes and rest. I'll keep Joy company while you go in." She ran her hand over the dog's furry head, and Joy rewarded her with a look of pure dog adoration.

"I'll be back in a minute. Text me if you think of anything else. And maybe text Charlie to see if she needs anything besides milk."

"Got it."

He crossed the sidewalk and hurried through the store, grabbing the dairy products and the root beer. His phone buzzed with a text from Emma, and he added bread, a carton of eggs, and a Snickers bar to his stack.

Setting the items down at the register, he was glad that he hadn't had a request for any embarrassing feminine items. Not that he wouldn't buy them, but he was glad he didn't have to.

He threw in a pack of gum for Emma, the green one that she liked, and couldn't help whistling as he walked out of the store. He was happy, plain and simple.

The whistle died on his lips as he saw Earl Purvis leaning against the side of his truck, talking to Emma through the open window.

What the hell?

"What do you want, Earl?" he asked as he approached the truck, looking in at Emma to gauge if she was okay.

She sat up stiffly in the seat, her expression grim as she gripped the dog's collar. The fur on Joy's back was up, and she stood in front of Emma, her lips pulling slightly back to bare her teeth in warning, as if protecting her. *Good dog.*

"I'm just having a little chat with my sister-in-law." A soggy toothpick clung to Earl's bottom lip, his mechanic's uniform dirty and sweaty.

"I thought Sheriff Johnson told you to keep your distance from Emma."

"We're just talking. Last I checked, there ain't no law against that."

"No, but there is a law against tampering with someone's vehicle and disabling their brakes."

"I wouldn't know nothing about that."

"Yeah, I'm sure you wouldn't." They hadn't been able to prove that the brakes had been intentionally cut, but a trained mechanic would have the knowledge to know how to make that look like an accident.

"I heard little Miss Emma had herself a new boyfriend. I was just asking her if the rumors were true."

"We don't bother paying much attention to rumors."

Earl's mouth turned into an ugly sneer as he looked Cash up and down. "Nope, me either. And I couldn't believe that Emma would go whorin' around while my poor brother

Leroy is stuck in a jail cell."

Poor brother Leroy, my ass.

"But now I see her sitting all cozy in your truck, I'm starting to wonder," Earl continued.

"I already told you," Emma spoke up. "Leroy is my ex-husband. And it's none of his business, or yours for that matter, who I see or don't see." Her voice was a little shaky, but she came off sounding stronger and more confident than the last time she had stood up to Earl.

And from the look on his face, it seemed Earl noticed, too.

Good for her.

"You heard the lady." Cash moved past him and opened the truck door then passed Emma the bag of groceries. "You all right?"

She nodded, and he slid into the truck next to her and slammed the door. "Looks like your chat time is over. There isn't anything more you've got to say to Emma." Turning the engine over, he put the truck in gear, anger bubbling up inside of him. He pressed his lips tightly together to prevent him from saying anything he might regret.

"See you around, sis." Earl spat on the ground.

Not if I have anything to do with it.

He put his hand over Emma's and noted the slight tremble in her fingers. "You sure you're all right?"

She took a deep breath. "Yes. He just caught me off-guard. I didn't even see him come up to the truck. Joy started to growl, and I looked up and there he was, leaning into the window."

"I shouldn't have left you alone."

"I wasn't alone."

"You did good, you mangy mutt." The dog had settled back into Emma's lap, and Cash ruffled her ear. "She must have sensed danger."

"Either that, or her asshole alert came on."

He busted out laughing. Emma didn't often swear or speak poorly of other people. Unless it was someone in the Purvis clan, apparently. And in this case, it seemed wholly appropriate.

"It could have been that, too. Either way, I'm glad you're okay." He squeezed her hand. "And you did a good job standing up to him. You sounded more confident, more in control. And he noticed."

She shook her head, her lighthearted expression turning to anger. "He would have noticed more if I'd gotten out of the truck and kneed him in the walnuts."

Another chuckle escaped him. "You are killing me, woman. I like this side of you. It's like part Sunday school teacher/part biker chick. It's kind of tough."

She laughed—just the reaction he'd hoped for. He had enough anger brewing in him for the both of them.

"I didn't feel tough. I still felt scared. On the inside."

"Well, you didn't show it."

"I just thought with the self-defense stuff I wouldn't still feel like such a wuss. I mean, I looked up to see him there, and my heart jumped to my throat. I don't want to feel terrified like that anymore."

"Don't be so hard on yourself. Everybody gets afraid sometimes, and Earl is a scary dude. I think you did great. What did he talk to you about anyway?"

"He wanted to tell me that Leroy's being moved this weekend to the State Prison and wondered if I wanted to go visit him at the county lockup before he left."

"Do you? Want to go visit him, I mean."

"Hell, no. I never want to see his face again. I haven't gone down to the jail to visit him yet, I'm sure as heck not gonna start now."

"Good." Her answer soothed him a little, but his anger

still bubbled under the surface, like the slow rolling boil of a pot of water. He tried to think of something to change the subject. "You heard from your dad lately?"

"Yeah, he called me this morning. It sounds like my uncle is still having a rough time getting around, even with the crutches. I think having my dad there has really helped, both with taking care of my uncle and keeping his spirits up. They get along really well, and I think this time together is probably good for both of them. You know, besides me, he's the only family that my dad has left, and I could tell that he wanted to stay. I told him not to worry, and that we'd been checking in on the farm every few days, and everything was fine."

Her dad didn't have much in the way of crops and had a hand that took care of feeding the few animals they still kept. They stopped in every few days on their way home from town, and everything always seemed to be in order.

"I told him I was still staying with Charlie, and that seemed to ease his mind enough to feel okay about staying another few weeks."

What would he think if he knew she wasn't actually staying with Charlie, but was instead spending her nights in his cabin, in his bed? Probably best not to get into that.

They pulled into the driveway of Tucked Away. A blue Volkswagen bug sat in front of the porch.

Emma stiffened next to him, proving that she hadn't entirely gotten rid of her fear of new situations. "Do you recognize that car?"

Chapter Sixteen

"Oh, yeah I do," Cash said, a smile tugging at the corner of his lips. "It belongs to my Aunt Patsy. I told you my mom was coming to the Fall Festival this weekend. I knew she was flying in today, but my aunt was picking her up. The way those two gab, I figured we wouldn't see them until tomorrow."

Emma's eyes went wide with fear, and she clasped her hands together in her lap. "Oh great. I thought it was scary seeing Earl. Somehow the thought of meeting your mother terrifies me more than facing five Earls."

He chuckled and wrapped an arm around her shoulders, drawing her to him and planting a quick kiss on her lips. "Don't worry. My mom's a sweetheart." He felt her shoulders relax and couldn't help teasing her a little more. "Now, my Aunt Patsy, she's a terror."

Opening the truck door, he slid out, narrowly missing the playful slap she aimed at him.

She climbed out behind him and smoothed her hair up toward her messy ponytail. "At least let me go get cleaned up and out of my uniform before I meet them."

The screen door slammed and two women in their fifties clamored down the front porch stairs, their hands waving as they called out to Cash.

"Too late." He offered her one of his most charming grins before turning to the women. Grabbing the petite brunette, he lifted her in his arms and swung her around in the air. "Hey, Mom."

The woman clung to him, kissing his cheek as he set her back down on the ground. "Hey, baby boy. It's so good to see you, son. You look great."

His aunt was taller and of considerable more girth than her petite sister, and she held up her hands as Cash turned to hug her. "You lift me up like that, and you'll throw your back out. I'm fine with a regular hug."

He hugged his aunt to him, thinking that he wrestled heifers that weighed more than her, but wisely chose to keep that comparison to himself.

"You are as handsome as ever," Patsy said, giving him a squeeze before letting him go and turning to Emma. "Now, this must be Emma. We've heard so much about you." She pulled Emma into a hug, holding her against her ample chest.

"I'm pleased to meet you, ma'am," Emma spoke, breathless as Patsy let her go.

Cash's mother held out her hand and shook Emma's. "Never mind my sister. She's never met a stranger. I'm Kathleen, but you can call me Kitty."

"It's nice to meet you, Kitty."

"It's nice to meet you. It sounds like you might be the first woman to actually capture my son's heart."

"Wow, Mom. Less than two minutes in, and you're already embarrassing me." He chuckled, noting the way Emma's cheeks pinked with color. "Let's let Emma get out of her work clothes before you start drilling her on her favorite color and how many fillings she has."

"You're right," Kitty said, checking the watch on her arm and winking at Emma. "I'll give you thirty minutes, then the interrogation will begin. And I want to know all about you and how you managed to snag the elusive Cash Walker."

"You staying for dinner, Mom?" he asked, trying to change the subject.

"I guess so. Charlie was a doll and invited us to stay. It sounds like we're grilling burgers."

He handed his mother the bag of groceries. "Will you give this to Charlie, and tell her we'll be in in a few minutes?"

Kitty took the sack. "But, what about—"

"There's ice cream in that bag, Mom. Better get it inside."

Even his mom couldn't argue with melting ice cream. "All right, we'll see you both in a few minutes. You're coming for supper, too, right, Emma?"

"Oh, I wouldn't miss it," Emma said as she hurried to catch up with Cash, who had already headed across the driveway.

They rounded the corner of the barn, and he stopped and wrapped an arm around her, pulling her into a tight hug. "Sorry about that. Be prepared for them to act like that all night."

Emma grinned up at him. "It's okay. They were cute. And you were right, I do like them."

"I like you." He leaned down and kissed her. A deep kiss full of heat and promise of more to come.

The kiss ended, and she looked up at him, a question in her eyes. "Was it true? What your mom said? Have I really captured your heart?"

If she only knew how true that statement was. "Darlin', you've not only captured my heart, you've netted, bagged, and taken it for ransom."

A broad smile lit up her face. "Good. And just so you know, I'm not giving it back."

"You couldn't if you tried." He tipped his forehead down

to rest against hers. "Because it belongs to you now."

...

Forty-five minutes later, they made it back to Charlie's for supper. Cash held her hand as they walked through the door, and Emma could feel the heat burning her cheeks, sure that they all knew what took them so long to return.

The kiss outside the barn had turned into more, and they'd barely made it into Cash's cabin before she had her hands in his shirt and he was peeling off her dress. Shedding their clothes as they moved through the room, they only made it to the living room before falling onto the sofa and succumbing to their passion.

She'd taken a quick shower and refreshed her light eye makeup, but now—seeing Charlie in the kitchen, looking gorgeous with her blond hair and stylish clothes—she wished she would have taken more time and washed her hair. She'd brushed it out and pulled it back into the same ponytail she'd been wearing all day.

Sophie squealed and raced across the room to hug her as if she hadn't seen her in a year, instead of just the day before. Snagging her from Cash, the girl pulled her over to the table to show her a funny meme that she'd just found on Facebook.

Thank goodness for Sophie. The teenager was oblivious, but Charlie gave her a knowing grin when she entered the kitchen and asked if there was anything she could do to help.

"I think I got it," Charlie said. "I was wondering if you all had changed your minds about supper. You must have got into quite a discussion over at the cabin."

She grinned at her friend, unfazed by her ribbing. Instead, her heart was full and happy that she had a friend to tease her. "Well, you know, we had a lot of things to *talk* about."

Charlie lowered her voice and added a note of naughtiness.

"It must have been a *long* talk."

Emma giggled and swatted Charlie with a towel.

"What are you two girls giggling about in here?" Cash asked, sauntering into the kitchen and leaning against the counter.

He was so good-looking, he took her breath away.

She still couldn't quite believe that he was with her, that he whispered sweet words of intimacy to her, and that she got to have "discussions" with him. Discussions that involved touching his hard muscled body and seeing him naked.

Charlie saved her. "Oh, nothing. Just a little girl talk."

Emma hugged her arms around her stomach, so dang thrilled to be having "girl talk" and another woman to laugh with. It had been so long since she'd had a friend, a real friend, one that knew about Leroy and still cared about her.

And now she not only had Charlie, but a whole bushel of friends, Sophie and Cherry and the guys, people who actually liked her and invited her into their "family."

"What's going on in here?" Kitty asked, crossing to Cash and looping her hand through his arm. "Did I hear something about girl talk?"

Once again, Charlie came to the rescue. What was she going to do when it was just her, and she had to actually be the engineer of the conversation train?

"We were just talking about the Fall Festival this weekend and what we were gonna wear," Charlie said, giving her a discreet wink.

"Well, it's supposed to be warm," Kitty said. "But bring a sweater just in case. You know how the weather can change in a second in Montana."

Oh, she knew. Thoughts of the sudden thunderstorm and the picnic under the tree with Cash flashed through her mind, and she hoped her cheeks wouldn't redden again and give her thoughts away.

Stupid blush.

"It's nice that you could come back for it, Kitty," Emma said. "I haven't been to one in years." Not since she married Leroy and moved to Great Falls.

After that her world pretty much became whatever grimy apartment they were renting at the time. She probably could have tried to come back more often, to spend time with her dad. But after a while, she couldn't take the look on his face when she was with him, the knowing looks, the pity, the confusion at why she stayed. Especially after he'd tried to convince her to leave him so many times before.

"Oh, I love the Fall Festival," Kitty answered, pulling her out of her dark musings. "It reminds me of the county fair, with the games and the music and the competitions. My sister enters her famous bread and wins every year. And one of her quilts almost always takes a blue ribbon."

"You should enter one of your pecan pies, Emma," Cash said. "You've gotten pretty good at them. That last one had a crust so flaky, it melted in my mouth."

She tilted her head, trying to decipher if he was being serious about her entering the contest or if he was making some kind of inside joke pertaining to their sex life. Knowing Cash, it could be both. They did eat a lot of pie while naked.

"I'm being serious. You should enter. What could it hurt?" he said, and she realized he was being sincere.

What *could* it hurt? "Well, why not? I used to be in 4-H when I was a kid, and the other kids were always entering stuff, like cookies, or drawings, or pictures they'd taken. I was always too bashful to submit anything."

"It sounds like it's about time you did then," Kitty said encouragingly, and Emma offered her a grateful smile.

"Yes, it is."

"I'm entering a few things, too," Sophie spoke up, obviously listening from the dining room table. "We can go down together with our entries on Friday."

"It sounds like it's settled then," Cash said. "Let's eat. I feel like I ran a marathon today. I'm starved."

They spent the next few hours lingering over the table, finishing their meal but staying to visit.

Cash and Zack made the root beer floats, and a huge mess, at the table, arguing over whether the ice cream went into the glass first or the root beer, then setting up a competition and a wager to prove who was right.

Emma hadn't laughed so hard in a long time. Cash's mom and his Aunt Patsy were a hoot, entertaining them with funny stories of the adventures they'd been on in the past few years.

Kitty had never remarried. Instead, after Cash finished school, she'd left the cold harsh winters of Montana and moved down to Florida. She'd gotten a job as a secretary at a travel agency, then worked her way up to agent, becoming one of their best sales associates.

The job offered her discounted travel, and she and Patsy often took off exploring different parts of the world, exclaiming that "the world has never seen the likes of two Montana gals like us."

They finally wound down close to ten o'clock. Emma and Cash waved good-bye as the two women drove off in the sporty little Volkswagen. Patsy gave a little toot of the horn as they sped down the driveway.

"That was fun," Emma said.

"Yeah? My family wasn't too much for you?" He wrapped his arm around her waist as they walked toward the cabin. "I know they can get a little rowdy. And they asked you a lot of questions."

"They were perfect. I loved your mom. And it's obvious how much she loves you." She tilted her head up, gazing at the scruff of dark beard on his chin as he grinned down at her. And Miss Kitty wasn't the only one.

Emma was in love with her son, too.

• • •

The afternoon sun shone brightly as they stepped onto the fairgrounds, a perfect Indian summer kind of day. The Fall Festival was in full swing around them, and Cash unloaded the extra table Cherry needed from the back of the truck.

She and her son, Sam, were running a booth sponsored by the diner and selling corn dogs and ice cream sodas, and she'd called earlier to ask them to bring one more table. They'd all committed to helping out for an hour at the booth, even his mom.

Kitty must have had the first shift, because she waved to him from Cherry's booth as he and Emma walked up. He leaned down and she kissed his cheek, holding up her batter-speckled hands. "Hey there, honey. You ready for a corn dog? I'm getting pretty good at them."

He glanced at Emma, who grinned and shrugged. "Sure, we'll take two." He pulled out the legs of the extra table and called over to Cherry, "Where do you want me to put this?"

"Now that's a loaded question," she said with a wink. She sashayed over, her hips swinging in snug pink capri pants. She wore a white blouse, the sleeves rolled up and the ends tied in a bow at her waist. Her red hair was pulled up into a loose knot, and she'd tied a pink scarf around her head. "It's a dang good thing you're on my good side today, or I might have a different answer for you," she teased.

He grinned back. He couldn't help it. Everything about today was shaping up to be a good day. And he had to admit, he was happy. Like down to his core, sunny rainbows and unicorns kind of happy.

And the woman who was making him this happy was giggling with his mother as she showed her how to dip hot dogs on a stick into a vat of batter.

Life could be funny sometimes. He didn't think he was ever going to have this. This chance at happiness. At love.

And he did love Emma.

He hadn't told her yet. Didn't know exactly what he was waiting for either. It wasn't like it was a big secret. He told her every night in the way he kissed her, the way he touched her, the way he caressed her skin.

But makin' love and saying the words "I love you" were two wholly different things.

He *would* tell her. When it felt right.

Although it felt pretty right *now*. With the sun shining and the smell of caramel apples and popcorn in the air. With the sound of her laughter ringing in his ears.

But he couldn't just pull her aside and whisper it in her ear.

A thing like that was big. It needed a moment. A special time when everything was right. Maybe some candles and soft music. Tonight. After the festival. He'd light a fire in the fireplace.

I'll tell her tonight, he promised himself.

For now, he was just happy to be with her. To watch her as she kidded around with Cherry's son and played with his dog, Rex, who was tied up under the table and taking advantage of any scraps that fell his way.

He bought them cups of fresh-squeezed lemonade from the next booth over, and they walked through the festival, checking everything out, as they ate their corn dogs.

It wasn't a huge event by big-city standards, but it had plenty of food vendors, a petting zoo, and a fairway of a few carnival games.

The school had a booth set up where you could pay to toss a pie in the face of one of the administrators, and Cash recognized the principal as he sat at the table waiting for the next pie. He must be a popular victim, because a stack of empty pie plates sat next to him, and a dollop of whipped cream clung to his eyebrow.

Making their way to the exhibition hall, he could feel Emma tensing next to him. "What's wrong?" he asked, as they tossed their empty cups and trash into a bin outside the doors.

She smiled—the shy smile that Cash loved. "I know it seems kind of dumb, but I'm nervous about the silly pie. I don't know how I let you all talk me into entering a pie, of all things, into a competition."

"I think your pie is amazing," he said, sneaking a pinch at her butt and sending her into a fit of bashful giggles as they walked into the building.

Dropping his arm around her shoulders, he led her toward the baked goods and wished he had a camera to capture the look on her face when she saw the ribbon stuck to the front of her pie plate.

Her hands flew to her face and the wattage from her smile could have powered an entire city. She looked up at him, wonder in her eyes. "A blue ribbon? I earned a blue ribbon on my pie?"

She reached out and touched the ruffled ribbon. "Wait. I haven't entered one of these before. A blue ribbon is still good, right?"

He chuckled. "Yes, a blue ribbon is still good. It means you took first place."

"First place? How could that have happened?"

"I told you that you made good pie."

"Me? I actually won?" She looked at the other two pies that were up against hers. "Okay, this one looks a little mushed and this one was made by a proud fifth grader named Tabitha, so it doesn't appear that the competition was too stiff. But you know what? I don't care. I still won. So suck it, Tabitha."

A burst of laughter erupted from his chest. "You are a

mean competitor."

"I guess I am. Who would have thought it? It's just that I've never won anything before."

He picked up the ribbon and held it out to her. "Hold it up, and I'll take your picture with your prize-winning pie," he said, digging his phone out of his pocket.

Her hand flew to her hair. "Oh no, I look a mess."

"You look beautiful. Now hold up the durn ribbon."

She held the ribbon and stood by the pie, and he snapped the picture, capturing her proud smile.

"Now, let's do one together," she said. "Our first selfie." She squeezed in front of him and smiled at the phone he held out at arm's length in front of them. Tipping up her face, she gave him a quick kiss on the cheek, and he tapped the phone again, capturing the kiss in the shot.

"Let's see them." She stood in the circle of his arms as he brought the phone to them and clicked on the photos.

The pictures were good. He was surprised at the smile on his own face, so different from the usual charming smile he offered when he got his picture taken. One had his lips parted in an actual laugh, and the picture expressed pure joy.

"Well now, isn't this cute?"

Cash looked up to see Tiffany Jordan standing on the other side of the pie display, her hands on her hips and one eyebrow raised.

"Hey, Tiff," he said, his arm tightening around Emma's waist as she tried to pull away. "You know Emma Frank?"

Tiffany was one of the women he'd sometimes take out to a movie or meet up with at a bar for a drink. She had big blond hair and ample hips currently encased in a pair of tight jeans. The neckline of her snug shirt dipped low, and her gaze traveled up and down Emma, obviously assessing her competition.

She held out her hand. "Nice to meet you, Emma." The

tone of her voice didn't convey that she thought it was nice at all. She looked back up at Cash. "I'd heard that you were dating someone new, but I didn't realize you two were an actual item."

He knew she was goading him, but he didn't take the bait. He could feel Emma shrinking into herself, and the next words popped out of his mouth before he could even stop to think about them. "Yep, we are an *actual* item. She's the one for me, the *only* one."

Like a violet in the warm sun, Emma's shoulder eased back, and she stood taller. He slipped his hand into hers.

"Well, what do you know about that?" Tiffany asked, her expression amazed. But like a dog with a bone, she wasn't quite finished with her questions. "Are you saying Cash Walker is officially off the market?"

"That's exactly what he's saying," Emma piped in, surprising Cash and probably herself a little.

He chuckled. "You heard the lady."

"Well, I never thought I'd see the day. Nice to meet you, Emma. I guess we'll see you around then." Tiffany gave them one final glance before offering them a wave and heading in the direction of the quilts.

"Well, I'll bet that news travels around town quicker than a hot knife through butter."

Cash tipped his head down and brushed a kiss against her lips. "Good, then I can cancel that ad I was takin' out in the paper next week." He held up his hands to illustrate the headline. "Cash and Emma, sitting in a tree, K-I-S-S-I-N-G."

A laugh escaped Emma's lips, and she playfully slapped his arm. "You're bad."

He slid his arm around her waist and growled into her ear, "Let's slip out to my truck, and I'll show you how bad I can be."

"Tempting, but your mom is at the festival, and the last

thing I want to do is get caught by your mother making out in your pickup." She grinned up at him, a naughty gleam in her eye. "But hold that thought, and you can show me when we get home."

He followed her out of the exhibition hall, a smile tugging at his lips at the way she said "when we get home." Pointing to the fairway, he asked, "How about if I win you a stuffed animal?"

She dragged him toward a shooting-gallery-style booth, with three toy rifles affixed to the counter. "How about if *I* win you a stuffed animal?"

He chuckled. "You pretty good with a gun?"

"My dad taught me to shoot," she said, handing the kid behind the counter a couple of singles. "Besides, I feel like I'm on a bit of a winning streak lately."

"Lately, huh? You win something besides the pie competition?"

"Yep—there's a rumor going around that I won a cowboy's heart."

Chapter Seventeen

Cash handed a freckle-faced kid a corn dog then turned to Cherry. "I think that's it for my shift. You need anything else?"

Cherry looked around the fairgrounds at the dwindling crowd. It was close to eight, and the festival was winding down. The sun had set, but the lights around the booths and down the fairway still gave off a cheery glow.

"No, I think I'm good. Taylor and his dad will come by in a bit and help me pack all this up. Thanks for your help though." She gave him a quick hug. "And tell Emma thanks again for me. We wouldn't have made it through the noon rush without her help."

"Will do." He tipped his hat and couldn't help the grin that snuck across his face. "She's pretty great, isn't she?"

Cherry grinned back, the knowing grin of a woman. "Yeah, she is. You two seem pretty cozy. I swear you're all that girl talks about at the diner." She patted his arm in affection. "I'm glad for you. You deserve this."

"Do I?"

"Yes, of course you do."

He shook his head. "I can't imagine a single thing I've done so right in my life that would make me deserve a woman like Emma."

Cherry blinked and pressed her hand to her heart. "Well, that right there is exactly why you deserve her. Now git outta here before you say something else mushy like that and make me smear my mascara from cryin'. Go find Emma, and tell her what you just said."

"All right, I'm goin'." He laughed as he stepped out from behind the booth and headed toward the exhibition hall.

Emma had said she was going over to pick up her pie and ribbon, and he'd told her he'd meet her over there after he finished up. His truck was parked behind the hall, and they were leaving from there to head back to the farm.

Walking across the fairgrounds, he thought about what Cherry had said.

Did he deserve this? This overwhelming feeling of happiness? Why? What made him so deserving?

He'd promised himself that he'd tell Emma tonight that he was in love with her, but now feelings of doubt were creeping up, surrounding his heart like the nasty vines of bindweed that snuck through the grass, clinging to every stalk.

She was so damn nice. And good—like good to her very soul.

He'd watched her today as she'd helped his mom and Cherry in the booth, as she'd smiled and greeted customers she knew from the diner, and as she'd gazed at him in adoration when she caught him watching her.

Adoration that he *definitely* didn't deserve. But for some reason she did act like she adored him. Like he was something special.

And he hated the fact that he knew he'd eventually let her down.

Today had been great. He'd felt on top of the world a

few minutes ago, but Cherry's words struck a chord with him, and those familiar seeds of doubt crept up so easily, causing a cloud of gloom to settle over him as he rounded the corner of the exhibition hall.

What the hell?

He stopped short at the sight in front of him. Then anger poured through him, propelling him forward, and he rushed ahead, his blood already boiling with rage.

Emma stood in the shadows of the buildings, her back against the wall, cornered like a trapped animal. Earl and Junior Purvis surrounded her, and he watched as she held out the pie to them, and Earl slapped it from her hands.

A shocked gasp slipped from her lips as the pie tumbled and spilled to the ground, and Cash heard Earl's mocking laugh.

"That's not the kind of pie I'm interested in," Earl sneered, his words drunkenly slurring together as he pressed Emma against the wall and roughly grabbed her breast as he shoved his knee between her legs.

Cash had thought that jeering laugh was the final straw, then he saw Earl touch her, and heard her cry out in fear, and that was it.

Something in him snapped.

In three steps, he made it to where they stood. Grabbing Earl's shoulder, he spun him around and slammed his fist into his nose.

A sharp crack sounded as Earl's nose broke, and blood poured down his face.

Earl howled in pain, then his fists came up, swinging wildly at him.

But he was obviously drunk, and his movements weren't as quick. Cash easily pulled back and avoided his sloppy attempts, then brought a roundhouse punch around that slammed across Earl's chin.

The other man's face snapped sideways. The blood from his broken nose sprayed through the air in an arc that left bright red droplets on the shoulder of his stained gray T-shirt.

Cash heard Junior charging toward him and kicked out his leg, connecting the heel of his cowboy boot with the other man's knee. Junior went down, clutching his leg, as he let loose a whine of pain followed by several descriptive swear words.

Earl shook his head, as if trying to clear it, then bent forward and charged into Cash's gut.

"Oomph," he gasped, as the air went out of his lungs. He staggered back, shoving Earl away from him. The other man hit the ground, falling on his butt. Grabbing a handful of dry dirt, he tossed it toward Cash's face.

Tears stung his eyes as the dust peppered his face, but the dirty move only fueled his rage. His head told him to pull back, but his anger had a mind of its own, controlling his actions as he drove his fist into Earl's face.

"Don't you ever touch her again." He spoke through gritted teeth as he landed punch after punch, using his fists to enunciate the words. "Don't even look at her."

"Cash, stop, please," Emma cried, reaching for his shoulder to pull him back. "That's enough."

He heard her words, but they sounded far away, and he shrugged off her hand.

Junior followed his brother's lead and started throwing dirt and trash at Cash from where he lay doubled over on the ground. An empty beer bottle grazed his forehead, and the shot brought him temporarily to his senses.

He backed away from Earl and his brother, his breath coming in hard gasps, then grabbed Emma's arm and dragged her toward the truck. "What the hell were you thinking? How could you let yourself get caught alone with those bastards? They could have killed you, or worse."

He wasn't making sense, and he knew he shouldn't be

yelling at her, but he couldn't seem to rein it in, couldn't control the temper that was pouring from him, seeping out of his pores like foul sweat.

Stomping up to the truck, he slammed open the door. "Get in," he growled as he turned to her.

He stopped short—frozen by the look of fear on her face.

Yanking his hand away as if her arm were on fire, the anger seeped from him like water from a sieve.

"Oh my God, Emma. I'm so sorry." He reached for her.

And she flinched.

And his heart broke in two.

He sunk to his knees. *What had he done?*

She *flinched*—from him—shied away from him in fear. He knew that look, had seen it a hundred times on his mother's face.

And on Gillian Carter's face in high school when he'd taken a tire iron to the back of a car.

He'd sworn to himself that he would never cause that look to appear on another woman's face, but he'd failed to keep that promise. Just like he'd always feared. Like he'd always been afraid that he would.

"I'm sorry," he said, his voice hoarse and rough.

He held out his hand, and bile rose in his throat at the dark smudges of Earl's blood that stained it.

Emma stood still, her arms wrapped around her middle.

Pressing up from his knees, he backed away from her. "I'm so sorry, Emma. I thought this could work. But I was wrong. I told you that you needed a better man than me. I should have never let things get this far."

A look of a different kind of fear crossed her face, this one an expression of alarm mixed with anguish. "What are you talking about?"

"You know what I'm talking about. You just saw for yourself. I'm a monster. I have a rage inside of me that I can't control. And I know you saw it. I just saw the look on your face. The same look I've seen on my mother's face when my dad went after her. It was fear, Emma. Pure terror. You were afraid of me."

"No, it wasn't. I was afraid of the situation."

"No, you weren't. I saw it in your eyes. You were afraid of *me*. And I swore that you wouldn't ever have to live like that again. And I won't let you. I'd rather let you go than have you ever be afraid again."

She stepped forward, and he backed away. "Cash, please. I wasn't afraid of you, I swear."

"I know what I saw." A pain like a vise grip squeezed at his heart.

"I was afraid of Earl and his brother. And I've been terrified of Leroy. But I've never been afraid of you."

"You should be. You saw me back there. I just beat the hell out of those two guys. I couldn't stop myself." He held up his hands. "This is Earl's blood on my hands. I'm no better than Leroy." He hung his head in shame.

"Bullshit."

His head popped up at the vehemence in her voice.

She took a step toward him, her back straight and her voice full of steel. "That's bullshit. You're nothing like Leroy." She came at him full force and shoved him in the chest. "I know the man I've been with the past several weeks, and I know you are *not* like him."

Her behavior stunned him, and he stood speechless as she shoved him again.

She spit out her words, her own anger now evident. "Do you feel like hitting me now? Do you want to teach me a lesson for shoving you in the chest, you bastard?"

"What? Hell no, I don't want to hit you."

"You sure? I just called you a bastard. What are you gonna do about that?"

"I'm not gonna do anything about that. It's true."

"What if we were together, would you let me have friends?" She shoved him again, goading him into a reaction.

"What are you talking about? Of course you can have friends."

"What about a job?"

"I *helped* you get a job."

"But that was before we were together. What about now?" She didn't wait for an answer. Instead, she looked around, her eyes wild as she grabbed the mirror from the side of his truck and broke it free then threw it at his feet.

"Hey, that's my truck."

What the hell was she doing?

"What are you going to do about it?" She came at him again, this time slapping her hand across his face. "You want to hit me now?"

The sting of the slap burned his cheek, but he still didn't bite. He knew what she was trying to do now, and it wasn't working.

He wrapped his arms around her and pulled her to his chest. "I'm not going to hit you. I'll never hit you. You can slap me a hundred times, and I won't ever hit you back."

She broke down, sobbing against his chest. Tilting her face to him, she reached up and touched his cheek. "See, you're nothing like Leroy. I could never have gotten away with doing any of that to him. He put me in the hospital once for calling *him* a bastard. I just slapped you, swore at you, and broke the mirror off your truck, and you didn't come after me. You didn't hit me back. Don't you see, you're nothing like him."

"I see what you're trying to do. And I appreciate it. But it won't work, Emma."

As much as he wanted it to. As much as he loved her, and so help him, he did. He knew that for sure now. Knew that he loved her with every fiber in his being.

Which was why he had to let her go.

No matter how much it tore him up inside.

No matter if it ripped his guts out and left them dragging behind him in a bloody trail of pain and anguish, he had to walk away.

Her test had proved nothing to him except that he was already hurting her. He might not have reacted tonight, but he'd already flown into a rage once, and his anger was spent. What would happen the next time his temper took over and all he saw was red?

He couldn't risk it. Couldn't risk her.

He had to leave—to walk away—before he did any more damage. "I'm sorry, Emma. It's over."

Chapter Eighteen

Over?

What was he talking about? How could it be over?

Emma couldn't believe it.

Hadn't she just shown him—*proved* to him that he was nothing like her ex. She knew it—knew in her very heart—that he would never hurt her.

She *wasn't* afraid of him.

Watching him beat up Leroy's brothers hadn't made her scared *of* him, she was scared *for* him. Scared that he would get hurt.

The situation was insane. Cash was acting crazy, and she might have looked scared when he told her to get in the truck, but that was just a knee-jerk reaction. A habit formed from years of abuse.

She knew he wouldn't hurt her.

Hadn't she just beaten him in the chest, slapped him across the face, swore at him—even torn the mirror off his beloved truck? And he hadn't raised a hand to her.

That proved it to her.

But he was still walking away?

His face carried the expression of a broken man—his eyes full of sorrow and anguish. And determination.

He pulled her to him again, hugged her tightly to his chest.

His voice broke. She could barely make out his words as he whispered into her ear. "I'm sorry. I'm so sorry. I never wanted to hurt you. I love you. That's why I have to let you go."

What? What did he say?

Did he just tell her that he loved her?

His words were so soft as he growled them against her hair. Maybe she'd just imagined he said that.

Because he sure didn't look like he loved her when he pushed her away and took a step back.

He picked up the broken mirror and tossed it in the bed of the truck. "Take the truck back to the farm. I'm not coming with you. I'll find another way home tomorrow."

Tomorrow?

What did that mean? Where did he plan to spend the night tonight?

Would he crash on a friend's sofa or find solace in the arms of another woman? One of the many in this town who'd be happy to have him in her bed? Like Tiffany.

The thought of Cash seeking comfort from Tiffany broke her heart.

And proved what she knew all along. That she was never really good enough for a guy like Cash.

She tried once more. "Please don't do this. Just come home with me, and we can talk about this."

"*We* don't have a home. Not anymore. Just take the truck, Emma. I'm not coming with you." He took another few steps backward.

"Where are you going? To find Tiffany?"

"Tiffany? Hell, no. I'm going to find a drink. A stiff one

followed by several dozen more. Enough to make me forget. Forget about this. Forget about you. Take the damn truck." He turned and walked away.

She watched his back as he rounded the side of the building, then he was gone.

Taking off after him, she stopped short as she saw the crowd of people gathering where Earl and Junior still lay on the ground.

Scanning the deserted fairgrounds, she saw no sign of Cash, but a deputy sheriff was heading in from the far parking lot, and she shrank back against the building.

That mess would catch up with her soon enough.

Hurrying back to the truck, she climbed in and grabbed the keys from above the visor where she knew Cash kept them. The big truck rumbled to life, and she drove a few laps around the parking lot looking for him.

Seeing no sign of him, she finally gave up and eased out onto the highway then drove toward the farm.

She considered driving around town, cruising through the parking lots of the local bars, trying to catch sight of him, but what good would it do?

He'd made it pretty clear that he was done with her, that they were over.

Instead, she drove back to the cabin and packed up her meager belongings. She was surprised at how many things she actually had at Cash's. Besides her clothes, she had gradually brought over more things from her dad's, making the cabin her home.

She pulled out her suitcase from where Cash had stashed it under the bed and tossed in her clothes, books, toiletries, and shoes. She grabbed the denim shirt she'd been wearing lately then stopped as she realized it actually belonged to Cash.

Sinking to the floor, she held the shirt against her chest

as she cried.

Huge wracking sobs tore through her body as she leaned against the side of the bed. The bed where only that morning they had made love, where she had thought her life had finally changed. Changed for the better.

Where she thought she had found a place to call home, not just at the farm, but in the arms of a man—a good man—one who treated her with respect and dignity. And love.

Had he really said he loved her?

The thought of it only ripped the hole in her heart wider.

Getting up, she felt like every bone in her body hurt, as she threw the denim shirt in her suitcase and slammed it shut. Zipping it closed, she yanked it off the bed and dragged it through the living room, not stopping as she banged out the front door, afraid that if she stopped again, she'd fall to the floor and never get back up.

The brakes on her car had been fixed. They'd picked it up a few days before, but she'd gotten in the habit of Cash driving her to and from work, so the car had just been sitting in the driveway next to the barn.

Opening the back door, she stuffed in her suitcase, then climbed in the front.

The lights of the farmhouse were on, and she didn't want to draw attention to herself. Didn't want Charlie and Zack to see her like this—broken, again. She didn't need their pity. Didn't need anybody but herself.

It was high time she realized that. Realized that she could only depend on herself.

The tears dried on her cheeks as she headed back to her dad's farm, not letting herself even glance in the rearview mirror as she left Tucked Away.

Five minutes later, she pulled up to the front of her dad's house. The porch light was on, but everything else was dark and uninviting. She grabbed her suitcase, dug her keys from her purse, and let herself in.

The house had been closed up for weeks and had that musty smell mixed with the scent of old bacon grease. She dragged her bag up the stairs and collapsed on her old bed.

The house was so quiet—no friends making popcorn in the kitchen, no kitten purring on her pillow, no rumbling laugh of a man—only the dry hiss of the radiator as the heat turned off for the night.

What the hell had happened to her life?

How could everything have changed in what felt like a split second?

She considered taking a bath, drowning her sorrows in hot bubbly water, but that felt like too much work. Instead, she unzipped her suitcase and pulled out Cash's denim shirt.

Stripping off her clothes, she wrapped herself in the faded cotton shirt that still carried his scent and crawled into bed. Except her bed didn't feel right. The plain sheets were rough and cold against her legs, not like the soft flannel sheets on Cash's bed.

She rolled over, but the other side of the bed was empty. And cold.

Curling into a ball, she hugged the pillow to her.

She'd been in a loveless marriage, she'd been single, she'd been lonely, but she'd never felt as utterly alone as she did right now.

At least she wasn't afraid. Cash had taken care of that. Earl and Junior were most likely at home nursing their wounds, or possibly at the hospital, but she was sure they weren't concerned about where she was tonight.

At least she had that.

...

Cash leaned forward on the horse, his hat low on his head,

as it galloped toward the barn. He'd pushed the animal hard, needing to feel the speed and the danger as they charged through the fields.

The sun was setting as they raced into the corral, and he pulled back on the reins. He'd been fighting a hangover all day, and his head pounded as he dismounted from the horse and led it into the stable.

Walking away from Emma the night before had been the hardest thing he'd ever had to do, and evidently drowning his pain in shots of whiskey down at The Dive bar hadn't been the best solution for getting over her.

He'd grabbed a ride home from one of the waitresses around two o'clock and had stumbled into the cabin and passed out on the sofa. Half of him had hoped that Emma would be there.

But he knew the minute they pulled into the driveway of Tucked Away, and he saw her car wasn't there, that she was gone.

As much as he spent the day today telling himself that he'd made the right decision, that what he did was best for everyone, his heart ached in his chest like an abscessed tooth.

Like a relentless, persistent throb that rivaled the pounding in his head.

Miserable and depressed, he'd spent the day alone, working in the fields fixing fence line and sticking to the barn where no one would bother him. And he could wallow in his own self-pity.

He'd taken the horse out for a run, hoping to blow off a little steam, but it hadn't worked. Nothing worked.

He pulled the saddle off Renegade and brushed down the horse's sweaty coat.

Keeping busy did help a little, but his mind kept going back to Emma. To time spent with her, to hearing her laugh, to thoughts of her naked and in his bed, moaning his name.

That didn't help either.

He'd crawled into the shower that morning and turned the water on as hot as he could stand it. She'd taken most of her things, but had forgotten her shampoo. Like a love-sick pup, he'd picked up the shampoo bottle, taken off the lid, and inhaled her scent.

Everywhere he'd looked today he saw reminders of her. He'd skipped having breakfast with Charlie and Zack that morning because he didn't want to face Emma's empty chair.

A noise sounded in the front of the barn, and his heart leaped at the insane hope that it was her. That she'd come back to tell him he was a fool and that she wasn't going to let him ruin what they had.

"Cash?" his mother's voice called out.

Not Emma. Which was probably a good thing. He wasn't going to take her back, but he didn't think he could handle breaking things off with her again today.

"Over here, Mom," he answered, stepping out of Renegade's stall and locking the gate behind him.

His mom crossed the barn and put her arms around his middle in a hug. "Hi, honey."

"Hey." He hugged her back, probably a little too hard and a little too long, but there was just something about a hug from your mom that always seemed to make things a little better.

She looked up at him quizzically. "What's wrong?"

Leave it to his mother to automatically know when something was up.

"I broke things off with Emma last night."

"Oh no." She gestured to a row of hay bales lined up against the wall. "You better sit down and tell me all about it."

They sat next to each other on the hay, and Cash leaned his back against the wall.

"What happened?" Kitty asked.

He let out a heavy sigh then told her what happened the night before. She listened intently, just like she'd always done, giving her whole attention to him when he had something to talk about.

Shame filled him as he told her about the fight with Earl and Junior, but he didn't downplay the anger he felt or the brutality of the brawl.

"From what you've told me about the things they've done to Emma, it sounds like those assholes had it coming."

A small smile tugged at his lips. It always struck him as a little funny to hear his mother cuss. "Yeah, they probably did. But that's not the point."

"Well, you're going to have to enlighten me, then, because it sounds to me like you protected Emma. If you hadn't shown up when you did, who knows what they might have done to her. This Earl character sounds like he's got a mean streak a mile wide, and mean and drunk are not a good mix."

He knew she spoke from experience. They hadn't really ever talked about it, just didn't bring it up, both preferring to focus on the here and now and forget about the past.

"I'm sorry, Mom. I shouldn't be talking to you about this stuff. I don't want to dredge up bad memories for you." He'd already hurt enough people; he didn't need his mother to fall onto his list of casualties.

"I'm fine, honey. I know we don't talk about it much." She gave her shoulders a little shrug. "Or ever. But I'm okay. I've had a lot of counseling, and I've worked through a lot of that pain."

He looked at her in surprise. "You have? Been to counseling, I mean?"

"Sure. Your Aunt Patsy made me go at first, but then I was glad I did. I used to have terrible nightmares and carried a lot of guilt."

"I know what that's like."

"What do you mean? What in heaven's name do you have to feel guilty about?"

Seriously? How could she ask him that?

"Mom, you were there. You saw what I did. That last night. I hit my own father with a baseball bat."

"First of all, he was your *step*father. And secondly, you probably saved my life." Tears sprang to her eyes, and a look of pain crossed her face. "Is that what this about? Does that night have something to do with why you broke things off with Emma?"

"That night has *everything* to do with why I broke things off with Emma." He leaned forward, cradling his forehead in his hands. "Don't you see? She's been through enough. She's spent the last ten years being abused by a man who was just like Dad, and she *just* escaped. I couldn't let her go back to living like that again."

"What are you talking about? How could starting a life with you be going back to that?"

He shook his head, the anguish pouring out of him, his throat hoarse from the sourness of it. "Because I'm just like him."

His mother froze, stunned, then reached out and took his chin, tilting his face to look at her. "Did you hit her? Have you hit a woman before?"

"No, hell no."

"Have you ever raised your hand to one?"

"No. But I'm afraid I might. You saw what I did. That same rage and fury that Dad had, that was in me that night. Mom, I think I could have killed him. I *wanted* to kill him."

"Oh honey, I think part of me wanted you to kill him, too. But that doesn't mean you are *like* him. We were the victims, and you were just finally fighting back. You were braver than I ever could be. You saved us."

"I wasn't brave. I was scared shitless. Terrified. But I was also fed up, and filled with hate and anger, and this beast inside of me came out, and I fought back. Just like I did last night when I beat the crap out of Earl and Junior Purvis."

He took her hand and held it to his chest, pleading with her to understand. "Don't you get it? I've got that rage inside of me still. That's why I never let anyone get close to me. Why I don't get involved with women. I can't take the chance that I might hurt them."

His mother lowered her head and tears rolled down her cheeks. She reached for him, pulling him into a fierce hug. "Oh, my boy. My precious baby boy. I'm so sorry."

He pulled back. "What are you sorry for?"

"That we never talked about this. That you've been living with this for years. With this guilt and a misguided understanding of what happened."

She took his cheeks in her hands, leaning her face toward his, her gaze solemn and her words stern. "Now you listen to me, Cash Walker, you are *nothing* like that man. Nothing. You hear me? I have known you from the day you were born, watched you grow up, grow into the man you are now. *No one* knows you better than I do. So you listen to me when I tell you, you are *not* like him. In any respect."

He wanted to believe her. Wanted so badly to believe what she was saying was true.

"But I have such rage inside of me. And I hurt him. Just like I hurt those guys last night."

"We *all* have rage inside of us. God gave us a whole passel of emotions and the ability to feel those emotions so strongly that you think they may take over your entire soul. We can feel grief to our very bones, we can feel joy with our whole spirit, we can feel a love so deep and wide that it feels as if our hearts may burst. And we can feel anger and rage so fierce that we may fear it will destroy us, but that doesn't define us. It doesn't define you.

"The rage you felt doesn't make up who you are. It doesn't consume you. I've seen you with your friends, with your goddaughter, Sophie, with the animals that you care for on this farm. I've watched you from the time you were a little boy. Even when we were going through the worst of it, you were still a good and caring person with a huge heart and an enormous capacity for love."

He couldn't speak; the emotions welling in him clogged his throat.

"You have always been loyal and fiercely protective. You watched out for me as best you could. And that was my mistake. I should have never put you in a position where you thought you had to protect me. I was the mother. I should have protected you. I should have left sooner, but I wasn't strong enough. We all feel angry when we are hurt or when someone harms a person we love, but that doesn't mean you have meanness and cruelty in you. And that's what it takes to hit a woman. Mean, vile, cruelty. And you do *not* have that inside of you."

He'd never thought of it that way, never had anyone tell him any differently than the way he perceived himself. "I don't know."

"I *do* know. And I know that the one thing—the most important thing—that diffuses anger is love. And I think you have a chance at love with Emma. I've seen the way you two are together. Even in the short time that I've been here, I could tell. That woman cares about you. And I've never seen you this torn up before."

"That's because this is the first time I've cared enough about anyone to risk it. But she saw me last night, saw me at my worst when I was beating up those guys. And when she looked at me after, I saw fear in her eyes."

"I'm sure you did. That sounds like a scary situation. But are you 100 percent sure that what you saw was fear of *you*?

Do you truly believe that she is afraid of you?"

He thought back to her baiting tactics of the night before. She sure hadn't seemed afraid when she was shoving him and yelling in his face.

"No, I guess not. She sure tested me last night. I think she was trying to draw that anger out of me, trying to get me to take a swing at her. She yelled and screamed, swore at me, and even slapped me across the face."

"And did you want to take a swing at her? Were you tempted to?"

"No, of course not. Never. Not even when she ripped the mirror off my truck."

"Your truck? Are you sure you didn't want to punish her for that? Even just a little?"

His head snapped back, shocked at the suggestion. "Punish her? NO. Not even a little. Why would you even say such a thing?"

Kitty offered him a gentle smile. "To prove to you, once and for all, that you're not like him. Your mind doesn't work the same way. Men abuse women for power and control. Your stepdad used to 'punish' me for what I wore or how I spoke or who spoke to me. Cash, you are *not* like him. That is not in your nature. You treat women with respect and as something to protect, not punish."

He let her words sink in.

What she was saying made sense.

Whenever he got angry, the bulk of his anger was either aimed at himself or at someone who was causing harm to another person. The angriest he'd ever gotten had been during times when he was protecting someone else.

"I feel terrible. I had no idea you were carrying this around inside you. We should have talked about this a long time ago," Kitty said. "Honey, what you did that night, the way you stood up to him, that's what gave me the courage to finally walk away, to be able to move out of Montana when you graduated, to build a new life for myself. You saved my life that night, in more ways than one."

"Really?"

"Really. And I'm so sorry you've been carrying around all that guilt. I'm sorry I never thanked you or made you understand that what you did was a gift to me. I want you to let all that go now. Just give it up. You don't have to carry it anymore."

Could he just let go of years of guilt? Of imagining himself as a monster?

What good was it doing him?

It only caused him pain. He'd lost the woman he loved because he was holding on to anger and guilt. But he didn't need it anymore.

His mother's words had set him free.

He inhaled deeply, held it for a bit, then released it, letting go of the burden he'd been carrying around all these years. His chest loosened, and it was like he could feel the weight lifting off his shoulders.

Leaning down, he pulled his mother into a hug, holding her tight against him. "Thank you, Mom. I'm glad you were here. I love you."

She pulled back and tenderly touched his cheek. "I love you too, son. And I'm glad I was here as well." Letting him go, she stood up and brushed the hay from her pants. "Now, what are you going to do about getting Emma back?"

He laughed, not because what she said was all that funny, but because he felt lighter. And he could imagine a chance with Emma again, like it was actually a possibility. "That's a good question. I hurt her pretty bad."

"Well, then you better think of something pretty good to make it up to her."

"You're right."

"I'm the mom. I'm always right." She pointed at his dusty jeans. "And as your mom, I'm suggesting you get cleaned up before you go try to woo her back. You smell like horse."

He took her suggestion, and after another quick hug and a promise to let her know what happened, he hurried back to the cabin. He took a hot shower, and as he was getting dressed, he came up with the perfect idea.

Forget flowers and chocolate. *Nothing says I'm sorry like a kitten.*

Emma loved the little gray kitten of Charlie's. It followed her around when she was in the house, and she'd brought it over to the cabin with her on several occasions. Hell, she probably missed the kitten more than she missed him.

Sending a quick text to Charlie, to make sure she was good with the idea, he pulled on his boots and headed over to her house.

Thankfully, she hadn't asked about what was going on with him and Emma.

Maybe she didn't know. She texted that she was staying over at Zack's, so she wouldn't see him that night, but that if he looked on the back porch, there was a kitty crate he could use to transport the cat.

Finding the crate, he lined it with a blanket then put the little kitten inside and closed the door.

After carefully inspecting the interior and clawing it around to his specifications, the kitten curled up on the blanket and closed its eyes.

Gently carrying it out to the truck, he secured the crate on the floor of the passenger side of the cab, and headed for the Frank farm, rehearsing his apology as he drove.

Chapter Nineteen

Emma sat on the sofa, trying to read a book, but not able to focus on the words. Her thoughts kept going back to Cash, and how everything had so quickly fallen apart.

Something hard thudded against the front door of the farmhouse, and it flew inward.

She screamed, then froze in terror, not able to believe her eyes, as Leroy barged through the door.

Too shocked to move, all she could do was stare wide-eyed at him as he crossed the room to where she sat.

"What are you doing here?" She shook her head as if to clear the apparition in front of her.

"Is that any way to greet your husband?" The sneer on Leroy's face told her that he wasn't feeling too loving toward her.

"You're supposed to be in jail."

"Thanks to you." He wore a blue cotton jumpsuit and soft-soled shoes, standard prison garb. She hadn't seen him in months and was surprised at the thick scraggly growth of beard covering his face. It made him look older. "But thanks to my brothers and a demolition derby style crash, I'm out now. And I've come to claim what's mine."

His face might look a little different, but his eyes were the same. Mean. And filled with hatred.

For her.

Still stunned at his arrival, she hadn't been prepared for the attack.

With the speed of a snake, he struck, catching her off guard with a sharp backhand across the face.

The hit knocked her from the sofa.

She cried out as she crawled on her knees, trying to get away.

Grabbing her ponytail, he yanked her backward. Screaming at the pain, tears stinging her eyes, she tried to remember what Cash taught her.

But she couldn't think, her body wrestling with her mind, as its only objective was to escape. To flee.

She kicked out her leg, connecting with his ankle.

He stumbled and swore, then retaliated by pulling her head back and smashing it into the side of the coffee table.

The blow rocked her head, pain radiating across her skull, and stars spun in front of her eyes. Fighting through the pain, she swiped at the blood running into the side of her eye, and kicked out again, this time connecting with Leroy's shin.

He let go of her hair. She scrambled to her feet, toppling the end table as she pushed it out of her way.

Ignoring the crash of the flower vase, she tried to run for the front door, but her heart sank as she saw Earl walking up the front steps of the porch.

Her purse lay on the floor, the contents spilling out—she spied her phone, but couldn't grab it.

Earl was coming from one direction, and Leroy was bearing down on her from the other.

She fought the panic rising in her chest as she raced for

the kitchen, hoping to make it out the back door.

Leroy must have anticipated her move—he cut across the room, grabbing her from behind as she ran into the kitchen.

She could smell alcohol and the sweet acrid scent of tobacco on his breath as he pulled her against him and breathed into her ear. "You didn't really think you could get away from me now, did you? Don't you know you'll always belong to me?"

Cash had practiced this exact scenario with her, and her body reacted on impulse, rearing back and slamming the back of her head into Leroy's face.

He howled in pain, releasing her to bring his hands to his face. She shot forward.

Her gaze darting frantically around the kitchen, she looked for a weapon. A block of knives set back against the wall, next to the ceramic canisters of sugar and flour.

Sprinting forward, she reached for a knife.

He grabbed her around the waist, yanking her back.

Her fingers circled the handle of a steak knife, and she knocked the canisters off the counter as he pulled her backward.

The crash of the canisters must have startled him just enough to give her the second she needed, and she slashed the knife across his forearm.

"You bitch!" he yelled, jerking his arm back and spraying the counter with blood.

He advanced on her, stepping through the mess of flour and sugar on the floor.

She braced one hand on the counter, the other holding the knife out, readying herself for his assault.

Not sure if it was the booze or the fact that she was fighting back, but she could tell he was off his game.

Good.

He narrowed his eyes at her. "You think you're gonna

fight me? Is that what this is all about? You think you're all tough now?"

"Just leave me alone, Leroy. Get out of my house and out of my life. I'm not your wife anymore," she yelled, trying to sound braver than she felt.

"Do you think a little piece of paper is gonna keep me from taking what's mine?"

A smear of blood ran across his cheek from where she'd slammed into his nose, and his eyes had a crazy gleam in them. His hair stood up around his head, and he looked insane.

The whole situation seemed insane.

How could he have escaped from jail? How could he be here, threatening her again?

Would she ever be able to escape this man?

The day before, she'd thought she'd had it all—a new relationship with a great guy who really cared about her, a job that she enjoyed, and friends.

All things that she'd never had before.

A thought struck her. She'd never had those things in her corner before, either. Cash might be gone, but she still had Charlie and Zack, and Cherry and Taylor to count on.

She tried a different approach, purposely lowering her voice to a calmer tone. "Listen Leroy, I'm sorry I upset you. You just startled me by showing up like you did. But things are different now. *I'm* different now. I have a new life and new friends, and a couple of them are on their way over here as we speak."

An ugly sneer crossed his face. He took another menacing step closer. "Yeah, the boys told me you took up with Cash Walker. Is he the one who's coming over? 'Cause I wouldn't mind showing him just how much I appreciate him taking care of my wife while I was locked up."

That hadn't worked as well as she'd hoped.

And the reminder that Cash *wasn't* on his way over ever

again had a stab of pain shooting through her heart that had nothing to do with Leroy. "I'm not seeing him anymore. I'm doing my own thing. I got a new job now, and I work for the sheriff's wife. And they're on their way over here now. The sheriff, too. So you'd better get out of here."

He laughed—an evil snicker that told her he saw right through her charade. "It's real nice the way you're so worried about me. And I am planning to get out of here. But I'm taking you with me."

The front door slammed, and Emma jumped, dropping the knife. Leroy kicked it away as Earl and Junior appeared in the doorway of the kitchen.

Earl's face was bruised, and his right eye was partially swollen shut from the beating Cash had given him the night before. "What the hell is taking so long? We've been waiting for you outside. I thought you were just gonna say your piece and get out of here."

Leroy sneered at his brother. "Yeah, well my piece is taking me a little longer to say than I'd originally thought it would."

"Well, your time's up. We gotta go."

"Just when did you put yourself in charge of this plan? I say when it's time to go. This is *my* plan, and I'm changing it. We're bringing Emma with us."

"What the hell? Are you crazy?"

Leroy shoved Earl back against the counter, pressing his forearm against his brother's throat. "Don't call me crazy."

Earl pushed back, his eyes bulging as he gasped for breath.

Leroy released him, then roughly grabbed Emma's arm. "If I'm gonna spend the rest of my days living in Canada, I want my loving wife by my side."

"Whatever, man. But for the record, I think it's a bad idea to bring her with us." Earl rubbed his hand across his throat, his voice hoarse.

"She said the sheriff is on his way over, so we gotta get outta here. We just need to stop by the house and get the rest of my stuff, then we can head for the border." Leroy pulled her through the house, and she stumbled down the front steps.

There was no way she could fight all three of them.

She just needed to go along with them until she could find another way to escape.

Earl's car sat in the driveway, and Leroy shoved her into the back seat then climbed in after her. They raced out of the driveway, heading for the Purvis farm.

. . .

Cash's carefully practiced rehearsal of his apology had been for nothing, because when he got to the farm, no one answered the door.

Strange. Emma's car was out front. He scanned the farm for any signs of her. Maybe she'd gone for a walk. Unlikely, considering it was already dark.

He put the cat back in the truck and crossed the yard to check the barn.

No Emma.

He knocked again and yelled out her name. A small knot of alarm formed in his gut, and he dug out his cell phone and called her number.

The alarm grew as he heard the familiar ring tone playing inside the house.

Screw it. He was going in.

Ready to bust down the door, he took a second to try the knob, thankful to find it unlocked. Pushing the door open, he gasped at the scene in front of him.

One of the chairs was tipped over, and the room was in disarray. He was no detective, but he recognized the obvious signs of a struggle. Emma's purse lay on the floor, the contents spilling out, including her phone, which had now stopped ringing.

The end table was overturned, and a vase of silk flowers lay broken on the floor, the flowers scattered, and a few of the pieces were crushed as if they'd been stepped on.

He took a step closer, trying to make sense of the clues in the room, already praying that she was okay.

"Emma!" Tearing through the room, he yelled her name. He knew in his gut that she wasn't there, but he still grasped that bit of hope as he flipped on the kitchen light.

His heart leaped to his throat.

The cheery kitchen with its yellow countertops had been trashed. The coffeepot lay on its side, and several of the drawers hung open. The ceramic canisters of flour and sugar were smashed, their contents spread across the counters and floor.

But it was the bright red spray of blood on the counter and the clear outline of a boot print in the flour on the floor that had him reaching for his phone to call the sheriff.

Before he could place the call, the phone rang in his hand.

Taylor's number came up on the screen, and he tapped the button and held the phone to his ear, his gut already churning with dread. "Taylor. Do you know where Emma is?" he asked, not even giving his friend a chance to say "hello."

"I thought she was with you. That's why I'm calling. I needed to talk to her and couldn't reach her on her cell phone."

"She doesn't have it with her. What's going on?" Cash gingerly stepped into the kitchen, not wanting to contaminate the crime scene.

Leaning forward, he examined the bloody handprint on the counter next to the spray of blood.

It was only a partial print, a palm and a few fingers, but

it was small, closer to the size of a woman's hand, and Cash knew in his gut that it was Emma's hand that had made it.

And Emma's blood.

"We just got word that Leroy Purvis escaped this afternoon. He was being transported today to the state pen, but they never showed up. State troopers just found the transport van. It was rolled over and smashed up on the side of the highway. The one guard was knocked out, and the driver was handcuffed to the steering wheel. Both of their guns were missing, and there was no sign of Leroy or the other prisoner they were transporting. The troopers said it looked like another vehicle had crashed into it, so my guess is those idiot brothers of his had something to do with this."

Cash wasn't guessing. He was sure of it.

"I'm at the Frank farm now. Emma's not here, and I haven't seen or talked to her all day." Now wasn't the time to get into the specifics of their argument or that she'd been home by herself. Or that the only reason she was alone was because he'd broken things off with her the night before. "But Taylor, Leroy was here. I'm sure of it. The place is trashed, and there's blood on the counter."

"Blood?"

"Yeah, and a size dumb-ass boot print in the middle of the floor."

"I'll be right there," Taylor said. "Don't touch anything."

He *wasn't* touching anything.

In fact, he wasn't even in the house anymore. He was already in his truck, turning over the engine, and throwing it in gear.

"And Cash, stay there. I'm heading over to the Purvis farm now, and I don't need you in the mix. I already know what happened at the fairgrounds last night. Earl and Junior wouldn't say who roughed them up, but I have a pretty good feeling about who the culprit was. I'll send a car and a deputy to you. And don't worry, we'll find her."

He'd find her.

He hung up the phone, his truck already barreling down the highway. It would take Taylor at least ten minutes to get out to Emma's and another fifteen to get out to the Purvis place.

He didn't have time to wait.

Images of the blood dotting the floor of her kitchen filled his head, and he prayed that he wouldn't be too late.

Feared that he would be too late.

Too late to save her.

...

Emma kept a watchful eye on Leroy as he paced the kitchen floor, swearing and yelling at Earl and Junior, who sat at the scarred and scratched kitchen table.

In their infinite wisdom, Earl and Junior decided to crack a few cold ones and make sandwiches while they waited, thus earning them the wrath of their brother's temper.

She sat still, trying not to draw attention to herself. Her hands were bound behind her back, and she reached them down the back of the sofa, using the metal frame to try to break through the layers of tape.

It was slow going, but at least she was doing something.

And one thing she had on her side was the fact that Leroy totally underestimated her.

He was used to the old Emma, the meek and trembling mouse who took his abuse. Not that she wasn't still trembling—hell, she was shaking like a leaf—but she wasn't meek anymore, and she wasn't going to sit back and just take it.

She was going to fight.

As soon as she had the chance.

Her smarts counteracted the stupidity of the Purvis brothers, and the alcohol they were consuming didn't add to their intellect.

Like Cash had taught her, she analyzed her surroundings, looking for what she could use as a weapon. Trying to free her hands, she also listened to their plans, trying to calculate her own strategy for escape if she ended up back in the car with them.

The sound of an engine coming down the driveway filled the air, and her heart leaped at the hope that it was the police. They had to know by now that Leroy had escaped, and only a bunch of idiots would go back to their own house.

Good thing she'd been kidnapped by a bunch of idiots.

If she were honest, she'd admit that she hoped it was Cash, riding in to rescue her, but there was no way he could know about Leroy's escape.

Earl jumped up from the table and crossed to the front windows, peering out the faded drapes. "Shit. It's Walker. I told you we shouldn't have brought her with us."

Emma's heart soared.

It *was* Cash. But how could he be here? How could he have known?

Taylor must have called him, told him Leroy had escaped, and he'd come looking for her. Which hopefully meant the police were also on their way.

Leroy slammed his fist against the kitchen table. "Shut up, Earl. I'm glad he's here. I've got a thing or two I want to say to him."

"Don't mess with him, Leroy." Junior rubbed the side of his leg where Cash had kicked him the night before. "He's one tough bastard. Let's just get out of here."

Leroy leaned down, his voice threatening as he spat the words, "I'm one tough bastard, too."

"I'm with Junior, let's just get out of here," Earl said. "We can leave her here, and slip out the back door. She's the only thing Walker wants anyway. If he has her, he won't bother coming after us."

"He's right," Emma said, her voice pleading as she tried to convince Leroy. "Just leave me here. I'll only slow you down anyway. Now's your chance to escape."

Leroy turned on her, anger flashing in his eyes. "You'd like that, wouldn't you? If we just left you here for your new boyfriend. Oh wait, you were just thinking of us, right? How nice of you." He crossed the room, bore down on her, his fist raised. "We'll see how this Walker guy likes you when your pretty little face is bashed in."

She cringed, pressing her back against the sofa, preparing herself for the blow.

Instead, the front door crashed in, banging against the wall—startling them all—as Cash charged into the room.

Chapter Twenty

Cash burst into the room, his adrenaline racing and his blood pounding in his ears. He'd seen Earl's car in the driveway and prayed he'd find Emma inside.

His gaze darted around the room, seeing everything at once—Earl standing guard at the door, Junior sitting like a lump at the kitchen table, Emma bound on the sofa, and Leroy standing over her, his fist raised.

"Get the hell away from her," he said.

Dried blood covered the side of Emma's head and streaked down her cheek. Seeing her scared and hurt only fueled his rage, and he wanted to tear Leroy from limb to limb.

"You can't just break in to our house. You're trespassing." Earl sneered as he rushed forward. "And that gives me the right to defend my home and kick your ass."

"I can't wait for you to try," Cash told him as he quickly assessed his surroundings. The scarcely furnished room offered little in the way of weapons.

Earl came at him, and Cash kicked out, his boot heel

connecting with the other man's kneecap. Earl went down, howling and clutching his knee.

Grabbing the lamp from the nearest side table and ripping the cord from the wall, Cash whacked Earl over the head with it. With a guttural cry, he crumpled to the floor.

Leroy took a step toward him, but Emma stretched out her leg and tripped him. He fell forward, landing on the coffee table, the cheap material breaking under his fall.

With a banshee scream, she kicked out at his fallen form as he tried to crawl away from her.

Cash rushed forward, grabbing Leroy by the collar and slamming a roundhouse punch into his face.

Leroy moaned in pain, holding his cheek, as he skittered backward.

Cash took one glance at Junior, who still sat at the table, his mouth hanging open and a half of a sandwich clutched in his hand. "You just stay where you are, Junior."

The other man must have remembered the beating he'd received from Cash the night before, because he nodded and stayed seated at the table, his focus returning to his sandwich.

"Don't listen to him, you lard-ass," Leroy yelled at his brother. "Get up and help me."

"No way, man." Junior shook his head. "This was your dumb idea to bring her here. All I wanted to do was go to Canada and see that big waterfall."

Cash crossed the room to Emma, pulling her up from the sofa and turning her so he could free her hands.

The tape was partially cut through. She must have been working on it the whole time she'd been bound.

"Good girl. You almost had yourself loose." He ripped the tape the rest of the way, and she shook out her hands, spreading her fingers to get the feeling back into them. "Although I'm not sure what you were gonna do if you got free."

"I was gonna do this." She stepped forward to where Leroy was cowered against the wall. Blood ran out his nose from where Cash had punched him in the face.

Grabbing an empty beer bottle from the end table, she swung it, trying to crack it across Leroy's head. "Don't you ever touch me again, you worthless piece of shit."

Before she could make contact, Leroy's hand shot out, catching her jaw in an awkward hit that sent her head reeling sideways.

That was it. Cash couldn't take it.

The fury exploded inside of him at seeing this man hurt the woman he loved.

He grabbed for Emma and pushed her behind him. "She said 'don't ever touch her again,' you little maggot." Crushing his boot down on Leroy's leg, he held him in place while he pulled him up by his shirt collar and pummeled his face with several punches.

The sound of sirens filled the air, and blue and red lights flashed through the room as the sheriff's cars sped into the driveway.

Cash shoved Leroy away from him, releasing his shirt and taking a step back. His breath came hard and fast as the adrenaline raced through his system.

He reached for Emma, pulling her against him in a tight hug. He wasn't ever planning to let her go again.

The front door stood open, and Taylor rushed into the room, his gun drawn. Two deputies followed behind him, weapons raised.

Junior dropped his sandwich and raised his hands. "I didn't do nothing. I was just sitting here eating supper."

One deputy stepped forward to cuff Junior while the other rushed over to Leroy to handcuff him.

Taylor crossed to Emma and Cash, his gaze obviously taking in her battered face. "You okay, Em?"

She nodded, a dazed look still in her eyes. "I'm okay." She looked up at Cash, her arms still circling around his waist. "How did you know to come after me?"

"I showed up at your dad's place planning to apologize and beg your forgiveness and found the house wrecked and blood in the kitchen. Then Taylor called me and told me that Leroy had escaped from the prison transport, and I figured these idiots would bring you here. So, I got here as fast as I could."

"Which, if I seem to recall correctly, was exactly what I told you *not* to do," Taylor said.

"Well, you should know by now that I'm not very good at following directions."

The deputy hauled Leroy to his feet. "You want us to take these two out to the car, Sheriff?"

Two? Wait.

Where the hell was Earl?

Cash scanned the living room and kitchen area. The spot on the floor where Earl had been previously passed out was empty. "Where's Earl?"

"Earl? I don't know. We didn't see him."

"He was here a few minutes ago. He was passed out on the floor." Cash let go of Emma and ran to the front door, squinting into the dark as he peered across the yard. "The little weasel must have heard the sirens and got away. He was here, though. He was part of this."

Emma nodded. "He *was* here. And he was bragging earlier how breaking Leroy out of prison had been his idea and how he'd been driving when he crashed into the prison van."

Taylor leaned down, speaking into the radio clipped to his shoulder. "I need an APB issued for Earl Purvis. White male, about six foot tall, two hundred pounds, dark hair. Last seen wearing—" He glanced at Emma for a description.

"Um, jeans and a green T-shirt," she said.

"Green with a little blood on it," mumbled Cash.

The deputies took Junior and Leroy out to secure them in the back of Taylor's car.

Emma and Cash spent the next thirty minutes going over the details of the night and filling Taylor in on what had happened. They sat next to each other on the dingy sofa, Cash keeping his arm around her shoulder the whole time.

He couldn't stop touching her. He'd been so afraid that something had happened to her or that he wouldn't get there in time to save her. Gratitude rushed through him that, despite a few bruises and cuts, she was still relatively okay.

Taylor shut his notebook and stuffed it and the pen into his front breast pocket. "I think that's about it for tonight. If you think of anything else, let me know, but I don't reckon there's anything else for you to do here. You all might as well head on home."

They stood, and Cash shook his friend's hand, and Emma gave Taylor a hug.

"You taking her back to her dad's place?" Taylor asked.

Cash answered before Emma could say a word. "No, I'll bring her home with me. We'll be at Tucked Away if you need us."

Taylor nodded. "All right then. I'll call you tomorrow."

Wrapping an arm around her waist, Cash guided Emma out the front door and down the porch steps.

As they neared the truck, she turned to him. "Thanks for being here tonight. It means everything that you came for me."

"Of course."

She leaned back against the side of the truck, crossing her arms and narrowing her eyes at him. "Now I believe I heard you mention something about an apology and you planning to beg for some forgiveness?"

He grinned. "Yeah, I believe I did mention something to that effect." He touched her cheek. "I'm sorry, Em. I was an idiot. It's not the first time it's happened, and I'm sure it won't be the last. But I screwed up, and I apologize. And I hope you'll give me the chance to make it up to you."

"What changed your mind?"

"Believe it or not, it was a visit from my mom. We had a long talk, and she set me straight about a lot of things. We talked about the stuff that happened back then, and a lot of it was what we probably should have talked about before now. She made sense to me and gave me a different way of looking at things. Including the way I was keeping myself away from you for fear of hurting you."

"Did you tell her that I'm not scared of you?"

"I did. And I want to believe you. But the fact is, I saw the look on your face. You were afraid of me."

"I was afraid, yes, I'll give you that. And my face probably reflected that. But that would have just been my gut reaction. I've had a lot of years of being afraid, and that doesn't just go away. You've got to give me a little leeway—it was a scary situation—I think anyone would be at least a little afraid. I've spent a long time being afraid—of everything. I need you to be patient with me, and give me some time to work through that. Can you do that? Be patient with me?"

He nodded, pulling her against him, his heart filling with joy that she still wanted to try to make things work with him. "I can give you all the time you need. Patience is something I've got plenty of. And I can wait until you're ready for a relationship with me. I've been waiting for you my whole life—I'm not about to give up now."

She grinned at him, and the sight of her smiling face made him so happy.

Tipping up on her toes, she circled her hands around his neck and pressed her lips to his. He tilted his head, deepening the kiss, capturing her mouth.

His emotions were going crazy, and he clutched her back to keep his hands from shaking. An intense sensation of love, mixed with a bone-deep feeling of relief, ran through him as he accepted that they were going to be okay. That she still wanted him.

He hadn't blown it.

Shots of desire darted up his spine as her tongue pressed between his lips. She tasted sweet and warm and felt so damn good. He needed to get her home. And into his bed.

Into *their* bed.

He pulled back, his breath ragged as he whispered, "Come home with me?"

"Yes. Yes. A million times yes."

He chuckled and reached for the truck door. "I brought a little something along to sweeten the deal, if you wouldn't have so graciously accepted my apology."

Opening the door, he revealed the crate sitting on the floor of the truck. The dome light in the cab gave off just enough brightness to illuminate the little gray kitten curled up and sleeping peacefully on the blanket inside the crate.

"Oh, it's Percy," Emma squealed, her hands reaching for her face. She lifted the crate into the seat and climbed in next to it.

"I asked Charlie if I could give him to you, and she said he already belonged to you. So if you want him, he's yours." The similarity to how he felt about his own heart wasn't lost on him. He picked up her hand and laid a soft kiss on her palm. "And the same goes with this cowboy's heart. It belongs to you, darlin', plain and simple. So if you want him, he's yours, too."

"I do. Yes, I do want him. Want you." She laughed as she stumbled over her words. "I want both of you."

"Good, then let's go home." He shut the door and crossed

to the other side of the truck. By the time he slid into the driver's seat, Emma had opened the door of the crate, removed the little kitten, and cuddled it to her chest.

He smiled at her and was surprised to see tears on her cheeks. "Hey, now. What's wrong?"

"Nothing. I'm just so happy." She squeezed the furball against her. "I've never had my own pet before."

Cash headed out of the driveway, leaving the Purvis farm in the dust. He squeezed Emma's leg and offered her one of his most charming grins. "I sure hope you're talking about the cat."

She laughed, and the sound was music to his ears.

...

Emma walked into the cabin, the kitten curled up and asleep in her arms.

Even though it had only been one day, it felt like it had been so long since she'd been here. Although, it *had* been one hell of a long day.

She should be exhausted—but she wasn't—instead, she felt exhilarated, full of energy. Unused to the feeling, she was fairly certain that she recognized it as happiness. Pure clean untainted happiness.

The man who was the main source of that happiness walked into the cabin behind her, stopping to stomp the dirt off his boots before he toed them off and left them in a heap by the door.

Her mouth went dry at the sight of him. He was one damn sexy cowboy. And he was hers.

He'd just offered her his heart, along with a kitten.

How could she resist?

She set the kitten in its favorite spot, nestled in the pillows on the sofa, and turned to Cash. "Are you hungry? You want me to make you a sandwich or something?"

His eyes darkened with desire. "I'm hungry, but not for a sandwich. I think I'm more in the mood for the 'or something.'"

"I think I can be persuaded into a little 'or something.'"

He stepped closer and slid his hand under the back of her shirt, caressing her skin above the waistband of her jeans and sending delicious shivers of need up her spine.

Leaning down, his breath warm against her ear, his voice husky as he said, "I don't want to push you, but I'd sure like to have you sleepin' in my bed with me tonight."

She grinned up at him, feeling flirty as she batted her lashes. "But I didn't bring any pajamas."

"You won't need any pajamas tonight. Or ever, if I have any say in the matter." He reached down, slipping his hands behind her knees, and lifted her up. Cradling her against him, he carried her to his bed and laid her gently on the mattress.

He pulled off her shoes and socks, then unzipped her pants and peeled them down her legs. Stepping back, he tugged his shirt over his head and tossed it to the floor. Repeating his actions, she pulled her T-shirt over her head and dropped it by the bed.

Her heart raced as she reached behind her back and released the clasp on her bra. Peeling the straps down her arms, she let it fall, then lay back against the pillows so she could watch him undress.

She'd never felt so brazen, leaning against the pillows wearing only her panties. But Cash made her feel beautiful and sexy and alive.

Yes—alive—like every nerve in her body was tingling with anticipation.

Keeping his dark gaze on her, he shimmied out of his jeans and left them in a pile as he crawled onto the bed next to her.

They hadn't turned on the light in the bedroom, but the

lamp shining in the living room brought in just enough light to see the expression on his face, while still being dim enough to mask the imperfections of her body.

And to highlight the perfection of his.

His chest was so toned and muscled, his pecs solid and hard. And they weren't all that was hard, as evidenced by the thick bulge in his white boxer briefs.

Her skin prickled with eagerness, every part of her craving his touch as his body molded against hers.

Running his fingers from her neck down to her middle sent delicious rivers of desire coursing through her, and she shivered.

"You cold?" he asked, pulling his hand away to reach for the blanket.

She reached for his hand and set it back on her stomach. "No. I'm not cold. I'm practically burning up. I feel like I'm on fire from the inside out, and every place you touch brings that fire to the surface."

He barely lifted his hand and arched an eyebrow at her. "Is that a good thing?"

"Yes, that's a good thing." She caught her breath as he set his hand back down and skimmed it up to cup her breast. "That's a really good thing."

Her nipple was pebbled and taut as he circled it with his fingertip then dipped his head to draw it between his lips. His mouth was wet and warm, and desire shot through her like a flame.

"How about this?" he asked, pulling slightly back and teasing her nipple with just his tongue. "Is this a good thing?"

"Uh-huh, that's good, too," she whispered as her hands gripped the comforter beneath her.

He trailed his fingers lightly down her skin, skimming her stomach, her waist, then slid his hand inside her panties.

She gasped at his touch, his long fingers finding her warm

center, and she thought she might melt into the mattress. His mouth found her breast again, and he drew her nipple back between his lips, his teeth gently grazing the tip.

Arching her back, she offered herself to him. Offered her body, her heart, her soul. Everything was his—his to claim and explore, to touch and tease.

Her body was on fire with want and need, but she wanted more—more of his skin next to hers, more of his mouth licking and nipping and sucking, and more of him inside her.

A moan escaped her lips as he rubbed and stroked her most sensitive place. A storm of feelings churned inside of her, building in intensity, as he took her to the brink of desire.

Forgetting everything else around her, she let the moment take her, let the feelings consume her, let herself get caught up in the passion that this man drew from her.

The circle of the storm grew, pulling everything into its center, into its core, until it reached the crescendo, and she cried out from the release, her body shuddering against him as the waves of feeling ripped through her body, again and again.

She fell back against the bed, her body spent and tingling as she tried to catch her breath.

Oh Lord, what had just come over her?

She'd given in to all of it, all of the feelings, and had cried out when they overtook her. And she was afraid she'd cried out rather loudly.

Was she supposed to do that?

Suddenly shy and nervous, she snuck a glance at Cash, then had to smile at his expression.

He wore a satisfied grin as he looked down at her, like he'd just won first prize at the county fair.

Before Cash, she'd never had a man put her desire first or spend the time to tease and tantalize her body. She finally understood what all the articles about foreplay in the women's magazines were about.

And Cash Walker was a master in the field.

She smiled up at him. "You look pretty proud of yourself."

He chuckled. "You just look pretty."

Her heart might burst with what she felt for this man. "You make me feel pretty."

"I want to make you feel a lot of things." He sat up and slowly slid her panties down her legs.

Her body woke up again as he tugged off his briefs then reached into the drawer next to the bed and pulled out a foil-wrapped packet.

He covered himself then lay down between her legs, his arms braced on the bed on either side of her shoulders as he supported his body over hers.

His expression was solemn, his eyes full of feeling as he stared into hers. "You make *me* feel a lot of things, Em. Things I never even dreamed were possible to feel. Things I thought I'd buried and let go of years ago. You make me feel happiness and joy, as well as the deepest sadness and regret at the thought that I had lost you. You make my skin itch, and my hands shake, and my heart feel like it's going to bust out of my chest. You make me feel alive. In fact, you make me feel *everything*."

It was as if his heart was speaking to hers. "I know. I feel the same way about you."

He shook his head. "I doubt that you do. I can't imagine anyone feeling the depths of emotion that I feel for you. I know it's kind of soon, and I swear I'm not trying to rush you, but I want you to know that I've fallen for you, darlin'. And fallen hard."

She couldn't speak, afraid that if she opened her mouth, she might start to cry. Hearing his thoughts spoken in his deep voice and with such tenderness and feeling told her how much this moment meant to him. How much she meant to him. Could this really be happening? She held her breath, waiting to hear his next words.

"You don't have to say anything, but I want you to know…" He paused, his voice choked with emotion. "I want you to know that I'm in love with you. So help me, as much as I've tried to fight it, I can't, it's bigger than me. It's bigger than anything I've ever felt before."

He raised his hand and brushed his fingers against her cheek. "I love you, Emma. Plain and simple, I do."

Her heart felt as if it were going to beat out of her chest. "I love you, too. I swear I do. And it's not too soon. Not too soon at all. It's perfect."

A grin broke across his face. "If I've learned anything over the past few weeks, it's that life is short, and finding someone to share it with is rare and a gift that should be treasured. I've found you now, Emma, and I want to share my life with you. I want to share everything with you. And I do see you as a gift to be treasured and cherished. How do you feel about sharing your life with me and letting me cherish you every day that we're together?"

"I feel pretty good about that, actually." She tried to laugh, but her laughter turned to a shudder and tears leaked from the corner of her eyes as the intense emotions became too much for her to contain.

"Hey, now. Don't cry, darlin'," he said tenderly. A teasing smile tugged at the corner of his mouth. "It's not gonna be that bad living with me."

This time she did laugh. The laughter burst out of her mouth, born of happiness and joy, but it was cut short as he leaned down and captured her mouth in a kiss—a kiss filled with feeling and passion and desire.

She kissed him back, pouring all of her love into the kiss. Then his hands were in her hair, and his weight settled between her legs.

Clutching his back, she was filled with a bone-deep, gut-wrenching, soul-shattering need. Need for him to be inside of her. Inside of her heart, her soul, her body.

He shifted, and then he was.

She moaned as he filled her. Filled her with love and need and a glorious feeling of completeness.

Moving with her, his hands touching and teasing, while his hips increased their rhythm with each stroke. Their passion surged and swelled, her core convulsing with need. Need for him.

The rest of the world faded away as he took her to the edge until she was panting and crying his name, her fingers digging in to the hard muscles of his back. Then she was soaring over—flying—as his arms tightened around her, and he moaned into her neck with his own release.

Then she was falling. Falling back to earth, to reality, falling into his arms.

And he was there to catch her.

He dropped onto the bed beside her and pulled her against him. She curled into the crook of his arm, wrapping her leg around his, still needing the contact of his skin.

Laying her head on his chest, she breathed in the musky male scent of his aftershave. He always smelled so dang good.

"That was incredible." She reached her arms over her head, like a cat stretching in the sun, then curled back against him. "I've made a decision."

"What's that?"

"I don't ever want to leave this bed."

He chuckled. "Not even for pie?"

"Well, maybe for pie. But that's about it."

He brushed her bangs from her forehead, looking down at her with love in his eyes. "I've made a decision, too."

"Yeah?"

"Yeah. I've decided that I want you to move in here. With

me. And Percy, of course." He touched her lips. "You don't have to decide yet. But just think about it. There's no reason for you to stay at your dad's when I'm going to want you here with me every day anyway." He gave her one of his flirty winks. "And every night."

She laughed. "I don't have to think about it. All I have to do is go back to the house and pack my stuff."

"So, you mean you want to? Want to move in here with me?"

"Yes, of course." She rolled on top of him, straddling his waist, amazed at how comfortable she felt, even in her nakedness. "Cash, I've wasted too many years of my life being unhappy and feeling like I didn't deserve any better. I'm in love with you. I know it in my heart, in my very soul. I will never love another man the way that I love you. So why wait? Why waste another day? Consider me officially moved in."

He grinned up at her and slid his hands around her waist. "I like it when you get all sassy."

She grinned and swatted at his chest. Before she had a chance to say anything, he flipped her over and rolled on top of her.

A smile nearly split his face in two, and his eyes were full of mischief. "I love you, too, Emma. So, as long as we're getting all sassy and making decisions, why not just make it official? Don't just move in with me. Marry me."

Her breath caught in her throat, and she was afraid her heart may have just stopped.

Could this really be happening?

"Are you really asking me to marry you while my hair is a tousled mess and I'm lying naked underneath you?"

"I can't think of a better time. And I kind of like your hair like that."

She laughed, then sobered. "Really, Cash? Are you sure?"

"I've never been more sure of anything in my life, darlin'."

He leaned in, kissing her softly. "But I'm also sure I can wait. If you don't think you're ready."

She kissed him back, a hard quick kiss. "Oh, I'm ready. I feel like for the first time in such a long time, I have something to look forward to. Something to dream about and plan for.

"I feel like the darkness in my life is finally fading away and the brightness is shining through. I used to see myself as weak and afraid, but now, thanks to you and the friendships that I've made, I feel brave and strong. And I feel stronger every day. Being with you and having the job at the diner have given me strength and a new sense of confidence. And I can feel myself changing every day."

"Well, don't change too much." He smiled at her, his own pride in her showing through his expression. "Seriously, I'm so proud of you. I can see the changes in you. It's like you've blossomed right in front of me. You're getting sturdier and more self-assured every day. And that's all I want for you."

"I want to feel like I'm strong enough in myself so that you feel like you're getting a whole Emma, not a partial shell of someone I used to be."

"I think you are braver than you give yourself credit for. I always have. But I hear you, and I'm willing to wait, to let you dictate this. I know I love you and want you to be my wife, but I'll leave it up to you to tell me when you're ready. You decide. You set the time and date and just tell me when to show up at the church. You're in control."

She'd never been in control of anything. Especially when it came to her relationships or her own life.

Except that wasn't exactly true.

She'd taken control of her life when she'd made the decision to leave Leroy. And when she'd filed for divorce. And when she'd moved back to Broken Falls and when she'd taken the job at the diner.

She hadn't decided to fall in love with Cash, her heart had

been in control of that, but he was letting her decide how their relationship would progress. He'd laid it out in front of her, and all she had to do was pick it up.

Which seemed to be the easiest decision she'd ever made. She loved him and she wanted nothing more than to be his wife.

"Okay, if I'm really in control, I'm making my first two important decisions."

"Lay 'em on me."

"First, I want to get married to you, and I don't want to wait. I'll talk to Charlie and Cherry, and we'll start working on plans tomorrow."

"Sounds good. Now what's the second decision?"

"I've decided I'd like some pie. And I'd like to eat it naked, right here in this bed with you."

He chuckled. "I like the way you think. I'll even volunteer to get the pie." He climbed out of bed and pulled on his jeans, zipping the fly but leaving the top snap undone.

She swallowed. He was undeniably the sexiest man alive. And he was going to be her husband. And was bringing her pie in bed. Life couldn't get much better than that.

"Wait right here, and I'll be back in a minute with a big ole piece of pie and two forks." He winked and walked out the bedroom door.

She leaned back against the bed frame, pulling the sheets up under her arms, and sighing with contentment.

Her contentment was interrupted by the sound of a crash and a dull thud coming from the living room.

Every one of her senses went on alert as her nerves tingled under her skin.

She was probably overreacting. Sensitive to sounds after Leroy breaking into her house earlier.

That noise could have been anything. Cash could have dropped something or tripped in the darkened room.

But she didn't think so.

No, something felt wrong. Very wrong.

Slipping out of bed, she pulled Cash's T-shirt on over her head and tugged it over her bottom. The shirt was so big on her, it fit more like a dress.

Padding barefoot across the room, she called out his name but got no answer.

"Cash?" Blood pounded in her ears, and her nerves tightened in fear as she stepped out of the bedroom.

Her gaze took in everything at once, and she saw two things that had her heart literally stop beating in her chest.

One was Cash lying passed out on the floor and the other was Earl Purvis standing over him, a piece of firewood clutched in his hand.

Chapter Twenty-One

"Earl. What are you doing here?" Emma's gaze swept the room, looking for an escape.

But she couldn't run, couldn't leave Cash alone with this maniac.

She had to stand up to him. Had to fight.

"Hey there, sis," Earl sneered and spit a thick stream of chewing tobacco onto the floor next to Cash's head. "I came to pay you and your new boyfriend a little visit. Or should I say fee-on-say?"

Crap. How long had he been there? Had he been listening to them talk?

Or worse — listening to them make love?

She straightened her shoulders. So what if he did? She hoped he'd enjoyed the show. Because it was going to be the last time he ever came near her — or Cash — again. She'd just been telling Cash how she was done being weak and vulnerable.

This was the new and improved Emma. The one who was strong and willing to fight for what she wanted.

Pretend to be brave.

Cash's words of advice—her mantra—came back to her, but as she whispered them to herself, she realized that she didn't have to pretend anymore.

She actually felt brave.

Like she could take on this loser.

Well, okay, she was still afraid, but it was like 80 percent scared shitless and 20 percent brave. But at least she felt it, and she was holding on to that 20 percent.

Her self-defense lessons came flooding into her mind, and she knew the first thing she needed to do was to get him away from Cash.

She took a deep breath. All she had to do was outwit this guy, get him into a place where she could overpower him, or at least put herself in a position where she could attack.

Outsmarting him seemed the easiest task, especially when his weapons arsenal in that department was sorely lacking.

She took a few steps toward the kitchen, motioning to the fridge. Anything to draw him away from Cash. "How about I get you a beer, and we can sit down and talk about it."

He took a step toward her, more of a stumble really, and she realized he must have already started the "having a drink" idea.

Which could work for or against her.

If he was already drunk, he might make even worse and more impulsive decisions than hitting Cash over the head with a log of firewood. But hopefully, his inebriated state would work in her favor if his reactions were slower and his focus blurred.

Taking another step into the kitchen, she searched her surroundings—just like Cash had taught her—for any weapons she could use against him.

This situation felt eerily familiar as she recalled facing off with Leroy only hours before. But this time she felt different—

felt like she could really do this.

She just needed to try a different approach with Earl—take her time then strike when she was sure she had him and could do the most damage.

He stumbled a little closer. "Yeah, I'll take a beer, but I'll take it for the road, 'cause I'm not sticking around here waiting for the cops to show up."

"Fine. Take it and go." Nothing would make her happier than to have Earl Purvis hit the road and never come back. "Just leave us alone."

"You'd like that, wouldn't you? For me to just disappear and leave you here to play house with your new boyfriend?" His face held an ugly sneer. "But I can't do that, and you know it."

"No, I don't know it. I don't understand why you even care what I do. I divorced your brother. Why do I even matter to you?"

He slammed his fist onto the kitchen table. "Because you don't get to just walk away. Not after you got my brother sent to jail and made him a laughingstock by divorcing him. You're a Purvis, and you belong to him, to us. And we take what's ours."

Actually, she had nothing to do with Leroy showing up drunk at Cherry and Taylor's engagement party and taking a shot at her father and the sheriff—he'd done that all on his own. But now didn't seem the best time to point that out.

"You think you can just go on with your fancy little life, acting all high and mighty and sluttin' it up with Walker, while my brother rots in a jail cell."

Too bad you're not in the jail cell next to him.

Earl spit another stream of tobacco onto the hardwood floor.

Emma grimaced in disgust. He was truly a vile human being.

He advanced on her, taking another step closer, the look of menace clear in his eyes. "We had everything worked out. You know how much planning went into breaking Leroy out of prison, and you screwed that up, too."

It couldn't have taken that much planning. How hard was it to find out the time they were transporting him and crash into the county vehicle? "You can't blame that on me. Leroy could have just left. I never asked him to come for me."

"But that's the point, ain't it? I *can* blame you. And I *am* blaming you. Leroy would have been just fine if you wouldn't have pressed charges against him then walked out on him."

"I didn't press charges against him. The state did. After he put me in the hospital."

He narrowed his eyes. "What he did to you was nothing compared to what I have planned." Reaching for his belt, he fumbled with the buckle and pulled open the strap. Unsnapping the top button, he partially unzipped his fly. "When I'm done with you, no other man will ever want anything to do with you. Walker won't even recognize your stupid bitch face. Then you'll be crawling back to Leroy, begging him to take you back."

Terror filled her at his words and the evil look on his face. She wasn't sure if he meant to rape her or beat her with the belt, but she knew he meant to hurt her and hurt her bad. Her heart raced as he advanced on her.

Cash's lessons filled her head as he drew closer, and she tried to tamp down her fear and focus on getting out of this alive.

He must have smelled her fear, because he suddenly rushed at her, grabbing her wrists and pulling her toward him. He certainly didn't smell like fear, and she tried not to gag at the scent of alcohol oozing from his pores along with the smell of body odor and unwashed clothes.

Twisting her wrists the way she'd practiced, she broke free

and kicked her foot into his kneecap. He bellowed in pain and swung his fist at her in a roundhouse punch.

Pulling back, she missed the full force of the blow, but the impact of his fist on her chin still sent her head snapping back and reeling from the shock.

Blinking back the tears of pain, she pushed the kitchen chair between them, trying to give herself another moment to regroup.

He knocked the chair out of the way, sending it crashing to the floor, and made another grab for her wrist. This time he pulled her in, wrapping his arms around her from behind and holding her back securely against his front.

The clasp of his belt poked into her back, reminding her that his pants were partially undone, and she gagged at the thought of him touching her.

She was all too aware of the fact that she was only wearing Cash's T-shirt, and shuddered to think what would happen if Earl realized she wasn't wearing a bra or underwear.

Fear rose in her, like a swell of lava bubbling to the surface, but instead of letting it freeze her into submission, she drew strength from it, pulled from the boiling mix of fury and terror that filled her.

His arm was locked across her chest, and his hand cupped her shoulder. She could see a thin line of grime under his thumbnail and remnants of grease or dirt in the creases of his knuckles.

Fighting her revulsion, she screwed up her courage, dipped her head and bit into the flesh of his hand. The coppery taste of blood hit her tongue as her teeth broke through his skin.

Ripping his hand away, he released his hold on her and she reared back, cracking the back of her head into his face as hard as she could.

Cash had most likely broken his nose during their fight at the fairgrounds, and her hit must have intensified the pain. He howled with rage and agony, and she took her chance while he was distracted to jab her elbow into his stomach.

Earl's job required physical labor so, unlike Leroy's flabby gut, his brother's stomach was hard with muscle, and her elbow did little damage.

She stomped down on his instep with her bare heel. But his boots took the brunt of her force, and she doubted he noticed much.

Yanking away, she turned to face him, and saw sheer hatred in his eyes.

His hands were holding his battered nose, and his teeth were smeared red with the blood that dripped from it. "You little bitch." His words were full of venom as he spat them at her. "You're gonna pay for that."

Her heart pounded against her chest, but she pushed back the fear.

I'm smarter than he is. I can do this.

She searched wildly around the kitchen, looking for something to use as a weapon. The counters were bare, except for the coffeepot and a toaster. A cast-iron skillet sat on the stove, the filmy white residue of bacon grease lining the inside of it.

The coffeepot was out, too awkward, and the toaster was too bulky.

Racing for the stove, she clasped her hand around the thick handle of the heavy cast-iron skillet.

Earl was right on her heels and grabbed for the fabric of her T-shirt, hauling her back.

But she already had the skillet in her hand.

She turned toward him, planting her feet and swiveling her hip—just as she'd practiced with Cash—then kicked her foot out sideways to connect with his crotch.

He let out an "oomph" as he doubled over in pain, then reached out and grabbed her leg before she could get her balance.

Standing on one foot, she grabbed the handle of the pan with both hands and swung with all her might—swung like it was a bat and she was trying for a home run with the bases loaded. But this wasn't a game.

This was her life she was fighting for.

Earl dropped her foot to lift his hands in defense of his head, but it was too late, and the force of the pan connected with his skull with a sickening thud.

The remnants of the grease flew in an arc, filling the air with the scent of bacon, and landed with a splat on the floor.

Clutching his head, Earl weaved on his feet, then reached out for her, swinging his fists as he swore. "I'm going to fucking kill you, bitch."

Charging toward her, his foot hit the bacon grease, and he slid forward, his arms now pinwheeling as he tried to regain his balance.

But it was too late. The force of his own weight carried him down, and his head hit the side of the kitchen table as he fell.

She held her breath, her body still in a defensive stance, ready to fight.

His whole body slumped to the floor, and she released her breath as she realized the last hit must have knocked him out.

The bastard was going to have one hell of a headache in the morning. Served him right.

Remembering that she'd spied a roll of duct tape there earlier that week, she yanked open the junk drawer and pulled out the tape and a pair of scissors.

Kneeling beside him, she wrapped the tape around his hands several times, then wound the ends of it around the legs of the kitchen chair. It gave her the willies to be this close to him, afraid he might wake up any second, and her hands were shaking so badly, she almost dropped the tape.

After one more loop around the chair legs, she twisted another layer around his hands, sadistically pressing it down onto his hairy forearms and hoping it would hurt like a bitch to pull it off. She probably used half a roll of duct tape, but she didn't care.

She wasn't taking any chances that he was getting away this time. And if he did, he'd be dragging this chair along behind him.

Grabbing the wireless phone from the counter, she punched in 911 as she scooted around his body and raced for Cash. Thankful for once for the terrible cell reception in Montana, she was glad the cabin had a landline available to call for help.

Sinking to the floor, she cradled Cash's head in her lap as the dispatcher picked up the phone. "911 operator. What is your emergency?"

"I need you to send an ambulance and the police to the Tucker Farm, on Route 2. Tell them Earl Purvis is here. He attacked us, and Cash Walker has been injured. Tell them to hurry."

"I've dispatched an ambulance to the Tucker Farm on Route 2 and notified the sheriff's office. Help is on the way. Is the intruder still on the premises?"

"Yes." She stroked Cash's forehead, pushing back his hair to reveal a nasty cut above his eyebrow.

"Is he armed?"

"No, he's passed out on the kitchen floor. I hit him in the head with a cast-iron skillet."

"Are you armed? Is there a gun in the house?"

"No, I mean, I don't know. I don't have one, but there probably is."

"Do you have a weapon? Besides the skillet?"

"No, I'm fine. But Cash is bleeding. Earl hit him in the

head with a piece of firewood."

"Is he breathing?"

"Yes."

"Is he conscious?"

"No."

The dispatch operator walked her through more questions, trying to determine how she could help Cash.

She looked back down at him, and gently touched his cheek.

His eyes opened, and he blinked up at her. His hand went to his forehead as he mumbled, "What the hell happened?"

"Earl knocked you out."

He tried to sit up, pushing against her. "Where is he?"

"Lie back. He's passed out on the floor." She smoothed his hair as he relaxed back into her lap. "You took a good hit to the head, too."

"What happened to him? I don't remember."

A grin of pride crept across her face. "I beaned him in the head with your skillet."

"You did?" He chuckled then grimaced in pain, and his eyes fluttered closed. "Good girl." He opened his eyes again. "I hope you didn't damage my skillet."

She laughed as she heard the sounds of sirens approaching the farm. "I'll buy you a new one." She couldn't imagine cooking with the dang thing again, but she might hang it on the wall to symbolize her newfound bravery.

A small meow sounded, and Percy raced out from under the sofa and pounced into Emma's lap. She grabbed the kitten and cuddled it to her chest. "There you are. I'm so glad you're okay."

The front door opened, and the sheriff and one of his deputies burst in, followed closely by the EMTs.

"You guys okay?" Taylor asked, his gaze traveling around the room. The corners of his mouth tipped up in a grin as he spied Earl tied to the kitchen chair with duct tape. "Looks like you found Earl."

"He hit Cash on the head with a log of firewood," Emma explained as the EMT squatted down to examine Cash.

He shined a light in Cash's now open eyes and picked up his hand to check his pulse rate. "How long was he out?"

She shook her head. The whole thing had happened so fast. Even though it had felt like it was happening in slow motion at times, the whole incident probably lasted only five minutes. "I don't know for sure. He was passed out when I came out of the room, then I fought with Earl and tied him up. It couldn't have been more than a few minutes."

"I don't think I was out that whole time," Cash said. "I was kind of in and out, but my head does hurt."

"You're showing signs of a concussion. We're going to take you in to the hospital to get you checked out." The other paramedic was already wheeling in the stretcher.

"I don't need a hospital, just get me up to the couch." He tried to sit up and swayed as his eyes fluttered with dizziness. "Well, hell," he said as he slumped back against Emma.

"Hospital it is then," she said, then looked up at the paramedic. "Can I come with him?"

He turned away to assist with getting Cash onto the stretcher. "Sure, but you might want to put on some pants."

Oh crap. She still wasn't wearing any underwear.

Hopefully, she hadn't just flashed the EMT guy. Heat flamed her cheeks as she stood up and pulled Cash's T-shirt down farther to cover her legs. "Good idea. I'll do that, then meet you at the ambulance."

She curled the kitten into the pillows, making a nest for it in the corner of the sofa, then stood just as Charlie, Zack, and Sophie burst into the room.

Sophie spied Cash being loaded onto the stretcher and cried out as she raced to his side.

Charlie hurried across the room and threw her arms around Emma. "Oh my lord. What happened? We heard the sirens and could see the lights across the pasture. Are you okay?"

For the first time since she'd come out of the room and found Earl standing there, tears pricked her eyes. She'd been so focused on survival and the fight, she hadn't had time for emotions. But having Charlie's comforting arms around her and hearing her caring words hit a spot right in the center of Emma's heart.

She fought back the tears, burying her face in Charlie's shoulder. She'd always felt alone, fighting her battles against Leroy in a solitary prison of isolation. But now she wasn't alone anymore. This is what it felt like to have friends, to have people who cared about you.

The enormity of it hit her like a ton of bricks in the chest, and she wanted to weep with the sheer happiness of having other people to share in her struggles, her joys, her life. "Yes, I'm okay. They think Cash has a concussion, though. They're taking him to the hospital to check him out."

A ripping sound followed by a yowl of pain had them turning toward the kitchen to see Taylor trying not to laugh as he worked to free Earl from the kitchen chair.

He looked up at Emma with a grin. "Do you think you used enough duct tape?"

She shrugged, the ball of emotion loosening in her chest as the humor of the situation hit her, and she grinned back. "I didn't want to take a chance on him getting away."

"You did good. He's not going anywhere except the county lockup. His brothers are waiting for him there."

Earl writhed against the sheriff's legs and cursed her name, but Emma ignored him as she turned back to Charlie. "I've got to get dressed so I can go in the ambulance with Cash."

"Pants would probably be a good idea. And I'd probably put on a bra, otherwise the EMTs won't be paying any attention to Cash in the back of the ambulance." She followed Emma into the bedroom, letting her get dressed while she searched the pockets of the jeans that lay on the floor. "I've got Cash's wallet in case he needs his ID or his insurance card."

"Good idea." She only had the clothes she'd arrived in, so she stuck with Cash's T-shirt, but added a bra, then pulled on her jeans and boots, before heading for the door.

Charlie followed on her heels. "I'm coming with you."

"You don't have to."

"Yes, I do. Cash was the first friend I made in Montana. He's like family to me." She put an arm around Emma's waist and leaned in conspiratorially. "And from the frantic call I got last night asking if he could give you the kitten and the looks of those rumpled sheets, I'd say you're going to be joining the family soon."

"Oh. What about Percy?" She turned back, looking for the kitten, then smiled.

Sophie had the little cat cuddled in her arms as she hurried over and gave Emma a quick hug. "Don't worry, I'm on kitten duty and will make sure he's taken care of. Dad and I will stay here until the sheriff's department leaves, then we'll meet you at the hospital."

"Thanks, kiddo," Charlie said, giving Sophie a quick squeeze before hustling Emma out the front door and into the ambulance.

So this was what having a family felt like.

She could get used to this.

Charlie waved. "I'll follow you in the truck so you have a ride home. Don't worry. I'll be right behind you."

Cash looked pale against the white sheet of the stretcher, dried red blood smeared on his forehead and crusted into his black hair. The EMT was administering oxygen, but Cash's eyes were open and alert, and he reached for her hand.

The feel of his strong callused hand in hers gave her strength, and she squeezed his palm, hoping to give some of that strength back to him.

They'd been through so much. But they'd gotten through it and come out on the other side.

Had it only been an hour ago that Cash had asked her to marry him?

This night seemed to last forever.

But as the ambulance pulled out of the driveway and sped down the highway toward the hospital, Cash tilted his head, pulled down the oxygen mask, and gave her one of his panty-melting grins. And she was thankful for every hour, every minute, every second of what they had endured.

Each moment had brought them closer together; whether they were fighting as a team against the Purvis brothers, or wrestling in the sheets, they'd done it together.

Except that last part where she'd taken on Earl alone, and she'd come out the victor.

She'd needed to do that by herself. And she had.

And now she was ready. Ready to stand on her own, strong enough to enter into a relationship with the ridiculously hot cowboy who lay on the stretcher in front of her.

Squeezing his hand, she grinned back.

Yes, she was definitely ready for that.

Chapter Twenty-Two

Several months had passed since the incident with Leroy and the Purvis brothers. Cash had only spent one night in the hospital and rested for all of about ten minutes before he was back to working on the farm.

Thankfully, the other ranch hand, Buckshot, had returned from his trip and could take more of the chores while Cash recuperated.

Emma had moved her things into his cabin, and they had spent the last few months learning about each other, in the bedroom and out.

But a lot of *in*. That was her favorite kind of learning.

And Cash Walker was an excellent teacher.

Everything was falling into place, and she couldn't be happier. She'd started classes at the community college in Great Falls to be a veterinarian technician and had been working part time in the afternoons as the receptionist at the vet clinic with Zack. She still spent her mornings at the diner, filling in for Cherry, who'd announced that she was pregnant the week after the Fall Festival.

She and Cash had planned a spring wedding, but after Emma discovered her own plus sign on the pregnancy test she took earlier that month, they'd decided a Christmas wedding would work just as well.

Keeping it simple, she'd told Cash that all she needed was a justice of the peace, a bouquet of wildflowers, and her dad to walk her down the aisle. She didn't care about the rest. She'd had the church wedding, and that hadn't worked out so well, so this time she was going a different route.

She'd still take her vows before God, and a few witnesses, but she didn't need the cake and the seven bridesmaids and the long train. Although, she was wearing a blue satin garter under her simple white dress, but that was for Cash to discover later.

Cherry and Charlie had become her best friends, and there was no way that they were getting left out of the ceremony. The two women, plus Sophie, planned to spend the morning pampering her, doing her hair and nails and makeup, and fussing over every detail.

"We're celebrating this wedding morning in style. I'm making mimosas," Charlie announced as she dropped her things on the coffee table in the living room of the cabin. She pointed to Cherry and Sophie who were already sitting on the sofa with Emma, the gray kitten cuddled in the teenager's lap. "You two get virgin mimosas."

Cherry laughed. "So, basically we're just drinking orange juice in a fancy-pants glass."

"Basically, yes." Charlie laughed along with her friend.

"I guess you need to make mine virgin, too," Emma said quietly.

Her friends' eyes widened, then they all broke into excited laughter as Emma nodded and confirmed that she was pregnant as well.

"Oh my lands," Cherry said in her typical down-home

slang. "I'll bet Cash is just beside himself with all these blessings. He's got to be happier than a pig in a fresh puddle of mud."

"He is," Emma answered with a laugh.

She'd been a little nervous to tell him at first. They'd talked about having kids before.

One night he'd asked her if she and Leroy had ever tried, and she'd tearfully told him that she'd been pregnant once and had miscarried. She never knew for sure if the miscarriage had been due to Leroy's treatment of her or not, but she was careful not to ever get pregnant again, sadly resigning herself to the fact that she would never have children.

How she was pregnant now was a miracle, and when she told Cash about it, he was over the moon excited. And if she'd felt that he'd treated her with care and devotion before, he now handled her as if she were a fragile teacup.

"He's being very careful with me, not letting me lift anything heavy or even do the dishes at night," Emma told them. "I told him I'm not infirm, but he insists I sit down all the time and let him take care of me."

Charlie covered her heart with her hands. "That's so sweet. You've brought out this whole different side to Cash that I've never seen. He's always come across as this tough-as-nails cowboy. But he's so tender with you. And he's always been sweet and gentle with Sophie."

"He's great with her," Emma agreed. "He told me that he's always wanted kids, but figured he'd never get the chance to have them. And getting to be Sophie's godfather had been enough for him."

"Ahh. I love that guy," Sophie said. "He's gonna be a great dad."

Emma believed that he would be too. Believed it with all of her heart.

"Well, hell," Charlie said. "Zack and I better get with it if we want all of our kids growing up together like the guys did."

Sophie's eyes widened, and a big smile broke across her face. "Yes. We're going to have a baby. I've always wanted a little brother or sister."

Charlie grinned and passed her a glass of orange juice in a fancy flute. "You might not say that when you have to change poopy diapers and the baby throws up on you."

"Ha. I'm tougher than that," Sophie declared. "I'm a born and raised Montana stock farm-girl. You think a little vomit and poop scare me? No way."

Leave it to the teenager to take a new sibling in stride, even welcome the change. She was such a sweet girl and had completely accepted Emma into the family, always greeting her with a warm hug. She hung out often at the cabin, playing with Percy and bringing Emma new recipes or nail polish to try.

Between Charlie, Sophie, and Cherry, she felt like she'd been given three sisters. And Taylor and Zack acted as protective of her as two older brothers would.

They'd even welcomed her dad into their fold, often inviting him over for Sunday dinner and including him in the Friday night pizza parties.

"Enough talk of diapers," Cherry declared. "We've got a bride to get ready. Charlie, you start on her hair. Sophie, you've got her nails, and I'm in charge of makeup. Somebody pass me that eyeshadow."

Three hours later, Emma smoothed the petals of the wildflowers in her small bouquet as she stood in the courthouse outside the doors of the justice of the peace.

"You ready?" her dad asked.

Taking a deep breath, she nodded.

She was more than ready. She'd been waiting for this moment her whole life.

Her dad looked at her, tears welling in his eyes. "You

know I don't say it often enough, but I'm real proud of you, honey."

"Thanks, Dad." He *didn't* say it often, but the love and pride shining in his eyes proved his sincerity.

"I mean it. You've really turned your life around the past several months. It's like you're finally turning into the woman you were always meant to be. You've got a job you enjoy, and you're going to school, and you've found you a good fella in Cash. I feel like you're finally in a healthy relationship, and I'm just real happy for you."

"Are you crying?"

"No, that's just my allergies acting up."

They'd been keeping the pregnancy mostly to themselves, but Cash had told his mom the night before, and she'd been waiting for the right time to tell her dad. This seemed as good a time as any.

"I don't want to make your 'allergies' any worse, but since we're getting all mushy anyway, I might as well tell you another big change that's about to happen in my life. You're going to be a grandpa."

His eyes widened, and he let out a whoop, then leaned down to crush her against him in a giant bear hug. "That's great news, Em." He squeezed her tighter.

She hugged him back, not even caring that he was smashing her bouquet between them. She'd had so few times that she got to share good news with him, especially concerning her life. "That's why we moved the wedding up. The baby's not due until next fall, but we figured there was no reason to wait."

"No, you've waited long enough to start living your life. I'm just awful happy for you." He let her go and dug in his pocket for a handkerchief. Shaking it out, he wiped his eyes and blew his nose. "Now you've really got my allergies acting up."

The door cracked open, and Charlie poked her head out. "You ready?"

Emma grinned. She couldn't help it—couldn't keep the smile off her face if she tried. She looped her arm through her dad's and nodded. "Yes, I'm *so* ready."

The sound of the wedding march filled the air, and prickles of excitement tingled down her spine. She was getting ready to marry Cash, and she couldn't wait.

Her friend opened the door, and Emma gasped.

They'd decided on a small wedding, with just their family and a couple of friends, but the little courtroom was full of people. It appeared half the town of Broken Falls had shown up, and they all stood as she and her dad stepped into the room and began to walk down the aisle.

Customers from the diner smiled and waved. Buckshot stood on the groom's side. The other receptionist from the vet clinic sat on hers. The three self-professed matrons of the town, Etta James, and twin sisters Millie and Willie May, were smooshed into one row, and Stan stood on the aisle, wearing his best tie-dye T-shirt and a broad grin on his face.

Sophie and Cherry's son, Sam, were in the front row, and Emma wouldn't have been surprised to see that Sophie snuck the kitten into the courtroom.

She thought her heart was full with the love and support she felt from the town, then her eyes lit on the dark-haired cowboy standing at the end of the aisle, and her heart overflowed with love.

Her breath caught in her throat at the sight of him, standing tall and heartbreakingly handsome with a grin meant just for her. Keeping her steps measured, it took all of her willpower not to drop the flowers and sprint down the aisle and into his arms.

After what felt like forever, they finally reached him, and her dad passed her off, putting her hand into Cash's outstretched one.

Her father held both of their hands in his for a moment. It felt like he was giving them his silent blessing through the firm pressure he used to squeeze their hands. He looked over at Cash. "Take care of my girl."

"I will, sir." Cash nodded at Clyde then smiled down at Emma as her father sat down in the first row. "Hey, darlin'. You look beautiful," he said, love shining in his eyes.

"So do you," she whispered and let out a small giggle. "I don't know why I'm so nervous. I guess I've just never been this excited for anything in my life."

He intertwined her fingers in his and squeezed her hand. Leaning down, he nuzzled her neck, his breath warm on her skin, as he whispered in her ear. "I'm a little nervous, too."

Chuckling at the way she drew back a little bit, he pulled her tighter against his side. "I'm not nervous about marrying you, that part's easy. I've never been more certain of anything than I am about my decision to make you my wife. I'm just a little nervous that I'm not going to measure up to the ideal husband in your eyes."

"You've already exceeded every measurement."

A large grin cracked across his face, and he got a wicked gleam in his eye.

She nudged him in the ribs as a smile pulled at the corners of her mouth. "I do love you."

"I love you too, darlin'. You stole my heart clean away the moment I saw you drive up to the farm with that silly goat sitting in the car next to you, and now that heart belongs to you."

"It's safe with me." She blinked back the tears that threatened her eyes. "You stole my heart away, too. And I can't wait to be your wife and begin our life together."

"Then let's get started." He turned to the justice of the peace and nodded.

She squeezed his hand and breathed in the excitement of the moment. Her heart pounded in her chest, and she thought it might burst with happiness.

She thought about how much her life had changed in the past several months. She'd walked away from Leroy with nothing but a few boxes and the tattered remains of her pride. She'd been prepared to have nothing, but now she had everything.

She had a home and a man who loved her. Who had shown her that she was strong and resilient. She'd seen herself as a timid mouse who was afraid of her own shadow, but she'd grown so much.

With the help of her friends and the tall cowboy who now stood beside her holding her hand, she'd blossomed from that timid mouse into a strong, independent woman.

The mouse part was still there, would always be there, but now she drew strength from that piece of her life, believing in herself and taking pride in what she had overcome, what she had survived.

It took all of the pieces—the fear, the courage, the nervousness, the determination—all of it swirled and spun inside her, combining to fuel the woman she was now. A woman about to embark on a new journey, a new life. A life filled with family and friends, and a man who loved her and respected her and made her feel safe.

That shy part of her would always be there, but now she had a brave part of her, too. A part that stood up for herself, believed in herself, believed that she was worthy and strong and that she really could accomplish whatever she set her mind to.

The justice of the peace began the vows, stating her name and asking her if she took this man, Cash Walker, to have and to hold, in sickness and in health, for richer and poorer, until death do they part.

Pushing back her shoulders, she stood tall and looked into the crystal blue eyes of the man she loved, the man who had made all her dreams come true.

"I do," she answered, her voice strong and true.

A thousand times I do.

Epilogue

One year later

It was Christmas Eve, and they were all gathered around the tree in the living room of Tucked Away. The whole big bunch of them, their friends, and the people they called family.

Cash looked around the room and marveled at how his life had changed in the past year. How all of their lives had changed.

Cherry and Taylor were sitting on one sofa, their son, Sam, on Taylor's lap, and their baby girl curled in his arms. Swirls of thick strawberry blond hair covered the baby's head, and her frilly Christmas dress matched the pink and white peppermint-striped sweater that Cherry wore.

Their dog, Rex, lay at their feet, intently watching the frosted sugar cookie that Sam was waving around as he told his parents a story.

Cash couldn't help but smile as Cherry let out a hearty laugh. Being a wife and a mom suited her, and he'd never seen her, or Taylor, so happy.

Zack and Charlie sat on the loveseat across from them, his hand resting casually on Charlie's swollen belly—their own baby due in the spring. Leave it to a veterinarian to plan his wife's due date around calving season. Although, knowing Charlie, he might not have had that much say in the timing.

Charlie, Emma, and Cherry had become the closest of friends, and they were determined for their firstborn kids to grow up together like he, Zack, and Taylor had.

Zack had insisted on giving Charlie the big church wedding, and they'd gotten married at the end of the past summer and had invited the majority of the small town of Broken Falls. They'd filled the new barn with music, food, friends, and laughter, and their reception had lasted far into the night. It had been the social event of the summer.

Charlie had settled in to country life and declared she was never leaving Montana. He could almost feel her grandma Gigi smiling down at her from heaven as she watched her only granddaughter laughing with her new husband.

Happy was the emotion of the night. Everyone laughed as Sophie carried in a tray of steaming mugs of hot cocoa to pass around. Snow swirled outside the windows, but the atmosphere inside was warm and cozy.

He looked down at Emma, holding their own child, a beautiful baby boy with dark blue eyes and a mass of jet black hair. A child who had already taken over their lives—with diapers, and two a.m. feedings, and toys scattered all over the house—and more love than he'd thought he possibly had to give.

Sometimes he walked into the room and saw Emma sitting in a chair, holding their baby, and it literally took his breath away. For so long, he'd thought this was a life that could never be his. Now he couldn't imagine what his life would be like without them.

He passed Emma a small box, the bright red bow almost bigger than the present itself.

Her eyes shone with excitement. "What's this? I thought we weren't doing presents until tomorrow."

An excited grin stole over his face as he watched her turn the small box over in her hand. He'd been working on this surprise for months and couldn't wait to see her face.

"It's not just for you. It's for us," he said. "Open the box."

She lifted the lid, and a gasp escaped her lips. Tears sprang to her eyes as she looked up at him, as if afraid to believe in the contents of the box. "Is this what I think it is?"

"It is." He took the box from her, reached into the layers of cotton, and pulled out the contents. He held up the silver key then set it gently into her outstretched hand. "It's the key to our new house."

The room had gone quiet as the others watched Emma's reaction. They'd all been in on the surprise and had been working on making it happen for months.

"Our new house?" Emma asked, her voice soft and full of disbelief.

The Tucked Away farm had been in the Tucker family for generations, so Sophie and Zack had moved into the farmhouse with Charlie after they got married. They'd spent the last several months in negotiations and secretly working out a plan for Cash and Emma to buy Zack's farm.

"I wanted to surprise you." He gestured around the room. "*We* wanted to surprise you. After Zack and Sophie moved in here, we started talking about how he'd be taking over this farm and needing to sell his. We hatched a plan for us to buy it."

She looked around the room at their friends. "You all knew about this?"

They nodded and laughed, and Emma looked back at Cash. "So, is it ours? Really?"

He chuckled. "Not quite. We close on the first of the month. I couldn't buy it without you. I had to let you in on the secret before I asked for your signature."

"My signature? On what?"

He gave her a surprised look. "On the deed to the

property. *I'm* not buying the farm. *We're* buying the farm. Your name will be on the deed same as mine, and you'll own the property with me. I wouldn't do this without you. I plan to build our life here and raise our son, and all of his brothers and sisters there. But it's your decision, too."

He picked up her hand and looked into her beautiful eyes. Letting everyone else in the room fade away, he focused only on her. "You have to want this, too, or we'll forget the whole thing. So, what do you say, Em? Do you want to buy a farm with me?"

"More than anything." A tear slipped from her eye and slid down her cheek as she nodded, and a joy-filled smile burst across her face. "I just can't believe it. I'm so happy right now, I can't speak."

The baby in her arms took that moment to gurgle and babble out a bubbly coo.

Cash chuckled. "I guess you don't have to. It sounds like he approves."

Emma cuddled the baby to her chest. "I think he just asked for his first pony."

"I can handle that." He felt like he could handle just about anything that life threw at him right now. As long as he had this woman and his child by his side, he could do anything, face any trial, overcome any obstacle.

He looked around the room again, his heart full with the blessings in his life. The joy in this room overflowed, as the people he called family and friends began to speak and laugh and congratulate them on their new home.

Home. Family. Love.

Things he feared he would never have, and now they filled this Montana cowboy's heart.

THE END...
AND JUST THE BEGINNING...

Acknowledgments

My thanks always goes first to my husband, Todd, the one who supports me and believes in me. I love and adore you. Thanks for taking this and all journeys with me.

Thanks to my sons, Tyler and Nick, for your love and support. You guys make it all worth it.

A special thank you goes out to my dad, Bill Bryant, for your technical support in farming, ranching, and all things veterinarian and animal related. I love having your contributions to the story.

Thanks so much to my amazing editor, Allison Collins for your hard work and dedication to making this book happen. And thanks to the whole crew at Entangled Publishing for giving your valuable time and energy to publish this book.

A big thanks goes out to my writing sprint partners, Cindy Skaggs and Beth Rhodes. Your support and accountability helped make this book happen—that and several late night writing runs.

My thanks always goes out to the women that walk this writing journey with me every day. The ones that make me laugh, who encourage and support, who offer great advice and sometimes just listen. Thank you Michelle Major, Lana Williams, and Kristin Miller. XO

I adore my beta readers and ARC reviewers that I know I can count on in a pinch—Terry Gregson, Denise Fritz, Shari Bartholomew, and Lee Cumba. Thank you—you are all the best!

My biggest thanks goes out to my readers! Thanks for loving my stories and my characters and for continuing to ask for more. I can't wait to share my next story with you.

About the Author

Jennie Marts loves to make readers laugh as she weaves stories filled with love, friendship and intrigue. Jennie writes for Entangled Publishing in both the Select line and Lovestruck, the newest line of romantic comedies. She's also the author of the romantic comedy/cozy mystery Page Turners series, which includes: *Another Saturday Night* and *I Ain't Got No Body*, *Easy Like Sunday Mourning*, *Just Another Maniac Monday*, and *Tangled Up in Tuesday*.

She is living her own happily-ever-after in the mountains of Colorado with her husband, two sons, and two dogs whose antics often find a way into her books.

She is addicted to Diet Coke, adores Cheetos, and believes you can't have too many books, shoes or friends.

Jennie loves to hear from readers. Follow her on Facebook at Jennie Marts Books, Twitter at @JennieMarts, or Goodreads.

Be the first to find out when the newest Jennie Marts novel is releasing and hear all the latest news and updates by signing up for her newsletter at: Jenniemarts.com

If you enjoyed this book, please consider leaving a review!

Discover more Entangled Select Contemporary titles...

BOUND TO THE BOUNTY HUNTER
a *Bound* novel by Hayson Manning

Harlan Franco lives by his own rules: be in control, be detached, and never mix business with pleasure. These rules are tested when he's being paid to secretly guard the sexy, unpredictable, pain in the butt, Sophie Callaghan—a woman determined to stay away from him. Sophie is on a mission. What she doesn't need is hot, broody, and controlling Harlan barging into her life. After a night where both live out their darkest desires, Sophie tries to fight the explosive chemistry between them. But the ties that bind her heart to this bounty hunter are tight and tangled.

KNOCKED OUT BY LOVE
a *Love to the Extreme* novel by Abby Niles

Brody "The Iron" Minton has been in love with Scarlett for as long as he can remember, but she's his best friend's ex, and only an ass would make a move. Except Scarlett wants help getting back in the dating game, and Brody's torn. If he helps her out, he can keep an eye on her and guard her vulnerable heart. But having the woman he's longed for for years in arms' reach is hell on a man's restraint. And the more time Brody and Scarlett spend together, the less innocent and safe the flirting and fun becomes.

A FRIENDLY ENGAGEMENT
a *Friends First* novel by Christine Warner

When Omar Esterly sets his sights on a potential, family-oriented client, his confirmed bachelorhood becomes a problem. Fortunately, his friend and employee, Devi Boss, has the perfect plan: she'll be his fake fiancée. Now they've crossed the line between friendship and...well, something more. But when their friendly engagement gets unexpectedly romantic, Devi realizes she's made the biggest mistake of all—falling for her fiancé.

Discover the **Hearts of Montana** *series…*

Tucked Away

Hidden Away

Made in the USA
Middletown, DE
07 May 2018